STILLWATERS

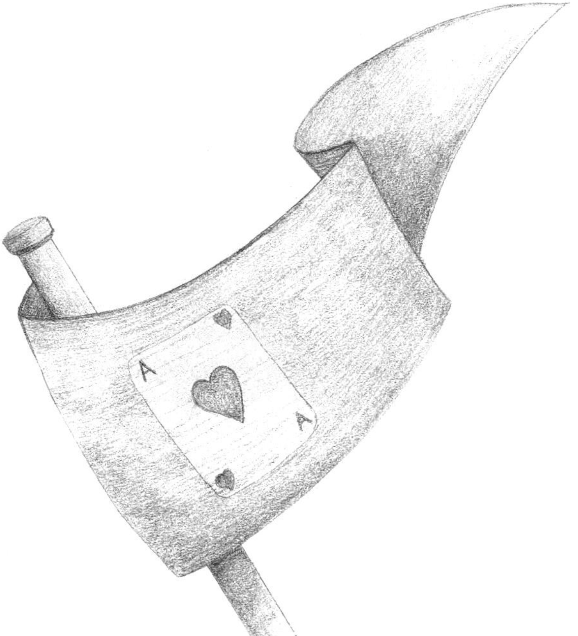

Chris Crowther

By the same author
BLADESTRIKE
WATERPROOF

British Library Cataloguing in Publication Data.
A catalogue record is available from the British Library.

ISBN 978 0 903094 24 5
EAN 9780903094238

First published this edition in 2009
by

Hamilton Publications,
9 Marine Parade,
Gorleston on sea,
Norfolk. NR 31 6DU.

www.chriscrowther.co.uk

Printed in Great Britain by
Barnwell Print Ltd, Dunkirk, Aylsham, Norfolk. NR11 6SU

Front cover photograph by David Burton *www.dbphoto.co.uk*
Sketches by Sarah Rogers *www.sarahrogers.co.uk*

Chapter One

Sally Beckett was already unlocking her front door before she sensed the men behind her.

Walking home through suburbia in the late-winter darkness, her thoughts had been deep as she tried to assess the life-changing events of the afternoon. Consequently, she'd hardly noticed the car parked outside her Victorian semi, or the two over-coated figures climbing silently out as she fumbled for her keys. Now, with sinister shadows joining her own, she turned to find dark figures blocking both the light from the street lamp and any line of escape. As the first chill of alarm froze both her thoughts and actions, the men reached into their coat pockets and Sally knew this strange day was not finished with her yet.

* * *

Only six hours earlier, the Piccadilly Line had been rattling her towards central London. In trousers and smart wool jacket worn for the first time in months, she had gained some satisfaction in comparing the white expressionless faces sitting opposite with her own bronzed complexion. Only momentarily though, for beneath her healthy tan lay a conflict of mixed emotions. Although very curious at the reason for this summons, she was also concerned that it might spell trouble. For the tenth time, she pulled the crumpled letter from her rucksack.

It was from a firm of solicitors in the city, *Landers, Simpson & Hedges*, and its message was simple: please telephone for an appointment to discuss urgent business. She had duly called and although enquiries as to the nature of this "urgent business" had met with professional silence, the secretary had given her an appointment for that same afternoon. The journey in had therefore been spent wondering what it could possibly be about and the more she wondered the more Sally decided it must be the work of Simon.

Simon had been her partner for a year. It had not been a totally happy relationship, brought to an even unhappier end with the revelation that he was seeing another girl on his frequent business trips to Birmingham. They had been living in Sally's own home, so throwing him out and changing the locks had effectively ended things months ago. In the few acrimonious telephone conversations since, there had been mutterings about compensation for work he had done on the house. She had never taken his money for keep or any of these threats seriously, but perhaps today's summons was the prelude to a bout of legal wrangling. Surely though, a simple letter could have explained that? Emerging into the drizzling grey of The Minories, she speed-walked towards the given address and an answer.

Around her, this centre of the country's economy seemed to throb with vibrant energy, while its bustling workforce scurried on missions of who-knew-what. Sally had spent her working life in the City of London, but was happy she was no longer a part of it. Three months exploring the more remote corners of the planet, she decided, had been a good antidote to failure in both romance and career. What she *was* unprepared for though, were the offices of *Landers, Simpson & Hedges*.

Illogically, their name suggested some Dickensian practice stuck in a side street. In reality, the chambers of this law firm occupied the whole centre floor of a modern high rise building. The receptionist sitting elegantly behind a state-of-the-art desk, smiled, told her to take a seat and said that "Mr Gathergood" would see her shortly.

The "shortly", though only twelve minutes, did nothing to ease Sally's building nerves. Gathergood, however, turned out to be a pleasant enough man in his early fifties who led Sally to his small but stylish office. Settled into the comfortable client-chair, she faced both solicitor and window. The former leaned forward, smiling.

'Did you bring some form of identification as requested, Miss Beckett?'

'Oh, yes.' Sally produced a well-thumbed passport from the pocket of her much-travelled rucksack.

While the solicitor flicked through the pages, she looked over his shoulder to the view beyond. Between the jungle of towering offices, the Thames was just visible, its grey flowing expanse flecked with small whitecaps as rain-laden wind blew in vain against the ebbing tide. But Gathergood's thoughts were far from winter London as he scanned the multiple stamps in Sally's passport.

'You've done a lot of travelling in the last three months, Miss Beckett?'

'Yes, I've been backpacking around the world. I only arrived home yesterday and found your letter.'

'Which would explain why Mr Blenkinsop, from our Norwich office, was unable to contact you a month ago.'

'Norwich office?'

Gathergood was studying the photo on the passport's final page before deciding that the pretty thirty-two year old sitting before him with short dark hair, brown eyes and a puzzled look, really was Sally Erica Beckett. 'Yes, we have offices around the country. Our Norwich branch asked us to contact you.'

'In what connection?' asked Sally, wondering when Simon had

moved to Norwich and more anxious than ever to know just how much that creep was trying to claim.

'The estate of your late grandfather,' explained Gathergood, opening the green-coloured file before him. 'Mr Blenkinsop acted as solicitor and executor for Charles McKenna-Hynes, until your grandfather's unexpected death a month ago…' Haverson paused as he detected the shocked look on the face of the young woman opposite. 'Miss Beckett, forgive me, did you not know of the death of your grandfather?'

'No…'

'Oh,' Gathergood shook his head in some embarrassment, 'I'm so sorry to be the bearer of such sad news but, if it is any consolation…' he forced a brightening smile, '…your grandfather has left the bulk of his estate to you.'

Over the years, Gathergood had dealt with a great many clients finding out, for the first time, that they had acquired new-found wealth. Some still carried the sadness of bereavement, some were left speechless, some simply asked "How much?". Never before had he seen a reaction like the young woman's opposite, whose well-tanned face was clouded with total bewilderment. Leaning forward, Gathergood said kindly, 'Miss Beckett, had you no idea your grandfather had made provision for you in his will?'

'Mr Gathergood,' said Sally, shaking her head, 'I had no idea I even *had* a grandfather.'

* * *

And now, as she stood on her doorstep, taking deep breaths and trying to decide whether to flee or fight, the men brought their hands out from their coat pockets. They were holding, not guns or knives, but leather-bound identification cards.

'Miss Beckett,' said the older of the two, 'I'm Detective Chief Inspector Hengrove and this is Detective Constable Bailey. We're from the Norfolk Constabulary and we'd like to ask you some questions regarding the death of your grandfather.'

* * *

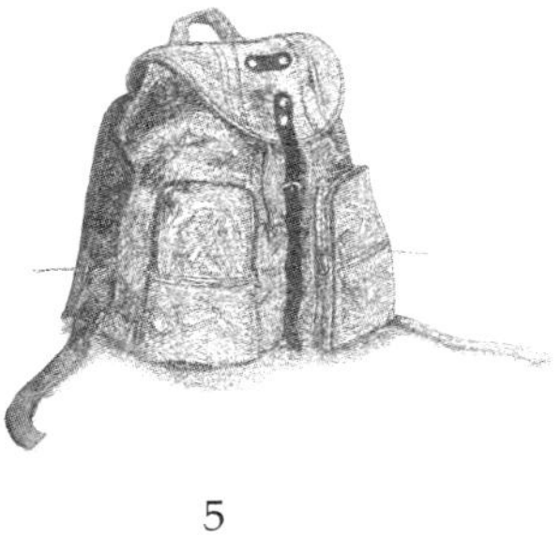

Chapter Two

'So, you're telling me you've been left a small fortune by a grandfather you didn't even know you had?' DCI Hengrove stretched his legs and took a gulp of coffee. All three were sitting around Sally's dining table and the senior detective was making no effort to hide his scepticism. 'Any idea why this generous benefactor should keep his presence such a mystery?'

Sally shook her head. 'I've no idea. I was hoping you could tell me.'

'But surely your family mentioned him?' queried Bailey at the other end of the table and busy taking notes.

'I haven't got any family,' answered Sally, taking a sip from her own mug. 'My mum and dad were killed in a car accident when I was just two. I was brought up by my gran who left me this home when she died.'

'Not done too badly out of grandparent deaths have you?' remarked Bailey in a neutral voice that could have meant anything.

Sally gave him her most meaningful look. This young DC might be quite good looking in a rugged sort of way, but that didn't mean she was going to take smart remarks. 'What are you implying?'

'Just investigating all angles,' intervened Hengrove, holding up a pacifying hand. He glanced around at Sally's lounge, homely and cosy but in a décor two generations old. 'What do you do for a living, Miss Beckett?'

'Nothing at present.' Sally was aware that all her answers so far had done nothing to inspire much esteem. 'Until four months ago I was a trader for a financial house in the City. When they made me redundant I decided I needed a change, so I cashed in my savings and went off backpacking in Asia.'

'No other-half to worry about then?' asked Bailey.

Sally couldn't decide whether the question carried just the hint of personal interest. Whatever, she answered candidly, aware they probably knew all about her already. 'I did have a partner living here for a year, but that all ended six months ago.'

'A bad few months,' observed Bailey with a touch of genuine compassion.

Hengrove stood up and made his way casually around the room, studying the framed watercolours of birds. 'You do these, Miss Beckett?'

Sally shook her head. 'No that was Gran's hobby. She was passionate about British birds, observing and painting them right until her death two years ago.'

'This gran of yours…' Hengrove sat down again and glanced at his own notes, '… Emily Halard … didn't she tell you about a husband?'

'Yes, of course she did.' Sally nodded towards the sideboard and the framed sepia print of a young naval officer. 'She always told me Granddad was killed on D-day, when she was pregnant with my mum.'

'And the name of your assumed grandfather was…?'

'Edward … Edward Halard, as far as I knew,' answered Sally, shaking her head in growing bewilderment. 'Now I'm told it was Charles McKenna-Hynes, a name I've never heard of before, and that he was alive until a month ago.' She looked up, meeting Hengrove's eyes and realising for the first time that the police never concerned themselves with ordinary death, no matter how confused the family history. 'How exactly did… *this* grandfather… die?'

'A boating accident,' said Hengrove, with no attempt at sympathy. 'Seems he was sailing his yacht on his own and fell overboard…' he glanced again at his notes, '… on February fifteenth.' Hengrove paused to let this date sink in. 'Would you mind telling me what you were doing on that day, Miss Beckett?'

'Why?'

'Procedure, that's all.'

'You mean you have suspicions about the way he died?'

'The coroner passed an open verdict, Miss Beckett, so we have to investigate?'

'Which includes suspecting *me* of having something to do with it.' Sally put down her mug with some force. 'I've already told you, Chief Inspector, I didn't even know of this Charles McKenna-Hynes, let alone that he was my grandfather.'

Hengrove's eyes narrowed slightly. 'So you tell us, but he obviously knew you so … where were you on February fifteenth?'

'Thailand backpacking. I can't tell you exactly where without checking my diary.'

'I'd like to see that and your passport, please.'

Sally went and fetched both, wondering if this was all a bad dream from which she would shortly wake. When she returned, Bailey took them from her. Sally sat down again and picked up her mug. Time, she felt, for some questioning of her own.

'You say my … "granddad" … fell overboard from his yacht; how old was he exactly?'

Hengrove checked his notes again. 'Eighty-six.'

'Eighty-six!' exclaimed Sally. 'And he was sailing on his own in winter?'

Hengrove nodded. 'Apparently he did quite often. A pretty fit man for his years by all accounts.'

'He must have been,' said Sally, almost to herself, before looking up and asking, 'So what were the exact circumstances of his death?'

'Went out alone in his yacht, for an afternoon sail,' explained Hengrove. 'The next morning, Mrs Jenkins, his domestic who'd stayed the night in the house, found the yacht still wasn't back on its mooring. That didn't surprise her, as apparently your grandfather often stayed out overnight if the fancy took him, and that morning there was thick fog. Mrs Jenkins just assumed he was anchored somewhere waiting for it to clear.'

'But he wasn't?' asked Sally, intrigued.

'No. Later on when the fog did clear slightly, a Navigation Ranger found the yacht drifting, its sails still up, but no one onboard. Your grandfather's body was found floating in reedbeds, hours later.'

Sally found herself giving a slight shiver. 'You say the coroner passed an open verdict; does that mean they suspected suicide?'

'Perhaps worse than suicide, Miss Beckett.' Hengrove sat back in his chair. 'The Navigation Ranger who discovered your granddad's yacht was convinced he hadn't been alone.'

'You mean someone pushed him overboard or something?'

'It's a possibility,' acknowledged Hengrove, obviously reluctant to give more detail.

'And you think I might have been that … that mystery person?'

'You stood to inherit a great deal of property, Miss Beckett.' The DCI looked at his suspect through narrowing eyes. 'Just how much, exactly?'

Sally felt like telling her inquisitor to mind his own business and realised, just as quickly that it *was* his business, so she said, 'A house and a business. Apparently my … my grandfather owned a small boatyard.'

'Money?' Hengrove could be as blunt as he was brusque.

Sally blinked, as though still coming to terms with revelations undreamed of until this afternoon. 'Apparently after probate, his liquid assets came to about four hundred and fifty thousand pounds. These were divided between me, Mrs Jenkins, and some chap called Ian Haverson.'

Hengrove nodded as though aware of these facts and only wanting confirmation from Sally herself. 'So, you've acquired another home, a business and a hundred and fifty grand,' stated the detective. 'Probably about a million all told. Not exactly lacking in motive were you, Miss Beckett?'

'Except she wasn't even in the country, sir,' said Bailey, holding up the diary. 'These show she was at some place called Phung Hu, which the passport confirms as being in Thailand.'

'Yeah, well you can write whatever you want in a diary,' responded Hengrove, 'and us Brits can always slip back into England without so much as a stamp from Customs.'

'But she'd get an exit stamp in Thailand,' countered Bailey.

Sally wasn't sure whether these two were playing the bad cop/nice cop game, but she still found herself warming to the young D.C. 'Would you like another coffee?' she asked Bailey, but it was his boss who answered.

'No time,' intervened the DCI standing up, 'and we've taken enough of yours already, Miss Beckett.'

At the door, Bailey smiled and shook her hand again and she mustered as sweet a smile as she could in return. To Hengrove she said, 'Goodbye, Chief Inspector. I'm sorry I couldn't be more help.'

'So am I.' He paused to give Sally his card. 'Give me a call if anything occurs to you. In the meantime, don't go backpacking abroad again without checking with me first.'

'And why not?'

'Because we might have some more questions we'd like to ask you.'

'Then you won't have as far to come for answers,' responded Sally, with not a little asperity. 'As from tomorrow I'll be up in Norfolk myself, trying to make sense of this whole crazy business.'

* * *

Chapter Three

'This is a very strange situation, Miss Beckett.' For the second time in as many days, Sally was facing a solicitor. Herbert Blenkinsop, however, was very different to his London counterpart. Nearing retirement age, with an avuncular demeanour that well-matched his portly physique, he smoothed back the few hairs left on the top of his head and looked over half-moon spectacles. 'You really had no knowledge of your maternal grandfather?'

'None at all. I always assumed my mother's maiden name was Halard and that Gran's husband, Edward, was her father. Now you tell me that Mum's birth certificate showed her father as this Charles McKenna-Hynes, whose existence I only learned of in your London office yesterday. I took the first train to Norwich this morning, hoping you could throw some light on the mystery.'

For someone who had recently traversed the globe, Sally had found that journey from London surprisingly exciting. Venturing somewhere you had never been before was always thrilling, but all the more so if the destination held secrets to your past that so far defied explanation. It also, of course, held the promise of considerable material gain, but that was something she refused to dwell upon until confirmation that this whole strange business was not just some dreadful mistake. With East Anglian countryside and farmland speeding past in the late winter sunshine, she felt that old tingle of anticipation for situations yet to be discovered. What would this new scene in her life be like? As the train trundled across a river before slipping into Norwich's Thorpe Station, she knew she would soon find out.

Outside the station concourse, Sally took a deep breath of invigorating Norfolk air. The journey had taken less than two hours, but already London and its manic energy seemed worlds away. Across the road she could see large boats moored alongside a quay. That must be the River Wensum which, according to her street guide, lead to the Cathedral. She crossed the road, walked over an ornamental bridge busy with morning traffic and down some steps to where a path led along the riverside.

Spring was only days away, but already there were three hire-cruisers moored on the far bank, alongside a building marked YACHT STATION. It reminded her that, supposedly, she was now the owner of a boatyard. She knew nothing of boats and boatyards and wondered what that could possibly involve. Before even imagining an answer, she arrived at an ancient flint watergate leading into a narrow road lined by buildings rich in period charm. Just beyond, the rising might of a magnificent spire pointed its medieval finger towards the Norfolk sky. Norwich Cathedral. Sally turned towards it and the offices of Landers, Simpson & Hedges.

Now, as she sat in Mr Blenkinsop's office, she thought what an altogether more splendid view he enjoyed than his London brethren. Framed in the small paned window was the whole south wing and cloisters of the Cathedral, a scene probably taken for granted by the solicitor who smiled and shook his head. 'I'm afraid I can't offer you an explanation,' he sighed. 'I was legal advisor to your grandfather for almost thirty years, but knew very little of his personal life. Only that he lived on his own and the only family he ever talked about was you.'

'Me?'

'Oh yes.' Blenkinsop lowered his head and looked higher over his specs, as though evaluating the merit of his client's devotion. 'He always talked warmly of "little Sally" and was obviously very proud of all you had achieved, especially when you graduated from Oxford with honours in economics. That must have been…?'

'… eleven years ago,' completed Sally, shocked and disturbed that strangers should be so familiar with her past.

'Yes, the years go by,' reflected the solicitor. 'In many ways you've hardly changed from when you were a little girl.'

'How could you possibly know?' Sally was finding this conversation increasingly bizarre. 'We've never met before today?'

'No, but I've seen photos,' responded Blenkinsop, smiling. 'Your grandfather liked to show me your latest school one and then, of course, your graduation.'

'But who sent him them?' asked Sally before answering her own question. 'It must have been Gran.'

'Possibly, though Charles very seldom referred to your grandmother,' said Blenkinsop. 'Presumably they separated at some stage, but he never discussed that aspect except to explain how their daughter and your father were tragically killed in a road accident just two years after you were born.'

'But why didn't Gran tell me the truth? The story she always related was that my granddad was called Edward and that he'd been killed on D-day.'

'Which is possibly half-true.' Blenkinsop lowered his head and looked higher over his spectacles. 'Wartime romances were quite common and, possibly, your mother's conception was the result of just such a liaison.'

'So, if her husband Edward was then killed on D-day, surely his death would have allowed Gran to marry this … this father of her love-child,' responded Sally, shaking her head, 'or was this "Granddad Charles" a bad sort?'

'Not at all. He was a charming man as far as my own contact with him went, but remember, Miss Beckett, that your grandmother came from an era when extra-marital affairs, especially while husbands were away fighting for King and Country, were far from accepted by general society. Your grandmother could well have decided that finishing the relationship, and the stigma it would have brought, were preferable to disclosing the truth.'

'Well, I intend to ferret out that truth one way or another,' stated Sally, with determination.

'And in the meantime, you are a very well-off young lady,' said Blenkinsop, taking some documents from his drawer. 'Here are the deeds to *Marsh Haven*, your grandfather's home.'

'*Marsh Haven*,' repeated Sally, 'what a lovely name.'

'And a lovely house too, I believe,' acknowledged Blenkinsop, opening some more legal documents. 'These are the business transfer papers relating to Full-deck Marine, the boatyard also bequeathed to you under the terms of your grandfather's will.'

'My goodness,' Sally gulped, as reality began to sink in, 'me a boatyard owner.'

'And a well-established boatyard at that.' The solicitor leaned forward again. 'Have you any experience of either boats or business, Miss Beckett?'

'Not really,' admitted Sally, 'but I'm a quick learner.'

Blenkinsop smiled. 'I'm sure you are, but don't expect too much help from Henry Higgs.'

'Who's he?'

'The yard manager of Full-deck. Sadly, there was some falling out, several months ago, between him and your grandfather.'

'But he's still working there?'

'Yes, and a very competent man, according to your grandfather but, increasingly, the two ceased to see eye to eye. Originally, he had made provision for Higgs in his will but, about six months ago, I was given instructions to cut him out.'

'Oh dear,' said Sally, anticipating the awkwardness, not to say bitterness, this would inject into future work relations. It also raised another, more sinister aspect of this whole business. 'The circumstances of my granddad's death, Mr Blenkinsop; I believe there was suspicion attached to how he died?'

'Yes, indeed.' The solicitor placed his hands together as though in prayer. 'Personally, I think the coroner would have been content to record "accidental death" if it hadn't been for the evidence of the man who found your grandfather's boat … one of the Navigation Rangers…' Blenkinsop checked a file which Sally guessed must be the Coroner's Report, ' … Jack Fellows. Based on his testimony, the coroner recorded an open verdict.'

'Which means…?'

'… that cause of death remains unclear: accidental or, possibly, suicide.'

'What's your opinion, Mr Blenkinsop?'

The solicitor continued looking down at the papers before him and lightly tapped the fingers of his right hand. 'It pains me to say it, Miss Beckett, but I'm inclined to think suicide. Your grandfather had been rather unwell of late. He actually rang me on February fourteenth to make an appointment to discuss what he termed "extremely urgent business".'

'So you actually spoke to him the day before he died,' confirmed Sally. 'How did he sound then?'

'Physically, much stronger and said he was feeling "fine again", but he was certainly very agitated about something. I told the coroner's court that something had obviously upset him, and they gave an open verdict, meaning they weren't sure whether it was accident or suicide…'

' … or murder,' added Sally, sensing the kindly solicitor's reluctance to even mention the word. 'It's alright, Mr Blenkinsop, the police have already interviewed me on the subject.'

'As they have to do.' The lawyer gave a reassuring smile. 'As the main beneficiary, they would see you as having the prime motive.'

'And, presumably, they will have already interviewed the other persons who benefited in the will…'

'… Ian Haverson and Mrs Jenkins,' completed Blenkinsop, before explaining, 'Haverson was an eco-engineer who had been working with your grandfather on a local project. Mollie Jenkins was your grandfather's housekeeper or, to be more accurate, his domestic for many years. She lives in the village and it's from her you will have to collect the keys to the house and mill.'

"Mill?'

'Oh yes, didn't you know?' smiled Blenkinsop. 'Just behind *Marsh Haven* is a lovely old windmill or, to be specific, a wind*pump*. Your grandfather and Haverson had been working on it together.' Blenkinsop sighed, before adding, 'I'm not too technically-minded I'm afraid, Miss Beckett, but I'm sure young Haverson will explain the project to you.'

'I shall look forward to hearing it,' said Sally, placing the documents in her rucksack and standing up. 'Could I ask your secretary to call a taxi for me please, Mr Blenkinsop.'

'Of course.' The solicitor smiled again. 'Off to see your new property, no doubt?'

'Oh yes,' nodded Sally, 'I can't wait.'

'I can understand that.' Blenkinsop stood up to see her out. 'Are you returning to London tonight or can we book you some accommodation locally?'

It was Sally's turn to smile. 'I'm definitely not returning to London for the foreseeable future, Mr Blenkinsop and, as for accommodation … I intend staying in my late grandfather's house.'

'*Marsh Haven*.' The solicitor seemed quite shocked. 'On your own?'

'Of course!' Sally was surprised at such a reaction. 'Why not?'

'Oh … er … just the association…' But Blenkinsop obviously felt he'd said too much and instead turned his attention to ordering Sally's taxi.

* * *

Chapter Four

Clouds sweeping in from the west now covered the afternoon sun, giving an edge to the wind and a mournful air to the collection of wooden sheds and moored boats that comprised Full-deck Marine.

'So, this is *my* boatyard,' thought Sally, before turning to watch her taxi disappear back through the village, leaving her feeling strangely alone. She looked back to the larger shed where a column of woodsmoke curled upwards from a battered stovepipe atop its corrugated roof. Beyond grimy windows, lights shone dimly, revealing some movement within. Warmth and life beckoned, but she decided to explore a little more before going inside. Shouldering her rucksack, she cautiously made her way along the quay heading, studying the many moored boats as she did so.

They were all motor cruisers, about forty feet long and in uniform grey and yellow. Instead of names painted on their bows, each one had a different playing card depicted. She'd wondered at the boatyard's strange name of Full-deck Marine, and surmised it must be some nautical expression. Now she realised it was a clever play on words. Walking along the quay heading, she found it fun translating the boats' names: *Jack of Clubs, Nine of Spades, Queen of Diamonds*. Through breaks in the cloud, the odd glint of escaping sunlight reflected off shining fibreglass hulls and stainless steel fittings. Peering through the cabin windows of *Ace of Diamonds,* Sally could see a tastefully appointed interior in light wood and modern fabrics. The boat's galley seemed equipped with the very latest appliances. She had never considered a holiday afloat on the Broads, but could now appreciate why so many people did. The walkway led her around the large shed to its far side. There she stopped, mesmerised by the scene.

Before her lay a wide expanse of open water, its edges fringed by encircling reedbeds which, in turn, appeared to stretch from horizon to horizon. This must be what they call "a broad", mused Sally as she wandered out along a wooden jetty, at the end of which, a small open dory lay tied with a single rope. How vast the sky looked here, compared to London. The surface of the broad was glistening now as the sun burst through the clouds, its fanning rays seeming to touch the sails of a towering windmill that stood sentinel-like above the distant reedbeds. I wonder if that's *my* mill, thought Sally, at the same time suddenly conscious of a strange whooshing of air above her head. She looked up in time to see a flight of swans winging overhead, the rhythmical beating of their wings slowing gradually as they translated into gliding descent to the white-flecked water. For a while she just stood there, entranced by the beauty of this timeless scene.

The whine of a power-tool from the shed behind her, brought Sally back to reality and the prospect of her forthcoming meeting with Henry Higgs, the yard manager. She was apprehensive, knowing as she did, that there had been bad blood between him and her grandfather in the last few months of the old man's life. 'Ah well, here goes,' she said to herself, taking a deep breath, opening the rickety door and stepping inside.

Here within, the aroma of wood, sawdust, engine oil and rotting marine life welcomed Sally to her new world. The shed was filled by the bulk of a motor-cruiser with the two-of-clubs depicted on its bow. It looked huge, sitting high and dry on a wheeled trestle that had obviously been used to haul it up the slipway sloping away under big double doors. Half a dozen men busied themselves around the boat at various tasks, but they all glanced around as a blast of cold air accompanied Sally's entrance. She didn't blame them; the only source of heat in the whole building seemed to emanate from a single potbelly stove that was glowing red-hot in the corner. A young man turned away from throwing more wood into its fiery innards. Suddenly meeting Sally, his face broke into a shy, but genuine, smile. 'Hello, Miss. What can we be doin' for yer?'

It took Sally a second to mentally translate the warm colloquial accent, before she smiled back. 'Hello ... what's your name?'

Obviously startled that anyone should take even the remotest interest in his being, the young lad stammered back, 'Me? I'm Tom Brewer, Miss.'

'Nice to meet you Tom.' Sally held out her hand. Tom glanced at his own, wiped it on equally grimy overalls and then gingerly took Sally's. She smiled again 'Now ... Tom ... Mr Higgs, the yard manager...' she glanced around the several inquisitive faces now peering at hers, '... is he here?'

Brewer nodded, seemingly relieved he could answer the question. 'Yeah, he's here. I'll show yer.' The lad led her around to the other side of the cruiser, where a big engine stood shackled to chains and overhead tackle, obviously ready for hoisting.

Two men were bending over it, one in overalls and the other, a huge bear of a man, in twill trousers and heavy parka. The latter straightened up. 'You've wasted enough time on this already; just get the thing in there.' He suddenly sensed Tom standing behind him. 'Yes, what do you want, Brewer?'

'A young lady to see yer, Mr Higgs.'

The big man turned round, his face unexpectedly handsome in a rugged sort of way, despite the deep-rooted scowl. He scanned Sally's presence with humourless eyes, said nothing and turned back to the engine. 'I want this in and running by two tomorrow. Get on with it.' He turned back to Sally. 'Right, what can I do for you?'

'I'm Sally Beckett, Mr Higgs.' She held out her hand.

'Yes, I know who you are.' Henry Higgs' hands went deliberately into his pockets as he nodded and said, 'The gov'nor's granddaughter?'

'Yes.' Sally looked around the workshop at yard hands seemingly intent on various tasks, but obviously straining to catch every word. 'Mr Higgs, is there somewhere we can talk in private?'

He grunted in reply and led Sally across the shed, but not before turning back to young Tom Brewer. 'So what are you standing around for? Get back to scraping that hull.'

The office that Higgs led Sally to was virtually a box in the corner of the shed, cluttered with boat bits and furnished with just two filing cabinets, a desk and two hard chairs. The yard manager squeezed into the one behind the desk, stretched his legs and again placed big hands inside his parka pockets. 'So *you're* the new gov'nor are you?'

This was all about as unfriendly a greeting as Sally could imagine. She looked around the office, more to collect her thoughts than show any interest in its state. Then she shut the door, pulled across the other chair and said, 'Mr Higgs, may I sit down?'

The yard manager gave another grunt that Sally was now recognising as the closest he came to an affirmative.

'Yes I am, as you put it, the "new gov'nor".' Sally had already decided that she would not even attempt a discussion on the mysteries of her strange inheritance with this man. Instead she met Higgs' cold eyes with her own and asked, 'Have you any problem with that?'

Higgs stuck out a petulant lower lip. 'You any idea what it takes to run a boatyard?'

'None at all...' Sally glanced through the office's small window onto the workshop floor. The men were busy again on the cruiser, chatting away as they worked. She guessed the arrival of the "new governor" might be one topic, though the odd burst of laughter showed their humour was the same as working men anywhere. Nevertheless, from the second she'd entered, she had sensed an underlying atmosphere in this workshop and had no doubt that its cause sat before her now. She turned again to Henry Higgs, ' ... but I do have experience of people and

I can tell you now, I will be making changes here.'

The yard manager looked at Sally through narrowing eyes. 'What sort a changes?'

'I don't know until I've evaluated the whole operation. First I want to look at the books. Who does the accounts?'

Higgs nodded in the direction of the unseen village. 'Jayne Howlett is the bookkeeper … comes in every Thursday.'

'The day after tomorrow … good…' Sally stood up. '… I'll come in then and go through them with her. Right now I'm going to walk into the village to collect the keys to Granddad's house from Mrs Jenkins.'

'The keys to *Marsh Haven*?' Higgs seemed taken aback if not downright shocked. 'You're surely not intending to *stay* there.'

'Of course; why not?'

Higgs shook his head. 'You got any idea how lonely it is out there?' He gave a scoff. 'You'll be scared to death, girl.'

'*Mr* Higgs,' emphasised, Sally, 'let me say again, I *will* be staying at *Marsh Haven* and, before you try and frighten me again, let me assure you I am quite capable of looking after myself without being "scared".' She turned towards the door. 'I'll be back in about an hour and then I'll need transport. Does Full-deck Marine have a vehicle that can take me?'

'To the house?' The yard manager threw back his head and laughed. It was a hollow laugh filled with derision. 'Just shows how you city types don't know much about these parts. There's only a rough footpath leading to *Marsh Haven* and that's too boggy to use during the winter months.'

'So how did my grandfather go to and fro?' asked Sally, conscious that Higgs was enjoying this exposure of her ignorance.

'By boat, of course.'

'Which boat?'

'His dory.'

'Is that the boat moored on the end of the jetty?'

Higgs nodded. 'Yes, but you can't have it. It's the yard boat. We need it here.'

Sally turned back and moved closer to the yard manager's desk, glad he was still seated. 'Mr Higgs, as this is now *my* yard, I presume the dory is *my* boat and as such, I will be using it from now on.'

Higgs paused for a second as he struggled to handle the phenomenon of having his word challenged. He nodded through the window. 'I've got work to get done out there. I can't spare yard hands to go running you around.'

'No problem…' Sally couldn't quite believe the words she heard herself saying next, '… I'll drive the boat myself.'

'You ever handled a boat before?'

'I've experience of boats, yes,' nodded Sally without explaining it was only as a passenger. 'I'll need one of the men to show me the controls and then I'll take it from there.'

'Not this afternoon you won't,' Higgs grunted, as he sat further back in his chair. 'I need it myself.'

'Then you've got one hour.' Sally picked up her rucksack with deliberate impatience. 'I'll be back by then and I expect the dory here and a hand standing by to check me out.' Then, without a backward glance, she walked out of her yard manager's office, slamming his door with a bang loud enough to make the whole workforce jump.

Outside, the fresh air smelt good as she breathed in deeply, took a few seconds to regain her thoughts and then strode off purposely towards the village. 'I can see this is going to be a barrel of fun,' she thought grimly. Just beyond the boatyard, hard by the water's edge, was a thatch-roofed pub. *The Steamboat* proclaimed the signboard, swinging and creaking in the now-gusting wind. Several open boats and one large cruiser lay moored in the pub dyke just outside. Smoke curled up from the tall chimney. The thought of warmth and a stiff drink were enticing indeed, but Sally stayed resolutely on course for Mrs Jenkins'. For that reason she didn't see the man in a hooded wax jacket who stood just behind the far pub wall, watching her with more than casual interest.

He continued watching Sally until she was out of sight.

* * *

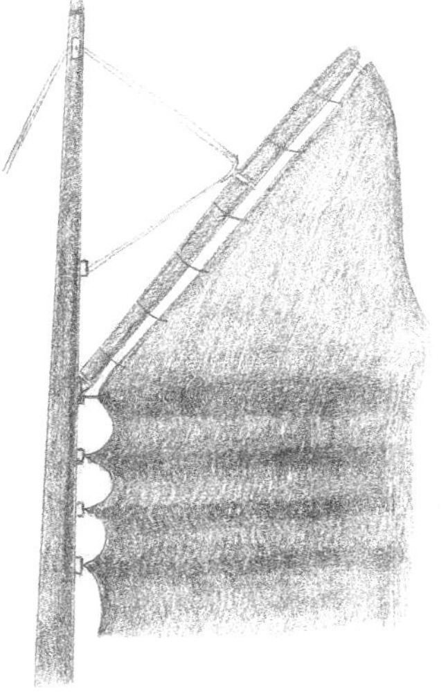

Chapter Five

Lichens was a small terraced cottage in the centre of the village.

'Miss Sally!' The late-middle-aged, rather short and stocky lady who opened its door, gasped and held a work-worn hand to her breast.

'And you must be Mrs Jenkins,' replied Sally, conscious that here was another who knew more about her than she did them.

'Oh, how wonderful.' Mrs Jenkins glanced around Sally to check she was alone and seemed pleased she was. 'Come in my dear and have a cup of tea.'

Lichens' living room was small and cosy, a crackling coal fire throwing a welcome warmth over shag-pile rugs and the armchairs either side of the hearth. One had knitting hastily dropped onto its well-indented cushion. Mollie Jenkins ushered Sally into the other, scooped up the knitting and sat down facing her, a glow of excitement colouring her cheeks.

'You have a very snug home here, Mrs Jenkins.' Sally looked around the ornament littered interior with its background aroma of coal-smoke and home baking.

Her hostess smiled. 'Yes, and it nearly is *mine* now. Rented it for years, me and Mr Jenkins did, but he's been gone these last ten an', with the job finishing an' like, I was wonderin' how I'd keep up the rent. But then your dear granddad so kindly remembered me in his will an' now I've done a deal with the landlord to buy it jus' as soon as I have my money.'

'That's wonderful, Mrs Jenkins.' Sally was genuinely pleased that some happiness could result from tragedy.

The housekeeper hunched her shoulders in a gesture of genuine glee. 'Fancy you being here again, Miss Sally, after all these years.'

'It's good to be here, but why do you say "again"? Have I ever been here before?'

'Not for many a year you ain't.' Mollie Jenkins gave another smile of sad nostalgia. 'A babe in your mum's arms you were, the last time you were here along with your granny, Emily. A year later and your dear mum had passed on an' I never sees you ag'in 'til today; only the photos that your granddad always proudly showed me.'

There was a genuine warmth in the way this simple woman spoke of a family, only one of whom Sally had ever known. She had no hesitation about laying her cards on the table. 'Mrs Jenkins, there are many things about my granddad and this whole situation that I know nothing of. For a start, have you any idea why he and my gran lived separate lives?'

Mollie Jenkins shrugged. 'Not really; your granddad was a very private man who never talked about such things. We did just get on the subject once but all he'd say was that there were "political reasons" why they din't, whatever that meant. He din't say no more an' Cap'ain Charles weren't a man to push on such things he din't want you to know.'

'"*Captain* Charles"...?'

The housekeeper raised her shoulders again and smiled impishly. 'Yer, we all called him that locally. He let drop once that he'd spent some time in the navy an' ran his house an' boatyard like it was some ship, so I called him Cap'ain Charles once, an' it caught on.'

'And he didn't mind?'

'Bless me, no! It started when we was talkin' 'bout nicknames once an' I asks him if he'd ever had one. "I was called Caloy once" he says but din't explain why. "Well, I'm goin' to call you Cap'ain Charles", I said an' it kinda stuck from there. Fact is,' she concluded with another nostalgic smile, 'I think he sorta liked it.'

'He sounds as if he was a lovely old man.' Sally was intrigued to know more. 'Do you have a photo of him, Mrs Jenkins?'

'Jus' one.' Mollie Jenkins wrestled out of her chair, went to the cluttered sideboard and returned with a framed colour print. 'Liked his pipe, did Cap'ain Charles.'

Sally took the photo, fascinated to see this image of a man who had brought such a dramatic yet emotional change to her life.

Pipe in mouth, Charles McKenna-Hynes stood beside his somewhat self-conscious housekeeper, a man with a tanned kindly face lined by life and the elements and framed by a mane of snow-white hair and a beard to match. Although stooped, there was still a hint of naval bearing in his tall thin frame and Sally could see why Mrs Jenkins had called him "Captain". 'He seems the sort of granddad every girl would want,' sighed Sally. She handed back the photo. 'You were obviously very close to him, Mrs Jenkins, but surely he had other family besides Gran and me?'

Mollie Jenkins shook her head. 'None that I ever knew nor heard of. I did ask him once but he said his own family were "lost in time" whatever that meant.'

'But where were his roots? Was he a local man?' quizzed Sally.

'From little things he let drop, I got the impression his family were from Scotland,' answered the housekeeper smiling nostalgically, 'His name were Scottish and his accent a bit as well.'

'So how did he end up in Norfolk?'

'Went to school here, he told me, and fell in love with the place.' Mollie Jenkins spoke as though that was only natural. 'Apparently he sailed on the Broads in those days an' promised hisself he would live on them one day and so he did,' she completed with a touch of sadness returning to her voice.

'And so he did,' repeated Sally wistfully, almost to herself, but the thought of her grandfather's home brought her back to reality. She had already decided that now was not the time to discuss the manner of his death, and there were other more pressing and practical arrangements to make. She stood up to go and turned to the homely lady beside her. 'Mrs Jenkins, I intend staying in *Marsh Haven* for at least the immediate future and…'

'Stay in *Marsh Haven…*' interrupted Mrs Jenkins before Sally could even explain further, '… are you sure?'

'Yes, quite sure … why not?' This was the third person today expressing surprise at the occupation of what was now her own home.

Mollie Jenkins paused and then said, 'Well, it's just that it ain't been lived in since … since the Cap'ain went and there ain't even any electricity connected now. I wouldn't like to say how much dust has piled up in all these weeks an'…'

'Well, I won't even see it if there aren't any lights,' responded Sally, feeling it was time to cut through the housekeeper's emotions, 'but that's what I wanted to discuss with you. I'm going to be busy enough sorting out the boatyard without worrying about the house. You obviously know it so well and, in a way, I'm sure it knows you. I never knew my grandfather, Mrs Jenkins, but having you back in the house would, at least, give me some continuity with the past.' She took her host's hands between her own. 'Will you come back to *Marsh Haven* as *my* housekeeper?'

For a few seconds Mollie Jenkins didn't answer, but just stood there with slightly watering eyes. Then, between enthusiastic nods, she said, 'Oh, Miss Sally, I'd love to. I thought I'd never see the old house again, but doing for you will seem just like old times. Besides,' she added, glancing around the walls of her home, 'I'll still need a job to pay the bills on *Lichens*, even though it is almost mine now.' Mollie Jenkins' face showed her obvious excitement. 'When would you like me to start?'

'As soon as possible. How would tomorrow be?'

'Lovely,' responded the housekeeper before some practicalities occurred to her, 'but how will I get in? Cap'ain Charles always picked me up from the staithe in the dory…'

'... and I'll do the same,' assured Sally without mentioning she had yet to handle this intimidating craft. 'What time?'

'Eight o'clock if that's not too early.'

'Fine. Now, I need the keys and what about the electricity...?'

'I'll call Ian Haverson right now and get him to come in and reconnect,' said Mrs Jenkins, taking a large ancient-looking set of keys from a drawer and handing them to Sally. 'It probably won't be 'til tomorrow though as he's usually off somewhere in that there boat of his.'

'Ian Haverson,' said Sally, placing the keys in her rucksack pocket and remembering this third beneficiary was someone she had wanted to discuss with Mrs Jenkins. 'Who is he, exactly?'

'Ah, a nice young man is Ian,' responded Mrs Jenkins enthusiastically. 'He's one of them engineers what specialises in new ways to make electricity without oil ... what do you call 'em...?'

'Eco-engineers?'

'Yes, that's right. The Cap'ain had a big interest in that sorta stuff. Together, him an' Ian had some scheme to get the old Broads' mills puttin' out electricity or somethin' like that.' Mollie Jenkins chuckled to herself. 'Ian had the technical know-how, Cap'ain Charles the money, an' they both had the enthusiasm, so they made a right pair with their bright ideas. Not jus' ideas either 'cos they got the old mill at *Marsh Haven* makin' electricity for the house, but that was switched off when....'

'But you'll get this Ian Haverson to switch it back on,' interrupted Sally, determined to keep things on track. 'It will be a good chance to meet him as well.'

'Yes, but, in the meantime, you'll need somethin' to light your way,' worried Mrs Jenkins. 'The cooker's gas from cylinders so you'll be alright there, but you'll need some candles and a torch.' She nodded down the road. 'Village store sells 'em. Get yourself plenty, my dear, an' I'll get on to Ian.'

'Right,' said Sally, choosing not to think too much about spending her first night in her late-grandfather's house in semi-darkness. 'Well, I'd better be going if I'm to get to *Marsh Haven* before dark.' She opened the door and Mrs Jenkins saw her to the gate.

'At least the parish lantern's working for you,' said the housekeeper, glancing up.

'The parish lantern?' Sally could see no form of street lighting.

'The moon; that's what we used to call it in the villages in the old days,' explained Mrs Jenkins, looking up again to where an almost-full moon peered through the rapidly breaking overcast.

'"Parish Lantern", what a lovely description. I love moonlight and I can see myself sitting up tonight just gazing over those marshes bathed in its glow.' It was said half-heartedly, but she was unprepared for the concern that clouded Mollie Jenkins' otherwise warm features.

'No,' she said, fixing Sally's eyes with hers, 'you don't want to do that, Miss Sally.'

'Why ever not?' Sally was getting just a little tired of local worries and warnings.

''Cos you see things you don't want to if you go lookin' out over them marshes at night.' Mrs Jenkins wore a gold cross on a chain around her neck and Sally noticed her instinctively fingering it as she spoke. Before there was chance for further discussion, the housekeeper hugged and kissed her, confirmed, 'Tomorrow at eight then, Miss Sally,' and disappeared back into *Lichens* leaving her new employer wondering again what a strange world she was finding herself drawn into.

* * *

By the time Sally reached the village store, the sun was already low in the sky. Less than an hour would see it disappear completely below the western horizon. Conscious she had a first trip in an unfamiliar boat to an equally unfamiliar house ahead of her, she spent only minutes inside the store buying a dozen candles, a box of matches, a small torch and some groceries which she stuffed into her rucksack. Even this simple transaction was accompanied by a slightly unnerving encounter, though it was innocent enough in itself. Leaving the shop, she noticed a man on the other side of the road. He turned abruptly as Sally looked in his direction, the raised hood of his wax jacket preventing any clear view of his face. He had a pair of powerful binoculars slung around his neck so, presumably, he was a birdwatcher or suchlike. Much as he appeared to avoid Sally's gaze, she was well aware of him following her along the street as she quickened her step back to Full-deck's yard.

It was with some relief that she found the yard lad, Tom Brewer, standing by at the end of the jetty to get her away in the dory.

* * *

'You ever handled one of these afore, Miss?' Tom asked, as he helped Sally aboard and stowed her rucksack on a thwart.

'Not one *exactly* like this,' answered Sally, settling herself behind the wheel and feeling the situation needed a little economy with the truth, 'so you'd better explain it all, starting with that engine hanging on the back?'

'Transom ... the back end's called the transom,' explained Tom, seemingly astonished that he could know more than someone else on any subject. 'Engine's warm so...' He leaned down and turned the key and the outboard purred to life. 'This is your throttle, Miss.' He leaned down and touched the lever by Sally's side, giving a couple of bursts of power to emphasise the point. 'Push it forward for "ahead" and back for "astern". Wheel steers it in the normal way. No more than five miles per hour on the broad an' keep clear of the shallows. Right, off you go,' he finalised, jumping ashore, untying the lines and throwing them into the dory's open interior. 'Have a good trip.'

'This must be the shortest checkout ever,' thought Sally, suddenly feeling horribly ignorant and alone. 'Is that *Marsh Haven*?' she shouted, pointing to the house and mill on the far edge of the broad.

'Yep; take yer 'bout fifteen minutes,' shouted Tom above the noise of the engine, as Sally pushed the throttle forward too hard and surged away at the head of a maelstrom of prop-wash.

'Just concentrate going the right way,' she said aloud to herself as she gripped the wheel and attempted to point the dory up the broad. After a few curving S-turns she managed to stabilise direction enough to scan the broader picture. On either side, curling waves were fanning out from the dory's fast-moving stern, causing the few boats lying at scattered moorings on either side to rock alarmingly. Clearly she was going too fast. Gingerly, she brought the throttle back, causing engine note, speed and wake to all reduce immediately. Perhaps too much, for now the dory was barely idling along and the engine seemed ready to stop. Using a little more *feel* this time, Sally eased the throttle slightly open again causing the engine-note to sound so much smoother and the wash behind, to only moderately increase. 'Looks good,' she told herself, feeling pleased that already she was learning new skills to go with her new life. She took a deep breath, sat back, eased her grip on the wheel and found time to even take in her surroundings.

On either side, the expanse of the broad stretched away, its surface broken by small wavelets that danced on the wind towards the surrounding marshes. From the dory's bluff bow, a moderate wave went to join them, with the little vessel responding to just the merest touch of the wheel. She knew that shortly she would have to bring this boat to some sort of landing but, right now, the feeling of control in an otherwise unfamiliar environment, was something she found utterly entrancing.

All too soon, however, she had crossed the mile-long broad and was approaching the pleasing aspect of her new home. It didn't front directly onto the broad and was partly hidden by encircling reedbeds, but the mill loomed high above them and glimpses of the house showed a fairly large building in the style of a chalet bungalow. The roof was thatched with attractive "eyebrowed" dormer windows worked into its craftsmanship in a way that seemed so at one with its surroundings. At one end, an intriguing framed structure rose even higher than the roof and must be some sort of lookout tower. Behind *Marsh Haven*, standing like some sentinel against the darkening sky, was the mill, its huge stilled sails seemingly forming a cross of remembrance to its late owner. The mill tower was brick and black in direct contrast to the house which, Sally noted, was of lapboard construction and painted white. She was wondering how to reach the house from the broad when she noticed a small gap in the reeds and steered towards it. It led her into a narrow channel that twisted slightly before emerging at the very front of the house.

Tongue in cheek and hands clenching the wheel, she cautiously brought the dory in. Ahead of her now, close to the house, was a wooden jetty with a lovely old sailing boat moored alongside it. Astern of this large boat, a small mast projected from the water, something else to avoid as Sally aimed the dory further along the jetty. She had closed the throttle as soon as she saw the mooring, but still the dory was moving at a fair speed with the jetty getting closer by the second. Tom Brewer hadn't explained anything about brakes, so how did you stop and park these things? "Pull back on the throttle to go astern", he'd said. Presumably that meant reversing which surely would have some sort of stopping effect. Sally pulled the small lever back to neutral and then even further back. The engine note rose again and a welter of propwash surged ahead of her. The dory, however, was duly slowing.

Slowing and then stopping and now, heaven forbid, going backwards! Not only that, she had turned the wheel slightly to steer in, but the wretched boat was turning the other way! Almost frantically, she returned the throttle to "forward" and the backward movement ceased and, once more, they were turning the correct way. 'Obviously, the steering reverses with the engine,' she said to herself as the boat once again moved ahead and she steered towards the ever-nearing jetty. It was time to stop the boat once again, but she wanted to put the jetty on her left-hand side. Trying to remember what she had just learned, she now gingerly turned the wheel to the left, at the same time easing the throttle into the 'astern' position. Once again, the dory slowed, but this time the back swung the way she wanted, with the result that the boat now stopped almost parallel to the jetty. There was still a gap of two feet or so between boat and landing, but a bit of pulling with the boathook soon had it reduced to nothing. 'Phew, I've done it,' thought Sally as she breathed a great sigh of relief before clambering ashore with the lines.

There were rings on the jetty's edge and she tied the ropes to these, realising as she did so that her knowledge of knots was about as limited as her seamanship. However, a few turns and a tangle seemed to have things reasonably secure. She reached into the dory, grabbed her rucksack and moved along the jetty to where the small mast stuck up suspiciously from below. Presumably, it belonged to a small dinghy now sitting unhappily on the bottom. This was another problem that would need sorting in the near future. She passed on to the larger boat that was moving slightly in the residual wind.

Sally guessed it must be at least thirty feet long, with a wooden mast seemingly tapering forever upwards and supported by a veritable web of rigging. Like the boats in the yard, this yacht had a playing card depicted on the ... what did Tom Brewer call it?... transom. *Ace of Hearts* had obviously been a loved and beautiful boat in her time, but now the sleek white hull was streaked by dirt, the varnished cabin dull with grime and the lovely little brass portholes, green with incipient verdigris. 'This must have been Granddad's sailing cruiser,' she thought, 'the one he...' Sally shuddered slightly and thought how sad he would be to see his beloved boat in such a state. She turned away, but not before promising herself that *Ace of Hearts* would, one day soon, be restored to her obvious former loveliness. It was the least she could do for a man she had never known, but who had so generously changed her life. The wooden walkway led towards the house and, almost reluctantly, she followed it.

She should have been feeling excitement and anticipation, standing on the doorstep of a dream-home and new life. Instead she felt sad and strangely down, as though the shades of her dead grandfather were still hovering around his beloved home, trying to tell her that the truth of his parting was something still to be discovered.

* * *

Chapter Six

Sally looked up at the mill. It stood about thirty metres beyond the house, its tapering black brickwork towering over all and surmounted by a white wooden structure that looked somewhat akin to an inverted boat. The open structure of the stilled sails had formed a handy perch for several large black birds, which sat with almost primeval brooding, as they surveyed this interloper to their domain. 'Cormorants,' thought Sally, deciding they did nothing to alleviate the sinister ambience that this whole scene instilled. Still following the walkway, she wound her way around the house, searching for the entrance and the source of the gentle, melodious notes that were causing her skin to prickle.

The wind chimes hung beside the green-painted main door, the bamboos producing a continuous random peel as they moved in the slight gusts of wind. She had grown used to them in Thailand and normally liked their cheerful greeting but, at this isolated home of the not-long dead, she found sound and movement produced without the touch of a human hand, something she could do without. Resisting the urge to head back to a room at the inn, she instead fumbled in her rucksack for the keys, placed the largest in the lock, turned the well-oiled levers and went inside.

Her first impression was the smell. It was not unpleasant, just the slightly musty odour expected in a house that had been left unoccupied for a few months. There was another smell lingering that Sally *couldn't* quite define, but which was causing a distinct feeling of unease. Probably nerves, she told herself and, knowing she had only a short while to get her bearings in the rapidly failing light, she moved swiftly from the small hallway into what must be the main lounge.

It was a large room that obviously combined the functions of sitting room, dining room and study, for to one side was a sturdy wooden desk, a large brass lamp and some papers piled beside it. Indeed, wood and brass seemed to be the dominant materials for the furnishings which, perhaps, was to be expected in the home of a man whose life had been boats and all things nautical. Even the floors were polished wood, which squeaked slightly beneath the homely oriental rugs that lay scattered throughout. They led Sally to the comfortable looking armchairs and sofas with flowered loose covers that surrounded a large black stove set against the room's long side. A wood-burner, she observed gleefully and knew that lighting a fire would be her second immediate job.

Her first was to find the kitchen. When she did, it was large and homely with a sturdy farmhouse-style table and chairs filling its centre. The units surrounding the sides were just as functional, their style dating back a good three decades. In one of the wall cupboards she found the crockery and selected six saucers. Returning with them to the lounge, she took the candles from her rucksack and placed a lighted one in each. Now, with the day all but gone, she at least had light.

Back in the kitchen, she lit the hob, put a kettle on to boil and then took the torch and went back out to the rear of the house. In a small lean-to shed, she found a pile of chopped logs and a stack of old newspapers beside them. An armful of both carried back to the lounge soon had her busy feeding them into the stove. Her nautical knowledge might be pretty limited, she decided, but months of backpacking and, sometimes living rough, had made her pretty practical when it came to establishing the basic comforts of life. It wasn't long before flames were licking the stove's interior, allowing her to return to the kitchen to make the mug of tea she'd been promising herself all afternoon. Back in the lounge before the now blazing stove, mug in hand, Sally instinctively huddled closer to its enticing glow.

Funny how fire and warmth could change your whole outlook on life, she pondered as she lay back on the thick-piled rug, sipped her tea and felt the coldness of the room and her own feelings being replaced by a warm glow of contentment.

In fact, the whole place seemed to be coming alive now, the flickering firelight causing shadows to dance across the walls and boarded ceiling. It wouldn't have taken a lot of imagination to see sinister shapes in those prancing forms, but Sally was determined to let nothing detract from the peace of the first evening in her new home. In fact, already she found herself *knowing* that this would be home from now on, her house in London seeming a world away and fast becoming just a distant memory. It had been a long day, full of emotions and new experiences. Now the relief of finally being here, coupled with the warmth of the fire, was causing her eyelids to droop.

It would have been very easy to simply curl up on this cosy rug and go to sleep, but it was too early for that. The coldness of the rest of *Marsh Haven* didn't exactly beckon, but Sally decided she should explore before having a bite to eat and settling down for the night. Taking one of the candles, she went back into the hall and slowly up the stairs.

It was a mistake. Once again, away from the fireside, the chilly interior created an altogether different atmosphere. Climbing the stairs, the flickering light of the candle reflected off paintings of mainly marine subjects lining the ascending wooden walls. Sally went up slowly, step by step, as the creaking staircase angled through ninety degrees to the landing, where a long corridor ran the length of the house. She turned right, peering through doorways at a sparsely furnished guestroom and a junk-filled box-room. Then she headed back along the corridor to find another guestroom and, opposite that, a bathroom. Facing her at the very end of the corridor was a door which must be the master bedroom. She gingerly eased it open as though, irrationally, she might wake some slumbering person within.

It was, of course, empty of life, but pleasantly furnished with the end wall virtually all French window. Outside was now total darkness, but Sally went to check the view anyway and just as immediately realised why this main bedroom of the house was situated here. Spread before her, bathed in moonlight, was the broad. The wind had died now, allowing the smooth surface to reflect the lunar light and seemingly illuminate the surrounding dykes and marshes as well. These seemed to stretch for miles around, a vista of enchanting desolation with just a cluster of twinkling lights a mile away, marking the position of boatyard and village. For the first time, Sally realised how isolated *Marsh Haven* really was.

This wonderful outlook was, however, not totally unobstructed: the French windows opened out onto a balcony with a surrounding handrail and a hefty wooden framework containing a vertical ladder. This must be the lookout tower she had seen when approaching *Marsh Haven*. If the view from the bedroom was breathtaking, what must it be at a higher level yet? Keen to see for herself, she turned the key already in the lock. As she did so, she recalled Mollie Jenkins' warning to "Never look out over the marshes at night". Stuff and nonsense thought Sally but, just the same, she found herself re-locking the French windows and deciding that perhaps daylight would be a better time to check out *Marsh Haven*'s further attractions. Instead, she turned her attentions back to the bedroom and its furnishings.

These were plain enough with no pretensions to style or glamour but, nevertheless, cosy. There were two large wardrobes along one side and, facing down the room, a large double bed covered by a colourful throw. Bedside tables held brass lamps and some framed photographs. Sally went closer and picked up the largest frame. By the flickering light of the candle she studied an old black and white photograph of herself as a little girl. Perhaps she should have been prepared for this, but it was still slightly unsettling to think of her image in the bedroom of a man she had never known, in a place she had never heard of. Alongside this photo was another of a young woman holding a baby. It was a photo she hadn't seen before, but something told her the woman was a young Granny Emily and the baby, Sally's own mother. On the other table was a photograph that she *had* seen before: her mother as a young girl. Next to this was a studio portrait of Emily when she must have been in her twenties. For the first time, Sally realised what a strikingly beautiful woman her grandmother had been, and a romantic one too, judging by the dedication written across the corner in her gran's distinctive hand.

To my darling E.

My love always.

E xxx

It was obviously a loving endearment, but why to "Darling E" and not "C" for Charles? "E" had to be Granny Emily's husband Edward, the man Sally had always been told was her grandfather. Why would this Charles McKenna-Hynes have a photo dedicated to another man by his lonely bedside? She picked up the third photo, a happy snap of a young bearded man smoking a pipe, arms entwined around a pretty girl, who Sally again recognised as her gran. That must be the young Charles, she thought, with an inward smile.

She looked again at the photo and suddenly recognised the strange odour lingering in every room of *Marsh Haven*. It was the smell of burned pipe tobacco. Even more unnerving, for the first time she noticed the indentation of a head in one of the pillows beside her.

She dropped the photo onto the bed and left the room, the candle flame spluttering at the speed of her departure.

* * *

Back in the warmth and glow of the fireside, Sally took a hold on her nerves and stock of her emotions. She had inherited a beautiful house, a working business and a sizeable amount of cash, *but* she was also away from her lifetime home and friends and a stranger in an area virtually unknown to her. The local people must be regarding her with curiosity and, possibly, some with resentment. Added to that, her first night was being spent in an isolated house full of mystery, and last occupied by a possible murder victim whose shades still seemed to be lingering within. Little wonder she felt disturbed. 'Well, do something,' she told herself, 'and take your mind off the situation. Find a book to read.'

There were hundreds of books in the cases lining the walls and selecting one of these wouldn't even require her leaving the comfort of the lounge. Candle in hand once more, she made her way around the room, examining the framed paintings on the intervening wall as she did so. The use of colour in these watercolours was very familiar and a glance at the artist's signature at the foot of each confirmed it to be Granny Emily. These studies were of woodlands, marshlands, sea shores and tumbling ocean waves, whereas the only paintings of her grandmother's that Sally had seen until now had been of birdlife. Emily was regarded with some high regard in that genre, but this was an aspect of her gran's talent unknown until now. Sally shook her head at another revelation and moved on to the books.

It was no surprise to find the majority of them devoted to the sea and ships. Finding a slushy novel was going to be a futile task but, amongst the rest of this impressive library, she did find several books relating to the Broads and Broadland. At least that was a pertinent subject. She thumbed through several works covering the history and ecology of the area, but all far too deep for a relaxing read. Then, right at the end, she found one that caught her eye and imagination in one ill-starred second.

Ghosts and Legends of Broadland

If there was ever a book that shouldn't be read on a dark night in a strange house, it was this one, but Sally felt the need for distraction from her own strange situation. Perhaps a bit of supernatural lore might be the escape she needed. She settled down in the firelight and soon found herself lost in the book's absorbing content.

The Broads, according to this work at least, were well-endowed with ghostly happenings. Perhaps the book was meant to be read with tongue in cheek, but some of the encounters, especially when related by eyewitnesses were scary enough. Here were stories of phantom wherries and Viking longships, strange lights, haunted abbeys with their even ghostlier monks and a whole chapter on a demon dog called Black Shuck, who promised death within a year to anyone encountering its spectral form. Stopping only to throw some more logs into the stove, Sally glanced at her watch and saw with surprise that it was nearing midnight. Apart from the crackling logs, the house was silent and suddenly she again felt very tired.

Until this point, she hadn't even given a thought to where she would make her bed for the night. Somehow, she didn't feel drawn to upstairs and this rug before the fire was cosy enough for a night's kip. Without even bothering to draw the curtains, she pulled some cushions off the sofa, simply curled up where she was, closed her eyes and let her thoughts mull over what had been a very full day. Those thoughts only lasted seconds before sheer exhaustion, combined with the warmth of the stove, lulled her into a deep and blissful sleep.

It would have also been a long sleep if the sound hadn't woken her.

* * *

Sally reached for the bedside lamp that wasn't there before the slow realisation came to her that she was far from her London home and suddenly awake in a strange house in Norfolk. She groped for the torch, shone it on her watch and saw it was three o'clock in the morning. Death's midnight, she'd once heard it called, but why had she woken at this unearthly hour? Just as quickly the answer came in the sound of timber percussion.

The wind chimes. Obviously the wind was blowing again, causing the bamboos to re-play their erratic composition. Sally got up, went to the window and looked out onto the mooring. The moon had moved far across the heavens now, but its light reflected off millpond-calm water. There *was* no wind.

Then, what had caused the chimes to sound? It was a question that caused a little shiver to pulse through Sally's tingling skin. 'Don't be silly,' she told herself, 'obviously a bird or something has caught the chimes.' But, even as she grabbed this lifeline of rationalisation she saw something outside that instantly transformed slight unease into pure, undiluted terror.

* * *

Chapter Seven

There, standing close by the water in the eerie moonlight, was a figure. A black cloak covered the body and a cowl, the face. It was as motionless as the reeds and waters behind, and projected an atmosphere just as chilling. Sally thought of the accounts of phantom monks from the abbey she had been reading about that very night and felt her blood turning to ice.

Slowly, the figure moved. Sally stood frozen, transfixed into immobility, but all too aware of this apparition's intentions: it was heading straight for the window where she stood.

What should she do? Scream was the reaction that seemed to be surging up her throat, but she managed to choke it back. She needed to do something, but what? How did you fight a ghost? Then she realised she was still holding the torch. As a weapon it had its limitations, but it was better than nothing. By now the phantom monk was right by the window and reaching for the frame.

With a racing heart, Sally decided that, if nothing else, she would get a better look at this … this "thing" which was manifesting itself outside. Raising the torch, she flashed its beam straight at the figure now virtually facing her on the other side of the glass.

She wasn't sure what to expect, but the result was all too predictable: the torchlight reflected straight back, producing an area of only framed blackness and her own horrified features.

But if vision had disappeared, sound hadn't and, from outside, she could hear the most *un*-ghostly thud of a figure running along the boards of the quay and, a second later, an outboard motor roaring to desperate life. Sally switched off the torch in time to see the propwash of a dinghy surging out of the basin. With adrenaline now replacing ice in her veins, she dashed to the door, around the house and out onto the quayside. Only the swilling water within the basin marked the presence of the water-borne trespasser.

Presumably, ghosts don't propel themselves around with outboard motors, she reasoned, relieved that her intruder was at least of earthly origin and that her own dory still lay where she had tied it. So, who was this phantom-like interloper of the night, and where had he come from? Or where was he going? It suddenly occurred to Sally that she might get a clue to the latter.

Running back inside, she raced up the stairs, lighting her way by the faithful torch, until she stood at the French windows in the master bedroom. The key turned easily in the lock and then she was out on the balcony and climbing the vertical ladder to the summit of the wooden-framed tower. At the top, she looked out onto a scene as cold as it was beautiful.

The moon was still high in a cloudless sky. "The Parish Lantern", Mollie Jenkins had called it, and that recollection brought back the housekeeper's warning. The cold lunar beams certainly cast an eerie light over the shining expanse of water, but Sally's priorities now were escaping intruders rather than local superstitions. In vain, she scanned the broad and the waters running into it for any sign of the fast boat and its mysterious owner, but not even a wash remained to evidence its passing. It was as if boat and crew had disappeared into thin air... or were simply skulking in one of those silhouetted reedbeds, Sally reasoned, forcing her train of thought back into more earthly likelihoods. Pausing to calm herself, she looked out again on the ethereal beauty of this dominion of moonlit broadland.

There were certainly plenty of man-made lights. Across the water, just a few village ones still burned but, to the southeast, she could see the loom of Great Yarmouth. Further up the coast, a lighthouse beam swept its regular warning while, from the deeper blackness of the North Sea, came the regular pinpoint flashes of navigation buoys. Sally turned her gaze back towards the broad and saw, for the first time, a single pulsating glow.

It was close by in the eastern reedbeds and her first thought was it must be her intruder, lying low in a dyke. Then she realised this light was not in a dyke but in the reeds themselves. Not only that, it was moving.

What was its source? Surely, in these wetlands it couldn't be a person: these marshes were too deep for wading and too overgrown to permit the passage of any sort of boat. Once again, Sally felt that chill of unease at the unearthly way this phenomenon was moving steadily and in a straight line directly across reed and water. For reassurance, she turned and looked once more to the southeast and the glow of Yarmouth. When she turned back to her strange light, it was gone.

Almost hypnotically, Sally made her way back down the stairs and into the lounge. Finding the matches, she lit a candle. The log fire had died to embers now, but she opened the door of the stove and threw in a couple more logs. Sparks flew and within minutes a reassuring flame was again producing heat and dancing light. She sat back in one of the comfortable easy chairs, pulling a throw about her, while she attempted to bring some sort of order and rationalism to the night's events.

Who was the intruder? What did he want? Was he a thief or someone with a more sinister intent? Suspicions that her new-found-grandfather had been murdered, triggered the uncomfortable thought that this visitation might somehow be connected.

That strange light had seemed unreal too, hovering along without, seemingly, any human hand to guide it. Was this the "thing you didn't want to see" that Mollie Jenkins had warned her about? Sally glanced at the book on Broadland ghosts and legends that she had been reading, and which had mentioned strange lights over the marshes. Had she just seen one? If so, it seemed harmless enough. Not like "Black Shuck" the phantom dog presentiment of early death.

Perhaps it was just the thought of that sinister creature which made Sally sit upright, one ear cocked to the outside. Perhaps it was understandable that the night's events were causing her imagination to run riot. Or was her instinct really telling her that, once again, something outside was not as it should be? Warily now, she got up and went back to the window looking out over the mooring.

Gliding with spectral silence into the basin, were a pair of glowing eyes. Worse still, Sally could hear the unmistakable bark of a dog.

* * *

Chapter Eight

Heart pounding, unable to believe that she was being "spooked" yet again in one night, Sally prepared herself for another nerve-strumming. Then she noticed that one of the "creature's" eyes was green and the other, red. Navigation lights!

In their glow, Sally could now distinguish the fine lines of a launch swinging skilfully round, its searchlight beam probing the darkness and temporarily blinding her as it swept the house. Even as it came to a stop alongside her granddad's old sailing cruiser, there was not the faintest sound of an engine, but she could still hear the rasp of a dog's bark. Yet, this was no sinister growl of a phantom beast, but rather the woofing of an excited pet. And the launch too, she now noticed, had a blue light on top of its wheelhouse and a uniformed figure coming out into the cockpit. With all-consuming relief, she ran out to greet this very welcome arrival.

By the time Sally reached the jetty, a burly, grey-haired figure in fluorescent yellow jacket was already clambering over *Ace of Hearts* to meet her. There was something immediately reassuring about this man and his powerful build. He paused for just a second, seemingly surprised at the figure of a young woman coming down the walkway to greet him. Then a powerful hand stretched out to take hers and an authoritative, but friendly, voice said, 'Jack Fellows; Navigation Ranger.'

* * *

'So, whoever he was, took off as soon as you shone your torch at him. Not too much nerve by the sound of it,' concluded the Ranger.

Out there on the jetty, after quick introductions, Sally had poured out her story of the "ghost monk", though even she now realised it had probably been a hooded jacket rather than a monastic habit and cowl, and that her imagination had been wilder than the man himself. But, whoever it was, Jack had seen nothing of him, or his boat, as he made his escape.

'Either he came from the other village down-river or was lying low in the reedbeds,' explained this big man who, Sally imagined, would have been only too pleased to catch an intruder red-handed. He nodded towards the house. 'That smoke coming from your stovepipe worried me. No-one told me *Marsh Haven* had a new occupant.'

'I didn't know myself until a couple of days ago,' admitted Sally, giving a little shiver and suddenly feeling the cold of the night air on her bare arms. It was good to be talking to someone though. She nodded towards the house. 'I don't know about you, but I could do with some warmth and a drink. Nothing stronger than drinking chocolate, I'm afraid, but you're welcome to join me.'

Jack smiled. 'A hot chocolate would be just great, if it's okay for Spike to come too?' He bent down and scratched the neck of the Border Collie, which had just leapt across the boats and onto the jetty beside them.

'Of course,' said Sally, wondering how she could ever have confused this good-natured pet with the infamous "Black Shuck", 'I love dogs.'

The Ranger smiled. 'Then lead on.'

* * *

'So, you're the new mistress of *Marsh Haven*,' said Jack, as Sally busied herself making the hot drinks.

'Only from this afternoon,' she admitted, and went on to briefly explain her inheritance and occupancy, but without mentioning that she had never known Charles McKenna-Hynes. She poured boiling water into large mugs and led the Ranger through into the lounge. 'What does a Navigation Ranger actually do?'

While Sally re-lit the candles, Jack briefly described his job with the Broads Authority and how it was pure luck that he was out at all this night. Patrolling the rivers and broads in his launch was mainly a daylight operation, but this was the start of the closed season for angling and the occasional night patrol was enough to deter the odd rogue fisherman from trying his nefarious luck. At the same time, he kept his eye on the riverside properties, many of which were empty at this time of year.

'Sounds a wonderful job to me,' said Sally, throwing more logs into the stove and ushering Jack into a chair. She was keen to learn more from this man who had known her grandfather personally. Soon the logs were blazing and a contented Spike lay between them. 'It was you who found Granddad's body wasn't it?' she asked, taking a sip of her beverage.

'Actually, it was his boat I found first.' The Ranger paused to scratch Spike's head and it was obvious the memory was a particularly painful one. '*Ace of Hearts* was just drifting with her sails up but mainsheets lying over the side. Captain Charles... your granddad... and I always enjoyed a chat so I was a bit worried when he didn't come up on deck. In the end, I boarded, found the cabin empty and feared the worst. An hour later ... well, you know the rest.' He took a sip of chocolate. 'Your granddad was a good man and I shall miss him.'

'Not the sort to kill himself then?' asked Sally, hesitant to raise this aspect of the discussion, but knowing she had to.

'Suicide!' Jack Fellows shook his head vigorously. 'Absolutely not. If there was ever a man who wasn't a quitter, it was your grandfather.'

'But Mr Fellows...'

'Please, call me Jack', said the Ranger, smiling.

'... but ... Jack ...you don't subscribe to the accident explanation either do you... that Granddad had simply fallen overboard?'

'No, I don't.'

' Why not? After all, he *was* a very old man.'

Jack sat back again and stretched his feet just a little nearer the warmth of the stove. 'Because your granddad was a careful sailor who realised he was past his most agile years. For that reason, whenever he was sailing alone, he wore a lifejacket but, when I checked, it was still hanging on its hook in *Ace of Hearts*' cabin.'

'Was it that which made you think there'd been someone with him?'

'Partly,' Jack frowned, 'but it was also the sails.'

'The sails?'

'More the knots that held them up than the sails themselves,' explained Jack. 'Your granddad, you see, had a special way of belaying his halyards...' he paused, noticing Sally's vacant look. He smiled and leaned forward. 'Forgive me Miss Beckett...'

' ... Sally...'

' ... forgive me Sally, but am I right in assuming you're not too familiar with nautical terms?'

'I know nothing about sailing and not much more about boats generally,' admitted Sally, 'but I'm determined to learn.'

Jack laughed. 'I can see you are. Well, "halyards" are ropes that hoist things including sails, and "belaying" means to tie something securely to any fixed object. With the sail hoisted, a halyard is belayed to a cleat which is a T-shaped fitting around which the halyard is tied by taking a turn, a couple of 8s and then secured by one or two half-hitches.'

'I'll take your word for that, but how did these...' Sally concentrated on remembering the correct terms, '... halyards and cleats and half-hitches figure in your suspicions?'

Jack relaxed a little further into the comfortable armchair. 'Because Charles McKenna-Hynes never used hitches. He simply wound the halyard a couple more times around the 8s. He always reasoned that hitches jammed under load and could prevent you dropping the sail in a hurry if you had to. He did the same when mooring the boat to cleats on the dock. Apparently, during the war, they often had to move their boats at short notice and hitches were never used.'

'But these knots were tied differently?'

Jack nodded. 'As soon as I'd found *Ace of Hearts* empty, my first job was to drop the sails. That's when I found the halyards belayed with a strange system of half-hitches I'd never seen before.' Jack paused and met Sally's intent eyes. 'Someone other than Captain Charles had hoisted those sails and, right then, I realised we were dealing with something more sinister than a plain man-overboard.'

'But surely, someone else might have been sailing with Granddad, hoisted the sails for him, and then got off the boat before the ... the accident,' suggested Sally, trying to bring some rationalisation into this disturbing scenario.

Jack shook his head. 'Unlikely. For a start, it was thick fog that morning with not a whisper of wind. Why would anyone hoist sails in a complete calm when you couldn't see further than your bowsprit? And, if someone had been sailing with your granddad, why didn't they come forward to give evidence at the inquest?'

'So, if it wasn't suicide or an accident, you think it was...?'

'... murder,' completed Jack, with emphasis. 'Those sails were hoisted just to make it *look* like an accident.'

'Are you sure?'

'As sure as I can be.' Jack took a final swig of his chocolate. 'Sally, I spent a lifetime in the Metropolitan Police investigating murder and serious crime. It gave me an instinct for such things and my nose tells me *that's* what we're dealing with here.'

'My goodness.' Sally clasped her hands together and leaned forward. 'Have you any idea why? Did Granddad have enemies?'

The Ranger shook his head. 'No real enemies. Generally, Captain Charles was a respected, much-loved character hereabouts, though in recent years, he had ruffled a few feathers with his increasing obsession with renewable energy. He wanted his whole fleet converted to electric propulsion, which didn't go down well with his yard manager, Henry Higgs. More unpopular still, with many locals, was his campaign to have this whole broad restricted to sail and environmentally friendly boats. You can imagine how that went down.'

'It seems that you knew him well.' Sally tried to keep the curiosity out of her voice. 'What of my granddad's early background, Jack? Do you know anything about that?'

'Nothing really other than he settled down here after the war and bought the boatyard. It had been Newson Boats until then. Your granddad changed the name to Full-deck Marine and took it from strength to strength.' Jack shrugged his shoulders. 'Other than that I can't tell you much. My chats with your grandfather were always about current issues; we never got down to personal ones.' He paused to fix the young woman opposite with an appraising look. 'Surely you'd know more about that than me, Sally. You were, after all, his granddaughter.'

'I know *nothing* about my grandfather,' admitted Sally. 'In fact, until a couple of days ago I didn't even know he existed.' She looked again at the stolid figure of the Ranger, sitting slightly puzzled before her. There was something about this man that bespoke trust and reliability and she didn't hesitate now to take him into her total confidence. After explaining her upbringing with Granny Emily, she went on to detail all that had transpired in the last few days, since she first discovered her new grandfather and his generous will.

'I hope Phil Hengrove didn't give you too hard a time,' said Jack, smiling. 'He's a good copper but, like all DCIs, his case files are bulging and this is one investigation he could have done without.' Jack had wanted to ease the atmosphere created by Sally's revelations, but now his expression became serious. 'Yours is a very strange story, Sally. The first question is why your grandmother ... Emily Halard ... never told you of Charles. Her husband, you say, was Edward Halard, who was killed on D-Day?'

'Yes, he was a naval officer and his photo stood on the sideboard at home in London. I was always led to believe that *he* was my grandfather.'

Jack sat thinking for a minute before asking, 'And your granny, Emily; did she spend the war in London?'

'No.' Sally was glad she could supply at least some firm facts. 'Gran was quite a highly regarded artist and amateur naturalist.' She nodded towards the framed works hanging in the lounge. 'You can see some of her paintings here. According to Gran, when Grandfather Edward went off to war, she got a job at a nature reserve on the Suffolk coast, replacing a warden who'd been called up. Apparently, she loved those years, living in a small wood shack amongst all the wildlife which was so much a part of her life.'

'Hmmm,' said Jack, 'it must have been a terrible blow for her when your ... first ... granddad was reported killed.'

'Yes, especially as she was pregnant with my mum.' Sally shook her head. 'I'd always presumed it was by poor Edward, but now it seems she may have been a bit naughty and had an affair with another sailor, Charles McKenna-Hynes.'

'So it would seem,' agreed Jack, 'but I wonder why she never married him after the death of her husband?' He mused again for a few seconds before turning back to his host. 'Sally, you've got me intrigued. I can't interfere with Phil Hengrove's murder enquiry, but I could investigate the personal side of this strange mystery for you if you like.'

'Oh would you!' exclaimed Sally, unable to disguise her relief. 'I've got so much on here just sorting the boatyard and this house, but I obviously want to know the true story behind it all. If you could unearth those facts I'd be so grateful.'

'Glad to.' Jack smiled, at the same time wondering what wife Audrey's reaction would be to him making yet another foray back into detection. 'Obviously, the first step is to try and get more information about Captain Charles' past life.'

'Where on earth will you start?' asked Sally. 'Nobody around here seems to have the foggiest about his background.'

'Well, we do know he was in the navy,' explained Jack, 'so I'll try them for starters. From what little Charles said, I gathered his service was wartime, though he didn't seem to want to discuss it further and I never pushed him. Anyway, I've still got friends at the MoD who'll pull out his naval service records and, while they're about it, I'll get them to look up Edward Halard's as well. You say he was killed on D-Day; what else can you tell me about him?'

'That he died a hero's death, according to Gran, who always spoke lovingly of him.' Sally paused before adding, regretfully, 'But, of course, I have no personal recollection because I never knew him.'

'But you knew him from his photo. Tell me what that showed.'

'A naval officer,' said Sally, ' quite good-looking with a kindly face.'

'What about the uniform; were there rings on the sleeve?'

Sally had to think for a few seconds before saying, 'Yes, just one on each sleeve, I think.'

'A sub-lieutenant,' said Jack, nodding. 'And was that ring straight or wavy or a combination?'

'Straight, I think,' answered Sally, curious at these strange questions.

'Regular navy, then.' Jack again noticed the bemused look on Sally's face and explained, 'In those days, Royal Naval Volunteer Reserve officers wore wavy rings – they called them the "Wavy Navy" - and Royal Naval Reserve officers wore straight with intertwining wavy. Only regular Royal Navy officers wore pure straight rings, so your assumed grandfather must have been a career man. Good,' he said, standing up, 'this gives me something to go on. We'll see what the records say about Sub-Lieutenant Edward Halard RN, at the same time they're checking on Charles McKenna-Hynes.'

'I'm really grateful, Jack,' thanked Sally as she followed the Ranger and the faithful Spike out of the house, 'I feel something positive is being done now.' Back on the jetty she looked towards the narrow entrance to the broad. 'Let's hope our night intruder has made his last visit too. I've got enough concerns without having to contend with burglars.'

'I shouldn't worry about him,' said Jack reassuringly. 'My guess is he was just a local hooligan with more mischief than nerve. If you still feel uneasy though, give Phil Hengrove a call; I'm sure he'd send that dishy young DC Bailey to ask a few questions.'

'Oh, I wouldn't want to put them to that trouble,' retorted Sally, hoping Jack Fellows hadn't noticed a slight colouring in her cheeks. She felt the need to change the subject and pointed to the Ranger's launch. 'That's a beautiful boat, Jack, and it's totally silent.'

Jack laughed. 'That's because it's diesel-electric which allows me to run on either. I mainly run on electrics at night. Silence comes in very handy when you want to surprise the wrongdoer.' He nodded towards the blackness of the mill. 'That sort of technology was right up your grandfather's street. He and young Haverson had some interesting eco-projects under development including power from the wind.'

'I know,' admitted Sally before adding, 'Let's hope it starts giving us power again very soon.'

Jack smiled. 'Don't worry, Ian Haverson will get it sorted for you.'

'Hopefully tomorrow.' Sally bent down and gave Spike a farewell stroke. 'Nice to meet you, Spike...' she stood up, '... and you, Jack; you'll keep me advised of progress?'

'As soon as I find out something.' Jack clambered back into his launch followed by the ever-enthusiastic collie. Sally let go the lines and then launch and crew were gliding away from the jetty as silently as they'd arrived, with just a slight ripple in the water to mark their passing.

Sally waved them goodbye. She'd almost asked Jack Fellows about the strange light she'd seen over the marshes but decided that might be one mystery too many.

In a way though, she wished she had.

* * *

In a small cut in the reedbeds, on the broad's western side, the lone occupant of a black-painted dinghy slid binoculars back into their case, pushed back the hood of the wax jacket and started the long row back to the village. The boat had an outboard motor but the figure rowed in silence.

A check of the time between strokes showed it to be nearly 5 o'clock.

Way to the east, beyond the unseen horizon, the first loom of a new day was starting to pierce the darkness. It was bitterly cold, but a good pull at the oars would soon restore circulation and see the boat back at the staithe before life stirred anew. A glance over the shoulder showed just a few lights burning in the village. They seemed to be getting closer with painful slowness. It had been a long, but interesting, night.

* * *

'One egg or two, Jack?' asked Audrey Fellows, as her husband stretched his legs under their kitchen table.

'Two please, love,' replied Jack, 'and perhaps a couple of rounds of toast to help it down.' This was always his favourite way of ending a night's duty. Dawn had just broken, the launch was back in its boathouse, he'd had his shower and, after bacon and eggs, would be slipping into a bed still warm from his dear wife's slumbers.

Audrey's thoughts, however, were along more practical lines. 'You need to keep an eye on that waistline of yours, Jack Fellows,' she scolded light-heartedly as she slid the enticing plateful before her husband. 'Mind you, it sounds as if you've had an interesting night. Tell me more about this unknown granddaughter of poor Captain Charles.'

'Certainly a girl not lacking in self-reliance,' answered Jack, tucking into his breakfast, 'but totally mystified by the circumstances in which she finds herself.' He went on to tell his wife the whole strange story.

'Finding yourself heiress to an appreciable estate isn't the worst of situations,' observed Audrey before adding, sympathetically, 'but I can see how disturbing it must be for the poor girl, discovering her family's history is not what she thought.'

'Yes,' agreed Jack. 'It must have been bad enough growing up without a mum and dad, but now she finds the man she thought was her grandfather isn't and a chap she's never heard of, is.'

'So, how do you think you can help her?' asked Audrey, already worried that her ex-detective husband was again allowing himself to be inexorably drawn into murky waters. 'Surely this is something best left to the police and nothing to do with the Rangers?'

'Phil Hengrove has enough real crime to solve without getting into family puzzles,' declared Jack. 'Besides, it will give me some interest in my off-time.'

Audrey knew only too well the truth of that under-statement. Mysteries and their solutions were irresistible to her husband and she knew better than to try and stop him. Besides, as a mother herself, she felt for this young woman, alone and away from home with so many problems. It was only right that they should help, but one aspect still worried her. 'Jack, you were convinced that poor Captain Charles was murdered, so do you think this family mystery and the night intruder are all connected?'

Jack shrugged between mouthfuls. 'Possible but doubtful. Tragedies invariably bring out family secrets. As for the intruder, with *Marsh Haven* empty, it was only a matter of time before some local villain tried his luck.'

'Which brings me back to my first suggestion: that this is a job for the police rather than the Broads Authority?'

'Helping solve crime is everyone's responsibility, Audrey,' admonished Jack before putting down his knife and fork and taking a sip of coffee. 'As for the Authority, I agree it doesn't fall within their remit which is why any investigations I decide to pursue will be in my own time... starting with a check on the service records of Captain Charles and Sally Beckett's other grandfather, this Sub-Lieutenant Halard.'

'Why are you concerned with him, Jack?' Audrey poured another cup of coffee for both herself and her husband. 'Surely, if the man she thought was her grandfather died on D-day, he had nothing to do with what happened after?'

'Just a case of verifying all the facts,' said Jack, spooning one sugar into his coffee but deciding to skip the second.

'You've got some suspicions already, haven't you?' Audrey hadn't been married to this erudite man for over thirty years without gaining some deductive skills of her own. But she also knew his reluctance to air theories before getting concrete facts, so his response didn't surprise her.

'We'll see...' Jack glanced at the kitchen clock, '... but not before I've caught up on some sleep,' he added, picking up his coffee, giving his wife a kiss and heading for the stairs.

'Yes, off you go. I'll wake you before lunch.' Audrey watched him depart with mixed feelings. She knew this puzzle would give Jack new purpose, but was afraid, as always, he would become far too involved.

* * *

Chapter Nine

Sally had often heard how boating was the perfect antidote for life's problems. Now she realised for herself just how true that was.

Ahead of her, in magnificent desolation, stretched the broad. In contrast to yesterday, this morning was a sparkling spring-like day with the early sun enhancing a scene of almost breathtaking beauty. Already, geese were squawking overhead in perfect echelon formations before gliding in to surging landings that cut swaths through the glittering water, creating enough turbulence to give even the dory a small heave. And that air! Sally took another deep breath and felt it clearing not only her lungs, but also her mind and spirit as well. London might be a mere hundred miles away, but this was another world.

After Jack's departure, she'd managed some sleep before waking with the dawn, reassured that at least some of her problems were now being shared. A light breakfast and then she was ready for the day ahead, starting with the collection of Mollie Jenkins from the staithe.

Pulling on her warm fleece as she strode out to the dory, her first concern was whether she could start the wretched outboard and not have to suffer the indignity of calling the boatyard. As it was, a little playing with the choke and a few turns on the starter had the motor running sweetly, and soon she was manoeuvring the boat carefully from the jetty and heading out through the narrow channel and onto the broad.

Now, with the main broad crossed, more immediate concerns were presenting themselves. With almost unwelcome speed, the boatyard and its jetty were drawing ever closer. Standing at its end, Sally could already make out the homely figure of Mollie Jenkins. Worse still, lounging outside the boatshed, were several of the yard hands enjoying a leisurely cigarette before their morning's labour. She would have to bring this craft alongside in front of an audience who were doubtless, just hoping she made a complete pig's ear of the whole operation. That would give Henry Higgs all the excuse he needed to regain possession of the dory. 'Right,' she thought, 'I'll just have to show them.'

Conversely, she realised, this was not going to be a time for caution, but rather a touch of panache. She'd learned last night how putting the outboard astern with the helm over the opposite way would have the effect of turning the dory and stopping it in one smooth action. Well, now was the time to try it, with a bit more speed and power to match.

Not slowing her speed, Sally headed at forty-five degrees to the jetty, noticing Mollie Jenkins moving back slightly from the edge and the yard hands standing up for a better view. Just one boat-length from this now very solid-looking structure, she closed the throttle, wound the wheel hard-over towards it and then went almost full-astern on the engine.

For a startling second she thought she'd misjudged and was going to demolish all before her. Mollie Jenkins thought so too because she now took some very definite steps backwards, and more than one cigarette dropped from the yard hands' mouths.

But the ample power had just the desired effect. Right on the end of the jetty, the dory swung level with it and stopped, its quarter-wave catching up and providing a dramatic surge, leaving the boat perfectly positioned just inches from the side. Sally quickly pushed the throttle back to neutral and breathed a sigh of relief that she hoped wouldn't be noticed by the men now running to take her lines.

'Blimey, miss, you've obviously done that afore,' said the one now holding the boat's gunwale.

'Just once or twice,' admitted Sally, with what she hoped sounded like false modesty rather than truth.

With Mollie Jenkins helped into the boat, lines were cast off, a handy boot shoved clear the bow and then they were powering away up the broad, the housekeeper obviously delighted to be back in her old life. For her part, Sally was just content that another small victory had been won.

*   *   *

It was an hour later that Henry Higgs sat in his office, feeling angry, frustrated and increasingly worried.

The day had started badly enough with that cocky little yard hand, Tom Brewer, delighting in telling him how well the new Beckett woman had handled the dory. Now he'd just put the phone down from the young woman herself, ringing to tell him to organise a meeting between her and Jayne Howlett, the bookkeeper, for tomorrow afternoon.

It was a further complication that Higgs could have well done without. By now the future of the yard should have been sorted, with him left to run it as he knew best. At the inquest on the guv'nor, he'd told the coroner there were no money worries in the yard, but that the old man hadn't been in the best of health for weeks. That should have settled it, but instead that Navigation Ranger Fellows had stuck his oar in, with the result that the police had been back nosing around. This was the last thing he needed with the season proper beginning in just a few weeks and only half the Full-deck fleet yet ready. And now this pushy granddaughter had arrived on the scene, all set to take over everything and delve into the yard's finances.

Higgs groaned, picked up the phone again and dialled a well-known number. To the voice that answered he said only, 'Problems. You and I need to talk.'

Arrangements made, Higgs rolled another cigarette and lit up. It was the only thing that stopped him putting his head in his hands. Slowly, the cigarette burned through, but the problems remained. Eventually he stubbed out the end, ran an agitated hand over the sweat on his brow and stormed into the workshop.

Two of the hands were on their backs beneath one of the cruisers, busy painting the underside with black anti-fouling. Higgs took one look before booting the whole oily tinful over the shop floor.

'Red,' he shouted. 'I told you I wanted it in red. Do it again.' Then he stormed off.

When problems were at their worst, you had to take it out on someone.

* * *

'You saw a Corpse Candle,' said Mollie Jenkins.

'Corpse Candles! What on earth are they?' asked Sally with a mixture of consternation and fascination.

Mrs Jenkins had spent a couple of hours cleaning and tidying, and now she and Sally sat at the kitchen table taking a mid-morning coffee break together. It seemed a good time to tell the housekeeper of the night's events and that strange light over the marshes.

'P'raps not somethin' "on earth" at all.' The housekeeper again fingered the small crucifix around her neck. 'Legend has it that the Romans, all them centuries ago, used to use the pools hereabouts as a burial place for children. They'd weight down the poor little souls an' just lower 'em in the water. Lights have been seen hundreds a times over the years an' most of us round here have not a doubt that it's the spirit of one of them dead kiddies still lingerin' on earth.'

'My goodness.' Sally wasn't quite sure how to respond to such an obvious believer as Mrs Jenkins. In the end she simply asked, 'Has no-one ever investigated it further?'

'Not really,' said the housekeeper, shaking her head. 'Some fishermen reckon they've been quite close to 'em some nights, but they jus' moves off afore they get near enough to see what they be.' Mrs

Jenkins noticed the little shiver that her employer had just given. 'I told you never to look over them marshes at night, din't I?'

'I know, but I wanted to see where that hooded figure was heading and, anyway,' Sally added, with a little emphasis, ' I don't subscribe to lore and fantasy.'

'Well, maybe you should,' said Mrs Jenkins, with just a little admonition of her own. 'A lot of strange things happen hereabouts.'

'Like intruders in the night,' responded Sally, feeling it was time to bring subjects back to a more earthly realm. 'Now that really *did* scare me.'

'As it would anyone.' Mrs Jenkins gave a little shudder of her own. 'I reckon same as Mr Fellows, that you won't be bothered no more now they know someone's here. Cap'ain Charles never had no problem with break-ins or nothin'.'

'But did he have *any* enemies, hereabouts?' asked Sally, taking advantage of the lead. 'Was there *anyone* who would … wish him harm?'

'Murder him you mean?' Mollie Jenkins obviously wasn't afraid to call a spade a spade. 'I know what they was all saying round here after that inquest.' She shook her head again. 'Well, like all business folk, he'd stood on a few toes over the years an' I know some of them local boatin' types weren't too happy at him tryin' to get motor boats banned from these waters, but nothin' as would want him dead.'

Sally nodded and then, remembering Jack Fellows' line of investigation, wondered if her housekeeper might enlighten them further. 'Mrs Jenkins, you mentioned before that you thought my granddad had been in the navy during the war. Was there anything else he told you about his service?'

'Like I said,' explained the housekeeper, 'it weren't somethin' he ever wanted to talk about. He wouldn't even tell the children.'

'The children?'

'The kiddies at the village school.' Realising more explanation was needed, she added, 'They do the Second World War as a topic and Anne, the teacher there, mentioned they needed someone who'd been in it to talk about it and wondered if I'd ask Cap'ain Charles.'

'And he agreed?' asked Sally, surprised.

'Well he did, af'er I spoke my mind an' said it was right that kids know what men fought for. Finally he said, "yes", he'd do it.'

'So what did he tell them?'

'Oh, the history of how it all started an' how wrong war was an' that they should give them politicians the guns in future an' tell 'em to get on with it.'

'Amen to that,' agreed Sally with feeling. 'But what did he tell them about his own service?'

'Not much,' answered Mrs Jenkins. 'Course, some of them kids asked what he did in the war, but all he'd say was he spent most of it at sea in small boats.'

'And the last hours of his life were spent likewise,' pondered Sally, sadly. 'When did you last speak to him, Mrs Jenkins?'

'The mornin' he went for that sail. I was here to do for him an' after our coffee he went off in *Ace of Hearts*.'

'Did he intend staying out the night?'

'Not as what I could judge, but he of'en did if the fancy took him. I slept the night here, as I usually did if he weren't here to run me in the dory. I wasn't surprised when he didn't return 'cos the fog had really come down that evenin' an' I jus' thinks he's anchored out there somewhere for the night. When he din't come back next mornin' I rang the Ranger, jus' to ask him to keep an eye out for the cap'ain.' Mrs Jenkins gave a little sniffle and brought out a tissue to wipe the moistening in her eyes. 'Never occurred to me I'd never see him alive ag'in.'

'So, how did he seem when he went off for this sail?' Sally was trying to avoid emotions clouding the issue. 'Was anything troubling him?'

'Not really,' admitted Mrs Jenkins, somewhat reluctantly. 'He'd been quite down for months, gettin' right grumpy and aggressive at times an' then all remorseful afterwards. Not like the nice old man I knew at all. Forgettin' things too an' becomin' real vague. I finally got him to see the doctor 'bout it.'

'And what did the doctor diagnose?'

'He din't tell me,' grumbled the housekeeper. 'At first, the doctor put him on pills, which I don't think agreed with him an' if anythin', made him even dozier. I said all he needed was some good food inside him, so we threw away the pills an' I started cookin' for him as well as cleaning. That sorted him.' Mrs Jenkins gave a smile of satisfaction.

'You mean he was cured?' asked Sally incredulously.

'Oh, yes. I'd said for a long time he didn't take care of hisself an' as soon as I started feedin' him right, he became healthier than he'd been for years. Somethin' was still worryin' him though, but I never found out what an' I guess it don't matter now anyway.'

'Perhaps it does,' thought Sally, but didn't say. The question of her grandfather's health *was* a relevant factor and she asked, 'Who was his doctor, Mrs Jenkins?'

'Doctor Newson.' The housekeeper cocked her head in the direction of the unseen village. 'She has a surgery here.'

'A lady doctor, then?'

'Yes *and* a village girl too,' explained the housekeeper with obvious local pride. Father was a boatbuilder, but she got a scholarship an' went on to study medicine. Did well did Helen.'

'Well perhaps I'll make an appointment to see her myself.' Sally, got to her feet. 'I need to register as a local resident.'

'Sounds like you're intent on stayin' on here then.' Mrs Jenkins was obviously pleased at such a prospect.

'Yes, I'm sure I am.' Sally glanced wistfully towards the broad. 'I think I'm falling in love with your Broadland, Mrs Jenkins. It will be wonderful to explore it further but...' she paused to pick up her notebook, '...there's so much to sort out first.'

'Including this house,' said Mollie Jenkins, standing up herself. 'Is there anythin' special you want me to get done today, Miss Sally?'

'Yes.' Sally remembered the hollow in her grandfather's pillows. 'I'd like you to strip and change the bed in the main bedroom.'

'But I did,' responded Mrs Jenkins, defensively, 'an' then made it up ag'in with all clean linen.'

'Oh... alright.' It wasn't the answer Sally expected or wanted, but she ignored its connotations and instead simply requested, 'But perhaps you could change it again, if you wouldn't mind, Mrs Jenkins.'

'Right.' The housekeeper gave a little sigh. 'I'd love to give the whole house a good vacuuming, but I can't until we get some electricity back on.'

'Ah, the power.' Sally, remembered the other thing she meant to ask. 'Did you get in touch with this Ian Haverson?'

'Not until this mornin',' admitted Mrs Jenkins, 'but he was moored locally in his boat an' promised to be here as soon as he could. In fact,' she said, looking out of the window, 'I think this is him now.'

Sally followed her gaze, to see a boat sliding into the basin. Its entry was as silent as Jack Fellows' the night before, but there all similarity to the Ranger's launch ended.

This boat was certainly bigger, about thirty-five feet Sally estimated, with a cabin at either end and an open cockpit in the middle. In that respect it was not unlike the hire cruisers she had seen at Full-deck Marine, but it was the two wind turbines that proclaimed its eccentricity, turning steadily in the morning breeze and obviously supplementing the energy stored by the solar panels that covered the cabin roofs.

'If this is the floating home of our eco-engineer, goodness knows what the man himself will be like, thought Sally, as she went outside to find out.

* * *

Chapter Ten

In fact, the young man at the wheel looked surprisingly normal; nothing like the eco-warrior stereotype that Sally had, for some reason, been expecting. Nearly alongside now, he held up his mooring lines with a questioning smile. Sally nodded back, and soon the head rope was snaking across and she was securing it to one of the jetty's cleats. The young man jumped athletically ashore, tied his own stern rope and then turned to meet her.

'You must be Sally, the long-lost granddaughter,' he said, his boyish face breaking into an even broader smile.

Sally liked that face. Somehow, it seemed to speak wordlessly of excitement and a life lived for life's sake.

'And you must be Ian Haverson.' She held out her hand and felt a firm, strong grip in return. For someone who lived his whole life afloat on a small boat, this young engineer was quite presentable. Fair, almost blond, hair fell over his collar, but it was clean, as were the well-worn designer jeans and faded Guernsey sweater. She turned towards the strange boat that had the name *Electrifier* proudly emblazoned on its side. 'And this is your boat-cum-home?'

'Cum-office-cum-workshop-cum just about everything,' answered Ian, laughing. 'Want to have a look on board her?'

'I'd love to later, but…' she turned and nodded towards the mill, '… I'd be very grateful if you'd restore my power first.'

'Glad to.' He indicated the house. 'In the first kitchen cupboard you'll find some key hooks. The big ancient looking one is the mill's. Grab that and meet me over there. I'll just fish out some tools and a torch.'

'Right.' Sally went off as ordered, content that another problem was about to be sorted, and by someone she found rather attractive in an easy-going, no-nonsense way. Besides, she was looking forward to seeing inside her mill.

*　　*　　*

This was Sally's morning for things being not quite as she'd expected. With the old mill being converted to a wind turbine, she'd imagined its interior to be more akin to a space-shuttle than a century-old drainage pump. How wrong she was. When Haverson turned the lock and led her inside, the ancient machinery within seemed much as it must have been since the day it was built, which was…?

'1907,' explained Ian, before Sally had time to ask the question. 'That's the pump.' He pointed to the substantial mechanism filling most of the ground floor. A huge shaft came vertically down to it through the floor above, obviously the drive from the sails aloft. 'You have to remember,' he emphasised, as they climbed the wooden stairs to the next level, 'that these were wind *pumps*, not mills in the true sense. Their function was to continually drain water from the marshes into the rivers. There were once hundreds of them covering the whole Broadland area.'

'They must have looked a wonderful sight.' Sally was fascinated by all she was seeing and hearing.

'Yes, and it's a tragedy they were ever allowed to fall into decay,' agreed Ian. 'A good one could shift fifteen tons of water a minute, but the late nineteenth century saw much of the pumping converted to steam and then, in the early twentieth, to diesel and electric which they all are today. Of course, the mill only produces energy when the wind is blowing. When it's not, you'll rely on these.' He pointed to the bank of batteries filling most of the floor of this second level.

'How long would they last?' asked Sally.

'Not long if you had everything on, so keep electrical loads to a minimum if the sails aren't turning.' He caught Sally's worried look. 'I'm actually working on an alternative system that could do away with batteries altogether. My plan is to use the mill's original pumping capacity to shift water to a higher level. During calms that could then be used to drive a water turbine instead.'

'Pretty ingenious.'

'Oh, just adaptations of old ideas,' admitted Ian, climbing the next flight of stairs and pushing open a trapdoor. 'Now let's show you where all that power comes from in the first place.'

Sally followed him up into the third level. Here, the technology was definitely twenty-first century. 'That's the control cabinet,' he explained, pointing to the bank of dials, lights and switches going almost from floor to ceiling. 'The original big gearwheel in the cap still turns the shaft which then,' he continued, indicating the vertical system below the gear, 'drives this modern gearbox and generator.'

'You mean *that* provides all the electricity for *Marsh Haven*?' asked Sally, pointing to the small unit, surprised that such an insignificant-looking component could produce enough power.

Ian Haverson grinned. 'And for half a dozen other houses as well, given the chance.' He gave the vertical shaft a slap of affection. 'Throughout Broadland there are dozens of mills like this, which, if converted, could supply not only several buildings but, more importantly, charging points for electric boats as well. With just a little forethought and investment, we could get all of the boats on the Broads wind-powered again, one way or the other.'

'And the mills restored and once more earning their keep into the bargain,' observed Sally, seeing the enormous potential of the scheme and the environmental advantages it presented.

Ian nodded and then picked up his flashlight. 'But first we need to get *Marsh Haven* generating its own electricity again.' He nodded higher towards the top of the tower. 'Give me fifteen minutes to check all the mill gear and then I'll slip the brake and get the sails turning. All being well, we can then bring the generator on line and you'll have all the electricity you need.'

'Wonderful!' Sally was truly impressed, not only in this union of old and new technology, but also with the dynamic young man who was, so obviously, its devoted advocate. She smiled and looked out at the mill's huge sails. 'When I see them turning, I'll get the kettle on and bring you a coffee.'

'Sounds good.' Ian grabbed the rest of his tools and disappeared up the vertical ladder, a man truly involved in a labour of love. He shouted back down, 'I'd show you up here but it's a bit cramped and the main gear wheel is pretty intimidating with more than one!'

'That's all right,' she shouted back up. 'I'll look another time.'

She could well understand why her grandfather had become so absorbed in this exciting project. Already, she could see herself becoming just as involved.

Perhaps in more ways than one.

* * *

'What a wonderful sight.'

Sally stood on the jetty beside the boats, looking up to where the huge sails of her mill turned majestically in the freshening breeze, to the accompaniment of creeks and groans from within. Ian had assured her that those sounds were totally normal for century-old mechanics and that she would soon get used to them.

'Especially as you've now got light and power thrown in,' he said, taking an appreciative sip from the mug Sally had just given him.

With his foot, he indicated the small electrical socket, mounted on the jetty. 'That's the charging point we installed for *Ace of Hearts*.' He nodded towards the yacht. 'It's sad that Charles died before we got round to converting his own boat to electric power. He was so excited at the prospect of pollution-free, silent cruising this summer, especially as he was finding sailing alone increasingly difficult recently.'

'I'm just amazed he kept sailing as long as he did.' Sally indicated the neglected state of her grandfather's boat. 'Poor *Ace of Hearts* looks like she needs a good clean.'

'You're right.' Ian stepped on board and fingered some of the dull, stained woodwork. 'But the varnish is still good beneath this grime. It won't take much to bring it back and have her gleaming again.'

'But I just won't have the time, Ian,' explained Sally, regretfully. 'I've got the yard to sort out first, so I was hoping they'd do the work.'

Ian shook his head. 'They won't have time either. They're way behind being ready for this season as it is, so I can imagine Henry Higgs' response to you turning up with this job.'

'Yes, he's not the easiest man to work with is he?' Sally frowned and then asked, 'But why are they so far behind anyway? From what little I know of my granddad, he seemed the sort who would have had work schedules planned to the minute.'

'Perhaps you don't realise,' explained Ian dispiritedly, 'that your grandfather and myself started a programme of converting all his hire cruisers to electric propulsion. Higgs was dead against the idea and since your grandfather's death, he's wasted hundreds of manhours reconverting them back to diesel again.' The engineer shook his head. 'After all that research and planning, we were well on the way to becoming the first boatyard on the Broads to have the entire hire fleet electrically powered, and now that bloody yard-manager has set everything back years.'

'On whose authority?' asked Sally, consciously bristling at just the thought of this waste.

'Landers, Simpson & Hedges, the executors.' Ian shrugged his broad shoulders. 'They meant well enough. Their first priority was to keep the business operating and, until they found you, they left its day-to-day running to Higgs.' The engineer gave a heartfelt groan. 'A heaven-sent chance to get one over on me, which he grasped with both hands.'

'I gather there wasn't much love lost between you two then.'

'You could say that, though mutual hatred might be a better way of putting it.' The engineer swigged back the dregs of his coffee. 'Put simply, I couldn't stand the man and his antiquated work ethics. "Change" was a dirty word as far as Higgs was concerned. On top of that, the man's an incorrigible bully. Even his wife has kicked him out after twenty-five years.'

'I'm amazed she put up with him for five minutes!' exclaimed Sally.

'Oh, a lot of women put up with him for five minutes.' Ian gave a mischievous chuckle. 'He's a notorious womaniser as well. It was common knowledge that no boat cleaner kept her job if she didn't agree to a bit of overtime with the yard manager.'

Sally shook her head. 'From what Mrs Jenkins has told me, Granddad was a man of high principles who surely wouldn't have condoned that sort of behaviour.'

'And he didn't,' said Ian. 'He always had time to listen to employees' sob stories of bad treatment by Higgs. But the man kept his job. The truth is,' admitted Ian, 'Higgs is a very good manager. Every business needs its hatchet man to maintain discipline and productivity, and Higgs filled that role magnificently.'

'But not the one of husband,' observed Sally. 'Why has Mrs Higgs taken so long to dump him?'

'Because, after years of casual philandering, apparently, Higgs' latest squeeze is something far more serious. So, Mrs Higgs is suing for divorce and a pretty hefty settlement.'

'Good for her,' said Sally with feeling, but at the same time wondering how this situation might have influenced other events.

'So…' Ian slapped the cabin top of *Ace of Hearts*, '… forget Full-deck Marine doing the work. I've got a better idea.'

'Which is?'

'You let me do it,' Ian offered. 'I'm not too busy at the moment and I could do with the money.'

'But you're surely not hard up?' asked Sally, surprised to hear that he was strapped for cash. 'You're coming into a small fortune from Granddad's will very soon.'

'Yes, but when the executors do eventually release it, it'll virtually all go in paying off my old debts.'

'Debts?'

'I'm afraid so.' He held out his hands. 'Fact is, I put a lot of my own money into the windpump project. Research doesn't come cheap and it will be years before I see any return.'

'That's too bad,' sympathised Sally, before smiling and saying, 'but, of course, I'd love you to renovate this boat. When can you start?'

'Straight away.' Ian glanced towards the broad. 'We need to have her ready so you can go sailing.'

'If I knew how! The sad fact is, Ian, I've never sailed before,' admitted Sally, before adding, 'but I'd love to learn.'

'Then, I'll have to teach you.' The engineer jumped ashore with enthusiasm. 'We'll use *Joker*.'

'*Joker*?'

'Your granddad's dinghy,' explained Ian, pointing to where the small mast stuck out of the water just astern of the cruiser. 'Rain has filled and sunk her but I'll soon get her up. The sails and spars are kept in the shed so they'll be okay.' He held up his hands to the blue sky overhead and the cool breeze that continued to turn the sails of the mill with invisible energy. 'The perfect day for it. Why don't we give you your first lesson this afternoon?'

'Wonderful!' Sally glanced at the only part of her proposed training boat yet visible. 'But are you sure you can have … *Joker* … ready for then?'

'No problem at all. Wooden clinker boats kept ashore often dry out and leak and have to be sunk to tighten up anyway. She won't need that, so I'll drag her out, clean things up, get her rigged and be ready for…' he glanced at his watch, 'one o'clock?'

'One o'clock it is,' confirmed Sally. 'That'll give me time to take Mrs Jenkins back to the staithe first.' She reached out and took his mug. 'Ian Haverson,' she said with a broad smile, 'you've earned yourself another coffee.'

* * *

'Thanks, Harry. That's another one I owe you.'

Jack fellows put down his telephone with a satisfied grunt. During his years at Scotland Yard, he'd formed a good relationship with the personnel department at the MoD. They'd sometimes needed the odd discreet police investigation and in return, helped out with information as needed. Service records were always a useful tool in assessing men's characters and Jack's police authority had permitted him access to all. Now retired from the force, his enquiries were limited to those no longer living and the helpful Harry had promised to dig out both names from naval records. He hoped to e-mail Jack the results in twenty-four hours.

Jack sat back in his small but cosy study and considered progress. Learning more of Charles McKenna-Hynes' background may not help find his murderer, but that was Phil Hengrove's problem anyway. All Jack wanted was to help Sally Beckett fill in the gaps of her own ancestry. A pity her granny, Emily Halard, hadn't been more forthcoming in confessing her little dalliance while husband Edward was away at war. Learning more about Emily's war could well fill in a useful piece to this enigmatic jigsaw.

Jack went to his bookcase and fished out the guide to Suffolk. One of the largest of the "Norfolk" Broads was actually in Suffolk and he always enjoyed the odd secondment to that pretty county. Sally had said her granny spent the war as warden of a nature reserve by the coast. He wondered which one that could be?

The weekend was only a day away and a run down to the Suffolk coast would go down well with Audrey. Jack flicked to the county map at the front and started making notes.

*   *   *

Chapter Eleven

'Wow!' yelled Sally, as the little lugsail dinghy heeled and accelerated to another gust of the now fresher wind.

Ian Haverson had been as good as his word, hauling the eleven-foot boat onto the quay-heading and emptying her of water. After a good scrub and clean, he'd pushed *Joker* back in and been correct in his prediction that immersion would have kept her seams tight. *Joker* floated happily astern of her larger consort and, while Sally ran Mollie Jenkins back to the village in the dory, he collected oars and rig from the shed behind the house. When Sally motored back into the basin, it was to see the little dinghy sporting a jaunty tan lugsail and a small colourful pennant at her masthead. Learning to sail this little boat suddenly seemed the gateway to so much joy to come.

'Well done, Ian,' she called as she walked up the jetty to join him. She glanced at the masthead. 'And I like the pennant.'

'It's called a burgee, actually,' he explained kindly, before adding, 'and it's not there to look pretty but to tell you where your wind is.'

'Ah, yes, the wind,' Sally sighed. 'Ian, you really will have to teach me from scratch.'

The young engineer smiled and nodded towards the house. 'Let's go and have a coffee first and I'll explain the mysteries of sailing.' His next glance was towards the broad. 'Then we'll go and do it.'

* * *

Joker seemed to be enjoying her new-found life as much as Sally, cutting an arrowhead of wash across the broad as she surged through the water.

''Right,' said Ian, pointing to a distant marker buoy in their eleven o'clock position, 'take us round that.'

Sally altered course accordingly but, as she did so, the edge of the sail began to flap noisily.

'You're luffing,' Ian said, calmly but firmly. 'You need to bear away again or harden the sheets and pull the sail in tighter.'

Sally hauled away and the flapping stopped, *Joker* surging ahead once more, though now with slightly more heel.

'Sheets, halyards, warps, lines; what funny names all these ropes have,' she observed, as the marker buoy drew ever-closer.

'Yeah, that's part of the language of boats and sailing,' agreed her instructor. 'In fact, the only rope on a boat that's called a rope is the bell-rope, and we haven't got one of those,' he added. They were almost at the buoy now. 'Get ready to go-about,' he warned. 'You remember the orders?'

'Yes... ready-about!' she shouted as the buoy drew level with their bow and then, 'lee-ho,' as she pushed the tiller away from her and little *Joker* spun neatly around the mark. She remembered to duck as the boom came flying over her head.

'Well done; you've just tacked,' Ian complimented, as his pupil eased the sheets to get the little clinker boat sailing at its optimum speed once more. He gave Sally an affectionate pat on the back. 'I must say, you've taken to this like a natural.'

'I love it, Ian,' she agreed with relish. 'I've always dreamed of being able to sail and now I'm actually doing it. I can't tell you how good that feels.'

'Well, you've got a lifetime of it to look forward to,' he said, at the same time pointing to *Marsh Haven*'s mill peeking just above the reedbeds. 'I think that will do for one day. Bear away and run for home.'

Sally brought the tiller towards her, at the same time easing the mainsheet. Beating to windward, the slipstream over the boat had come with a decidedly chilly edge. Now, as the wind came from astern and *Joker* sliced through the following wavelets with ease, it virtually disappeared and the chill with it. 'Ah, what heaven!' she exclaimed, relaxing her hold on the tiller and finding time to take in the magic of what had been the setting of her first sail. On the channel marker posts, cormorants with outstretched wings, sat watching. 'They always look so sinister, don't they,' she remarked as *Joker* went gliding by.

'They've found cormorant bones fifty million years old,' explained Ian, 'so there's a good reason for them looking so prehistoric.'

'Especially when they sit with their wings out like that. They look a bit like pterodactyls.'

'They do that to dry out. The poor old cormorants, you see, don't have oily feathers so when they dive to catch fish they get gradually waterlogged.'

'Oh, poor things. Badly designed really...' Sally smiled as she gave her little boat a playful slap on the gunwale, '... unlike *Joker*.'

'Yes, but there are fifty-two variants of the cormorant in the world,' went on Ian, 'including a non-flying version in the Galapagos Islands, which fuelled Darwin's theory of evolution.'

'My goodness, a natural history lesson thrown in as well,' acknowledged Sally, grinning. 'You're a wealth of knowledge, Ian

Haverson.'

'Not really. Everyone around here knows the ways of nature, but I had the advantage of learning mine virtually from the cradle.' He turned and smiled his own entrancing smile. 'My own granddad was quite a renowned Broads naturalist.'

'No wonder you have such a crusading approach towards eco-technology then,' conceded Sally, wondering how many more surprises this young man had to spring. 'Presumably, unlike me, you knew your granddad well?'

'Very well. He brought me up or, at least he did until his death.'

'So, being brought up by grandparents seems to be is something we've got in common.' Sally hardened the mainsheet slightly as they approached the top of the broad. 'You must tell me all about yours sometime.'

'How about tonight,' he said, without any hesitation. 'Let's have supper together at *The Steamboat*.'

They'd reached the entrance to the basin now and were sliding in between the reedbeds. Another evening alone in *Marsh Haven* wasn't actually beckoning and this afternoon's new-found experience was certainly worthy of celebration. Besides, already she was finding herself drawn to Ian Haverson and his idealistic ambitions, in more ways than one. The jetty was coming up and she concentrated on judging when she should swing *Joker* into wind, but she still found time to say, 'Yes, I'd like that.' Then she let fly the mainsheet, put the helm over and brought *Joker* neatly alongside.

* * *

'Right, my round, Jack.'

Detective Chief Inspector Phil Hengrove picked up Jack Fellow's glass and went to the bar. Both he and the Ranger enjoyed their irregular meetings at *The Steamboat*, where a large log fire threw warming flickers over the beamed ceiling and glass-cased monster pike lined the walls. This evening's clientele represented the usual mix of friendly locals, frustrated anglers and the young crews from two cruisers moored outside, who were glad of this waterside tavern in which to spend the evening. The DCI was soon back with the drinks.

'Cheers, Phil.' Jack, raised the pint of lager and took an appreciative sip. He wasn't an ardent "pubber", but these informal chats with the head of the local CID gave a short nostalgic glimpse back into his old life and Hengrove, for his part, was glad to allow Jack's experience and instincts to play over the latest case. There was little doubt what this evening's discussion would be about.

'So, any theories about this McKenna-Hynes' death now you've spoken to the granddaughter?' asked the DCI, as he took a sip of his own beer.

'I'm afraid not,' admitted Jack, ' but I've got feelers out for some background on Captain Charles.'

'Any results?'

'Not yet, but hopefully tomorrow. It'll be good to know what we're dealing with here, Phil.' Jack put down his glass and licked his lips. 'I'm also planning a trip down to Suffolk to try and suss the girl's granny, this Emily Halard.'

'Any point?' asked Hengrove, sceptically. 'The old girl's been dead for two years, so surely she'll have no real bearing on the case.'

'No, but I promised Sally I'd try and unravel the mystery of her family, and Granny Halard might give me a lead on Captain Charles.' Jack fingered his glass, thoughtfully. 'When a suspicious death victim has an unknown past, Phil, you always have to consider whether some old enmity has come out of the historical woodwork to cause it.'

'But, you know as well as I do, Jack, that any murder enquiry always exposes some family skeletons.' Hengrove took a longer swig of his beer. 'All right, the victim had a romance with Emily Halard and the two kept quiet about it. That must have happened a million times during the war. It's probably just an incidental, Jack...' the DCI nodded in the direction of *Marsh Haven*, '... like that attempted break-in was just some local villain trying his chances.'

'Yes, and she's determined not to let it phase her. A very independent girl is Sally Beckett.' Jack gave a smiling shake of the head before asking, 'But the murder enquiry itself, Phil. Any leads? Any theories?'

Hengrove shook his own head wearily. 'Nothing of any consequence. Like any enquiry, my initial suspicions have to fall on those benefiting from the old boy's will. For starters you've got Mollie Jenkins, the housekeeper, who reckons she was alone at *Marsh Haven* awaiting her master's return, but has no independent witness to prove it.'

'Not your typical homicidal psychopath, though,' replied Jack, with a wry smile.

'Not really,' agreed the DCI. 'I imagine the most daring thing Mollie Jenkins has ever done is to put two sugars in her tea.' Hengrove stuck up a thumb and forefinger as he counted off his suspects. 'Then there's that young engineer, Haverson.'

'By all accounts, the apple of the old man's eye,' Jack cut in. 'That eco-project of theirs was a mutual fascination which Captain Charles had already poured thousands into, so what would be Haverson's motive?'

'More thousands,' answered Hengrove bluntly. 'Haverson has a mountain of debt and no alibi for that night and morning. Reckons he was alone on his boat with no corroborative witness.' The DCI met Jack's eyes and lowered his voice a level. 'How about this scenario, Jack? You have creditors starting to push you and you're out sailing with an old man, who you know has left you a bundle in his will. The old man falls overboard and you make the quick decision that a speedy rescue isn't exactly to your financial advantage. Instead, you hoist the sails to make it look like an accident and do the disappearing act in the dinghy or something. And that's putting the most generous slant on things,' completed the DCI cynically.

Jack shook his head. 'Feasible, but not likely, Phil. If that had been the case, Haverson would have had nothing to lose coming forward. Keeping quiet was only going to arouse the interest of the police, which could easily be avoided by reporting the accident in the first place.'

'Which therefore leaves your Miss Beckett.' The DCI swigged back the dregs of his beer. 'She stood to gain more than anyone and you've admitted yourself, she's a very resourceful young lady.'

'And a very honest one as well, who was on the other side of the world at the time,' countered Jack, firmly. 'Take it from me, that girl is as much in the dark about all this as we are.' The Ranger placed his own glass firmly back on the table. 'But you're missing one other suspect with a motive, Phil.'

'You mean the yard manager?'

Jack nodded. 'Henry Higgs, not the most endearing of characters and we know, from what the solicitors told you, that he originally stood to inherit a quarter of the estate, including a share of Full-deck Marine. Apparently, Captain Charles had him excluded from the will just a month before his death.'

'Which is certainly a reason for personal animosity,' admitted Hengrove,' and I wonder what he did to get cut out like that?'

'Did you ask him?' questioned Jack.

'Of course, but all he'd say was that the old man became cantankerous due to ill health in the last months of his life, and made all sorts of screwball decisions.'

'Well, I know Higgs was dead against electrification of Full-deck's hire fleet and is now busy putting back all the old diesels,' said Jack. 'That must be incensing Ian Haverson, whose project it was.'

'No love lost between those two anyway,' observed the DCI. 'Higgs regarded Haverson as a young upstart and is doubtless enjoying undoing all his good work.'

'But technical differences are hardly reason to lose a legacy and face life in nick. Any evidence of embezzlement in the yard, Phil?'

'We weren't concerning ourselves with fraud, but I must say their bookkeeper, Jayne Howlett, seemed pretty nervous and on the defensive when we questioned her.'

'And word is, Higgs' wife has chucked him out over some other woman,' offered Jack. 'Perhaps it's Jayne Howlett and, together, the two got their fingers into Full-deck's till.'

'So why didn't the old man just fire them?' asked Hengrove, tapping his empty glass on the table.

'He might have been going to before Higgs worked out his own solution.' Jack stood and picked up his friend's glass as well as his own. 'Higgs had motive, Phil. How about opportunity? Did he have an alibi for the time of death?'

Hengrove shook his head. 'No, just said he was alone in the yard on the fleet boat he was living on.'

'Well, he's my number one suspect until someone else sticks their head above the parapet,' stated Jack, indicating the DCI's glass and getting a nod in return.

'And mine's still Haverson or the girl…' Hengrove indicated towards the bar. '… and a pint of the same, if you please.'

The DCI couldn't divulge all his findings, thought Jack as he went for the drinks. Perhaps Phil Hengrove knew things he didn't.

* * *

Little did DCI Hengrove realise that his two prime suspects were approaching *The Steamboat* even as he sipped his beer within its amiable walls.

Halfway down the broad, *Electrifier* purred along, the only sound, the swish of her stem cutting through still water. At the wheel, concentrating on steering them along the marked channel, Sally found it easy to show enthusiasm for Ian Haverson's pride and joy. 'She's so quiet, Ian. I can actually hear the birds around us.'

Standing beside Sally in the boat's open centre cockpit, the young engineer smiled and nodded. 'Not only silent but also totally free from vibration and the smell of fuel. Add to that, the elimination of worry about water pollution, coolant-water, and the cost of diesel ever-rising, and you have an almost perfect propulsion system…'

'… that leaves no ecological footprint,' completed Sally, altering course slightly to avoid a pair of sleeping swans, seemingly unperturbed by their silent approach. She nodded down to where the electric motor hummed beneath their feet. 'This electric power seems to allow you to be far more at one with nature, but there must be some negative issues with it, Ian. Why, for instance, was Higgs so opposed to it?'

'Because it's different, that's all.' Ian slapped his hand on *Electrifier*'s cabin top in mock frustration. 'But yes, you have to accept some limitations with a boat like this. Endurance is one. A full tank of fuel for a diesel engine will give you a week's cruising, whereas a full charge on this boat will be good for only a day. It then takes a few hours to recharge, whereas a refuel of diesel is done in minutes.' He shrugged. 'All of which simply means a bit of pre-planning which is half the fun anyway.'

'How about cost?' Sally was sure that money had to be the overriding argument against this technology.

'Well, yes,' admitted Ian, 'it is expensive to convert any existing boat but, once it's done, you have probably ten years of very cheap boating before the batteries have to be replaced. In that time, the cost of fossil fuels will, of course, have continued to soar.' He shook his head. 'But, can I get the industry to see that?' His voice carried the near-despair of one who has constantly preached logic. 'If just the hire fleets alone converted to electric power and charged their batteries with alternative sources like my turbine mills, we could save the world almost three thousand tons of CO_2 emissions annually.'

Sally gave her own smile of encouragement. 'It'll happen eventually, Ian. It has to.' The staithe and *Steamboat* were coming up now and she indicated the wheel. 'You show me how it's done. I'd hate to set electric boats back a decade by crashing this one into the pub.'

He smiled, took the wheel and brought the power lever back to STOP. *Electrifier* continued to glide close to the quay where only a little astern power brought her neatly alongside. 'Well, here we are on eco-fuel.' Ian nodded towards the old thatched inn. 'Lets go and get ourselves some supper.'

* * *

'Jack! … fancy meeting you here.'

Sally had noticed the Ranger as soon as she and Ian had entered the bar and her greeting was warmed by the surprise of finding a friendly face in strange surroundings.

'Good to see you both.' Jack stood up and shook the engineer's hand. 'How are you, Ian?'

'Well, thanks, Mr Fellows.' Ian turned to Jack's drinking companion. 'How are *you*, Mr Hengrove?'

'Okay.' The DCI remained seated and took another swig of his beer.

'Will you join us for a drink?' asked Jack, sensing a slight atmosphere and indicating the two empty seats.

'No thanks Jack, we're eating and it's a bit late already,' explained Sally, before saying goodbye and following Ian into the dining room. 'That Chief Inspector would make a nun feel guilty,' she groaned as they chose a window-table overlooking the broad.

'I know,' agreed Ian, laughing, 'I think they must teach them that at police college.'

'Anyway, let's forget all that for one evening.' Sally took in the room's twinkling candles and intimate atmosphere, picked up the menu and scanned the appetising fayre. 'And remember, this meal's on me.'

'Oh that's hardly fair,' protested her escort as he made his own selection, 'I asked *you*, remember?'

'I know, but I owe you for getting power back on and then giving me my first sailing lesson.' The waitress came and took their order leaving Sally to sit back contentedly. 'You know, Ian, that hour in *Joker* this afternoon was one of the most thrilling experiences of my life.'

'Well, like I said, I think you're a natural,' encouraged Ian. 'You know the basics now, so just go and practise on your own as often as you can.'

'I will,' promised Sally. 'I love challenges and this is such an exciting one.'

The engineer smiled and leaned closer. 'I've been thinking about that, Sally. Little *Joker* is great for learning the basics, but you'll soon be yearning for something bigger.'

'Meaning?'

'Meaning, that I reckon we should get you sailing *Ace of Hearts*. Not on your own, but we could go out together for a few trips and let you see what a real boat is like.'

'But I thought she needed a good overhaul?'

Ian shrugged. 'The rigging will all have to be checked, of course, but that won't take long and I'll soon have the paint and varnish cleaned up. Let's sail and enjoy her.'

Their meals arrived and, for the moment, they savoured good food and wine, but Sally's thoughts kept returning to the possibly of handling *Ace of Hearts*. Between mouthfuls she asked, 'So, when can we sail her?'

Ian laughed. 'Allow tomorrow for me to check her over. How about the day after?'

'Mmmm, sounds great.' She looked outside. The near-full moon was high again, casting a gleaming ribbon of light across the placid expanse of the broad. It was a truly beautiful scene, but she hoped there would be more wind for *Ace of Hearts* in a couple of day's time. 'What have you in mind?'

'An expedition.'

'Expedition?'

'Yes,' he explained, enthusiastically. 'All you've seen, so far, is this minute corner of Broadland. It's time you explored further afield, so what I'm proposing is that we head downriver.'

'How far?' Sally asked, thrilled at the idea, but still unsure what this attractive, fast-working young man had in mind.

'Not far. Everything is very relative with sailing and just a few miles may seem like a substantial passage.' He looked out to where the sun had long-since disappeared below the horizon. 'Just over there is an old abbey called St Benet's. Not much left of it, but plenty of atmosphere and a great place to walk and relax. We could make it there and back in a day.'

'And I could do us a picnic,' Sally enthused. 'Ian, I can't wait.'

'Nor me.' He looked into her eyes and held up his glass close enough for their fingers to touch. 'To our first voyage together.'

'To our first voyage,' she responded, not quite sure whether to be happy or alarmed at the feelings galloping their way into her ever-cautious soul. It was almost a relief when the waitress chose this moment to clear their plates. Waiting for cheese and biscuits, Sally put her hands together earnestly and said, 'Now, about your family, Ian. You said you were brought up by a grandfather. What of your real parents?'

'Both wasters in their way,' he replied, without apparent rancour or self pity. 'Father, Granddad's son, died of alcoholism shortly after I was born. Mother was something of a hippie and took off to California shortly afterwards, never to be seen again. So, my dear granddad took me on and here I am.'

'Oh, that's sad,' responded Sally with genuine concern. 'Memories of youth should be ones of happiness, whereas yours must be quite painful.'

'Not really. I was very young when all that happened so, like you, I can't remember my parents and, therefore, never missed them. Besides, in spite of the big age gap, my granddad was great fun to grow up with.'

'You said he was a Broads' naturalist…?'

'Yes, and historian.' Ian was obviously pleased to get the conversation on more positive lines. 'In spite of his politics, Howard Haverson was well-regarded in his day. Before the war he'd conducted a full survey of the Broads and written a guide for boaters, plus several works on the ecology of the region. It made him quite famous and rich as well but, not long after I went to live with him, he went bankrupt so life at home was pretty frugal.'

'I'm sorry,' said Sally, thinking of her own comfortable upbringing with Granny Emily and feeling concerned that she'd raised a painful subject.

'Don't be.' Ian sat back with a reassuring half-smile. 'Lack of money didn't mean life was uninteresting. Quite the contrary, growing up with Howard Haverson was one adventure after another.' He nodded towards the broad. 'Granddad had a small rowing boat and every week we'd go out on some expedition to research an aspect of nature or history.' Ian's smile broadened into one of genuine nostalgia. 'He had the knack of making anything totally fascinating, whether it be the life-span of a beetle, history of some boat, patterns of vegetation or the migration habits of our birdlife. He could talk about it all and I just loved listening and learning.'

'You were obviously very fond of him.' Sally put her head on one side, sympathetically. 'Have you been without him long?'

'Oh, since I was a teenager,' replied Ian, trying not to sound bitter. 'He committed suicide when I was just sixteen.'

'Suicide!' she exclaimed, genuinely shocked. 'How terrible for you.'

'Yes.' He gave a shrug of the shoulders. 'At the time it was devastating but, in later years, I came to understand. In spite of professional success, he'd had a life of tragedy really, getting lots of stick for his politics, losing his wife and son, and, finally, all his money. I guess, he came to feel he couldn't handle the stigma of it any more.'

'Well, I'm sure he would have been so proud of all you've done to preserve the environment he loved, Ian.' The cheese and biscuits and coffee had arrived and pouring the latter gave Sally the chance to change tack. 'And you must keep up that wonderful work. How do you plan to go ahead from here?'

'I'm not sure. There are so many old ways to change.' He took a sip of his coffee and made a positive effort to brighten. 'But it can ... and *will* ... be done. It'll take money to implement all my ideas and a lot of effort too, but...' Ian paused and touched Sally's hand again, '... so much easier if you have someone to share the battle.'

Their backgrounds were so similar, thought Sally, and his ideals were so akin to her own views of the world. It wasn't difficult to imagine sharing life with this enthusiastic young engineer, but for now, she just smiled and savoured the moment.

* * *

Jack Fellows and Phil Hengrove had departed homeward and *The Steamboat*'s bell rung "time" before Sally and Ian finished their last lingering drink and exited into the chill night air of the staithe. Lights glowed behind curtains in the two cruisers ahead of *Electrifier*, and music and laughter from within showed the youngsters' party was far from over.

'I've got a couple of bottles on board,' said Ian, putting his arm around Sally's waist. 'Why don't we join them?'

'Because I've to be up early for an appointment with the doctor in the morning,' she answered firmly, but with a smile.

His face was suddenly one of concern. 'Nothing wrong with you, is there?'

'No, just registering and trying to learn a little more about Granddad at the same time.' Sally stood on her tiptoes and gave him a reassuring kiss on the cheek, but then realised she was being held in that position by Ian's strong arms and that her lips were moving towards his with all the fire of mutual attraction.

That embrace felt so heartfelt and natural, but finally she said, 'We must go,' and eased away.

They boarded *Electrifier* and minutes later, navigation lights shining, they were backing silently into open water and sliding away.

Enveloped as they were with their own smouldering emotions, they failed to notice the secretive figure watching them from the darkness of the staithe. It continued watching them until only a trail of disturbed water along the moon's path, marked their passage.

* * *

Gliding homeward, with the full moon lighting their way and only the chuckle of the bow-wave to break the infinite peace of the scene, Sally felt the enchantment of her new world enfolding around her.

But even enchanted worlds pose unanswered questions and, in this ethereal darkness, Sally sought the answer to a phenomenon that had been bothering her for some time.

'Ian, have you ever heard of Corpse Candles?'

'You've been talking to Mollie Jenkins,' was his immediate but slightly amused reply.

'Not just talking,' she assured him. 'My first night in *Marsh Haven*, after that incident with the intruder, I saw ... well, a strange light, like a flickering flame, moving across the marshes.'

'That was a Corpse Candle all right,' confirmed Ian, casually. 'Will-o'-the-wisp or Jack-o'-lantern are other names for them around the country. I've seen them once or twice myself and, of course, in old times, local folk believed they were the spirits of the dead.'

'Mrs Jenkins still does,' said Sally. 'She says they're the spirits of children the Romans buried in the pools hereabouts.'

'Yes, well, Mrs Jenkins would.' Ian gave a cynical laugh. 'With all her strange beliefs and superstitions, a few centuries ago would have seen Mollie Jenkins burned as a witch.' He turned and faced Sally with a reassuring grin. 'The fact is, no-one is really sure what causes them, but they have to have some scientific explanation.'

'Such as?' asked Sally, intrigued.

'Well, the fact that they are usually only seen in wet and marshy areas seems to indicate they are probably caused by the spontaneous ignition of swamp gas or methane. However, my grandfather's opinion was always that they were an electro-chemical luminous phenomenon. Some trees have phosphorescent fungi growing on them which may be picked up by birds' feathers. We know owls' wings often appear luminous at night and this would explain why they are sometimes seen in wooded areas as well. Don't worry,' he said, cheerfully, 'there are no ghosts and goblins around here.'

'Well, it looked pretty spooky to me,' Sally shuddered. 'After what I thought was a ghost, the last thing I needed was a phantom light drifting through the reedbeds.'

'*Marsh Haven* is a lonely place,' agreed Ian. 'I can understand you being a bit nervous.' He paused for a few seconds, as though unsure how to phrase what he had in mind. He turned and looked out ahead as he finally said, 'If you like, I can stay with you tonight.'

Sally smiled to herself. It was a suggestion she wasn't totally adverse to on this night of burgeoning feelings, but a determination to think twice, if not three times, before she jumped into a man's bed again, made her say words she didn't really want to.

'I'll be fine, thanks Ian, but knowing I can call you if I need help will be a great comfort.'

He appeared to accept her brush-off with good nature and continued to steer them up the moonbeam.

* * *

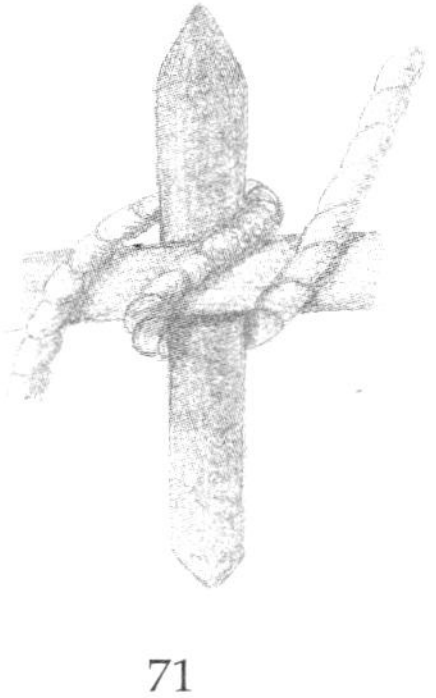

Chapter Twelve

The surgery was less than a mile from the staithe, and Sally enjoyed her stroll along the village street, studying the varied architecture. Thatched cottages seemed to predominate, but there was also a good assortment of modern houses and bungalows, all with well-kept gardens. One building, however, was first on her list to visit.

All Saints Church was quite large for the small village it served. Walking through the lych-gate and up the pebbled path, Sally found the round Saxon tower particularly enchanting, its small portholes and belfry openings in contrast to the beautiful gothic windows that were reflecting the morning light with an almost spiritual candescence. She wondered at the logistics needed to create such a beautiful place of worship all those centuries ago, and all the good people since who had lavished so much love and care in maintaining it.

The graves of many now lined the path she was walking along. It was a place of death, but in the surrounding trees birds sang in joyful celebration of life while, just visible through gaps, the broad itself glistened in the morning light. The atmosphere was one of blissful tranquillity, the perfect setting for her nature-loving grandfather to rest his bones for eternity. By the far edge, she could see some graves with fresh flowers. She made her way towards them.

Sure enough, at the very end was a simple wooden cross. Sally leaned down to read the name on the brass plate.

CHARLES McKENNA-HYNES

She stood for a few minutes, wishing she had brought some flowers. There were still wreaths scattered around, fast decaying and their inscriptions barely readable. One caught her attention. It was written in a bold hand and contained one word.

Sorry

Who had written this plaintive message and why the apology beyond the grave? It was a sentiment she felt herself, for never having met this man who had taken such an interest in her life. Sally gave her fingers a gentle kiss and placed them on the cross. 'I wish I'd known you,' she said aloud. Then she left.

Back outside the lych-gate, Sally paused to make a note of service times, particularly evensong which she and Granny Emily had always attended together in suburbia. She'd become a somewhat spasmodic worshipper since, but sensed it would be good to feel the peace of the church as part of her new life.

Walking on through the rest of the village, Sally was grateful for the calming influence All Saints had imparted. It had been the perfect antidote for the mixed emotions she'd been feeling since rejecting Ian's romantic overtures of the night before. 'Just too soon,' she'd kept telling herself. She glanced at her watch. 'But not for my appointment,' she realised, as she left All Saints behind and quickened her step towards the surgery.

Set on the edge of the village, the modern single storey Health Centre stood in direct contrast to its picturesque neighbours. There were several vehicles parked outside, including a police car and a glazier's van, the owner of which was busy fitting a new window beside the centre's entrance. At the desk inside, the receptionist appeared to be distracted.

'Sorry, we're not quite up to speed this morning,' she apologised, 'as we got broken into last night.'

'Oh dear,' sympathised Sally, sad that even rural villages were not immune to common crime. A young man was talking to the senior receptionist, and as Sally took her seat he turned, appeared to recognise her and came over.

'It's Miss Beckett, isn't it?'

'Yes…' For a second, Sally suffered that common embarrassment of being recognised by someone she couldn't place herself. But then she remembered the jet-black hair, tall strong physique, same smart no-nonsense suit and well-shined shoes. He looked exactly the same as he did that recent night in suburbia. 'Of course… it's Detective Constable…'

'… Bailey,' the young policeman completed for her, smiling pleasantly. 'Didn't expect to meet you here, Miss Beckett. Nothing ailing, I hope?'

'No, just registering,' explained Sally before enquiring, 'and you…?'

'Duty,' he said before cocking his head slightly towards reception and almost miming, 'break in last night.'

'Yes, they just told me.'

Bailey glanced around and then sat down on the seat beside her. 'So, how are you settling in here?' he asked with more-than-average interest.

'Oh, I love it,' she responded with equal sincerity, 'in spite of the odd incident.'

'Yes, the intruder,' said Bailey with a roll of the eyes. 'I have made some enquiries, but no results as yet.' He seemed to brighten with an idea. 'Perhaps you could give me more details some time?'

'Oh, I don't want to waste police time on something that was probably nothing,' she responded, lamely.

'We take intrusion very seriously,' Bailey assured her in his most authoritative voice, before lowering his tone again and almost whispering, 'but, if you don't feel like a formal interview, perhaps we could meet socially some time?'

There was no mistaking the invitation. 'Oh, gosh, I'm not sure…' she stammered. 'Perhaps…'

'Miss Beckett?' A tall, well-dressed lady was standing at the entrance to the consulting rooms. She smiled when Sally stood up. 'Please come this way.'

'Here's my card,' said Bailey, thwarted but undefeated. 'Let me know if I can help in any way or … you just want a chat.'

There was such sincerity in his voice, that Sally had no difficulty remembering the attraction she'd initially felt for this young officer. As she slipped the card into her pocket, she was disturbed to realise that feeling was with her still. Quickly murmuring a hasty, 'Thank you,' she shook his hand, at the same time knowing it was a rather inadequate response to someone showing such kind interest. Then she was following Doctor Newson to the consulting room, only too aware that she was running away.

'Hello, I'm Helen Newson,' said the doctor with outstretched hand.

Sally, took her seat opposite. Probably because of Mrs Jenkins' reference to Helen Newson as a "village girl", she'd imagined her to be much younger. This doctor was an undeniably attractive woman, tall and slim with well-styled, but greying hair, that hinted at an age nearer sixty than fifty.

'I'm sorry for all the disruption,' she apologised, nodding towards the splintered frame of the door, 'but we had visitors last night.'

'Yes, I'm sorry.' It was probably a stupid question but Sally asked it anyway. 'Does that sort of thing happen often around here?'

'First time.' Doctor Newson indicated the filing cabinet beside her desk that had obviously had a jemmy taken to its drawers. 'Looking for drugs, no doubt.' She leaned forward and smiled. 'Now, I understand you've just moved into the village and want to register?'

'Yes, I'm out at *Marsh Haven*,' explained Sally.

'Of course, you're Captain Charles' long-lost granddaughter.' The doctor smiled sympathetically. 'I'm sorry it was such a sad circumstance that brought you here.'

'Yes, thank you. I wish I'd known him, as he seemed to be such a lovely man.'

'He was,' agreed the doctor. 'Quite a character who will be sadly missed.' Having, seemingly, dispensed with pleasantries, Helen Newson reverted back to business. 'The practice manager will give you a form to be completed,' she said in her ever-charming voice with its hint of Norfolk dialect, 'but I'll just check your blood-pressure for the record.' She popped on her stethoscope and, like all doctors, seemed to have the knack of conducting a professional and casual conversation in effortless tandem. 'I hope you like boats,' she said between glances at the reading, 'because, you'll already have gathered, that's the way of life around here.'

'Well, I'd never sailed before,' answered Sally, 'but I'm learning on Granddad's little dinghy.'

'Good, that's normal,' smiled Doctor Newson, releasing the pressure and removing her stethoscope. 'That must be *Joker*,' she said, picking up Sally's answer. 'I learned to sail in her myself, as a little girl, when my dad owned the yard.'

For a moment, Sally was confused and then the realisation came. 'Of course, it was Newson Boats before my grandfather took it over. I hadn't put the two names together.'

Helen Newson nodded. 'Yes, my father built that yard up before the war. I was only eight when he sold out to Captain Charles, but I'd loved growing up amongst it all.' She smiled nostalgically. 'I can still smell that wonderful aroma of wood, glue and varnish that went with boat-building in those days.'

'Fancy both of us learning to sail in *Joker*?' declared Sally.

'She was called *Popkin* then,' explained the doctor, 'because Dad built her especially for me and I named her that. She was renamed when Captain Charles bought out everything and called it Full-deck Marine, which I always thought was a very funny name for a boatyard,' she added, with just the hint of asperity.

'Why did your father sell then?' asked Sally, anxious to dilute any raw memories.

'He was determined I should make a career in something other than boatyards and decided to put everything into my education.' Doctor Newson said it with obvious affection for her father if not, perhaps, gratitude. 'Charles was working in the yard at the time and indicated he'd like to buy, so Dad sold it to him and here we are.'

'Well, you certainly returned your dad's investment,' said Sally, continuing to be upbeat. 'How long did Granddad work in the yard before he bought it from your father?'

'As long as I could remember, but Dad said he came to the yard looking for a job soon after the war. Apparently, he had a great knowledge of boats and was an excellent worker so Dad was glad to have him.'

'But going from worker to owner is a big jump. Where would Granddad have got the money to do it?'

'I've no idea,' replied the doctor, 'but I think Dad assumed he'd inherited it or something.'

'I see,' Sally murmured, almost to herself. She wasn't sure if she should ask her next question. 'Doctor Newson, everyone tells me Granddad was unwell for the latter part of his life. What was his condition actually?'

The doctor didn't look up immediately and when she did there was just a touch of exasperation in her voice. 'He'd been suffering short-term memory loss and uncharacteristic mood swings for some time. I initially diagnosed mild cognitive impairment and put him on a course of treatment. In the end, it turned out he just hadn't been feeding himself properly, with resulting simple vitamin deficiency. An improved diet supervised by Mrs Jenkins soon put him right. He was virtually fully recovered when…'

'… he was murdered,' completed Sally, deliberately coming to the painful point.

'I think you'll find the coroner recorded an open verdict, Sally.' Doctor Newson spoke with renewed kindness in her voice.

'But could Granddad's medication have triggered any depression or other mental problems?' asked Sally, feeling she had to press her points while she had the chance.

'MCI itself can induce depression,' explained Doctor Newson, 'but I saw no such symptoms in your grandfather. I rather got the feeling there was something on his mind, but I put that down to concern over his condition. Full details of his medication are, of course, detailed in his medical records and available for inspection…' she glanced towards her filing cabinet, '… or were, before they were stolen.'

'Stolen!' exclaimed Sally.

'Yes.' Doctor Newson gave a shake of her head. 'For some reason, our thief of the night decided to steal patient medical records.'

'What, all of them?'

'No, only about a dozen.'

'But including my Grandfather's?'

'Yes.'

'But why would any thief want those?'

'I have no idea.'

'But aren't your records also on computer now?'

'In the process of, but not complete,' said Doctor Newson.

'So, what was my grandfather's general physical condition?' asked Sally, determined to find out as much as she could in the brief time available.

'Excellent,' replied Doctor Newson, without hesitation. 'I gave him a full medical examination just twelve months before his death and, apart from the scars, found him to be in perfect physical shape.'

'"The scars"?' queried Sally.

'Yes, he had some very long scars on his upper torso. The injuries that caused them must have been quite severe at the time,' explained the doctor with a grimace.

'Did he say how he got them?'

'Only that it was during the war.' Doctor Newson glanced at her watch. 'Sally, I've got a stack of patients to get through and...'

'Of course.' Sally stood up to leave. 'You must be very busy.'

'That's general practice for you,' agreed the doctor with a sigh. She gave Sally a warm smile. 'Good luck with the yard.' There was note of genuine regret in her voice when she then said, 'There are times I wish Dad had never sold the business and that I could be doing what you are now. I envy you, Sally.'

'Thanks.' Feeling she should make some gesture, Sally turned at the door and said, 'If you'd ever like to sail your old boat again, Doctor Newson, you'd be welcome...'

'That's very kind, but time is always a problem for me now. I've got a small kayak, so on the odd day off I can still get afloat.'

'Well, I hope I see you out there sometime,' answered Sally, sincerely.

Back in reception, DC Bailey had gone and the window was repaired. Sally completed her registration forms and also left.

Outside, the air was clear and fresh after the slightly sterilised atmosphere of the health centre. She had never liked hospitals or anything medical so she certainly didn't envy Helen Newson her profession and the doctor, herself, had almost admitted she would rather be running a boatyard. 'A strange world,' thought Sally.

Walking back through the village, she mentally recapped the conversation. She'd learned new facts about her grandfather but, in a way, the doctor had raised more questions than she'd answered. And why would anyone steal medical records?

Was she getting neurotic or was Helen Newson yet another person around here who knew more than she was admitting?

* * *

'So, you've got the new gov'nor coming to check your books this afternoon?' Henry Higgs had stuck his head through the doorway of the small yard office where Jayne Howlett was checking some recent invoices.

'Yes, she wants to go through everything,' the young bookkeeper said nervously. Jayne Howlett was a very pretty girl, not much younger than Sally, and the object of constant admiration by the workshop hands who knew better than to chat her up when Henry Higgs was around.

'Well, you just be careful what you show her,' growled the yard manager, threateningly.

'I'll try, but if she has a specific agenda, what can I do?'

'Tell her to go and find out herself,' was Higgs' abrupt answer. Then he slammed the door and left Jayne to her anguish.

She ran an agitated hand through her long fair hair. How she wished she had never been talked into that dreadful financial manipulation. Her aunt's warning never to mix business with pleasure had been ignored and now both her personal and professional reputation had been compromised to the point of jeopardy.

She had come to Full-deck Marine as a contract bookkeeper with a reputation for hard work and high morals. Captain Charles had been so good to her and paid more than the going rate for her service. He was the last man in the world she would want to cheat and yet, she had done just that, and willingly, for the man who had seduced her in every way. And now poor Captain Charles was dead and she had her own dreadful suspicions as to the reason.

Once again, she scanned the computer printouts of Full-deck Marine's accounts and hoped this Sally Beckett wasn't as assertive an auditor as she was a manager. Judging by what Henry Higgs had said about her first visit, the omens weren't good and if she got just an inkling… Jayne resisted the temptation to put her head in her hands. She might have coped better if she hadn't also been going through the agonies of emotional turmoil. As it was, she seemed to have lost control of a life now seemingly bent on a course of total self-destruction.

How she wished she had never come anywhere near this boatyard.

* * *

With twenty minutes to spare before her meeting with Jayne Howlett, Sally decided to enjoy some sunshine at the staithe. Because of her doctor's appointment and this meeting, she wouldn't be taking Mollie Jenkins to *Marsh Haven* until the afternoon, so it was a good time to relax on the public bench, think things over and, perhaps, feed a few ducks at the same time. As it was, when she reached the staithe, she found not only the two cruisers of the night before, but also the

Navigation Ranger's launch moored just astern.

'Hello, Jack,' she shouted cheerfully from the bank.

The Ranger was sitting in the open aft cockpit of his launch filling in a report form, but he looked up immediately on hearing the familiar voice. 'Sally! Come on board.'

She stepped across the gap onto the launch where neatly coiled ropes and carefully stowed equipment spoke of ordered practicality. 'Busy, Jack?'

He shrugged. 'Not particularly, but we had some complaints about the noise from those boats last night.' He indicated the hire-cruisers ahead. 'Apparently they had a bit of a party into the early hours that you could hear in the village.'

'Oh dear,' grinned Sally. 'They were already into their shindig when we left and it did seem to be warming up well.'

Jack gave a smile of his own. 'Just youngsters letting off a bit of steam, but we have to warn them. Nice kids, actually, and they took the rollicking in good part.' He looked into Sally's eyes. 'How about you? Good time yourself?'

Sally nodded. 'Yes, lovely, thank you. I had a fascinating evening learning about Ian's own grandfather.'

'Howard Haverson, a renowned Broadsman in his day,' nodded Jack. 'A great shame he ended his life as he did.'

'Yes indeed,' agreed Sally. 'Poor Ian's had a fair bit of tragedy to deal with in his life, one way or another.'

Jack smiled and there was just a twinkle in the Ranger's eyes as they met Sally's. 'You two seem to be getting on quite well.'

'Yes, we are,' she admitted, before adding, 'but it's early days yet.' Never having had a man in her family who she could talk to like this, Sally was pleased to air her feelings.

'Best not to rush into things,' agreed Jack and then, sensing a subject change might be welcome, continued, 'So, what have *you* been up to this morning?'

Sally explained her time at the doctor's, including meeting DC Bailey investigating the break in.

Jack shook his head. 'Drugs. The root of most of the evil they have to deal with now.'

'That's the strange thing,' said Sally, and went on to explain the medical records being stolen.

'Including your granddad's?'

'Yes.'

'Hmmm.' Jack didn't say any more for a while, but Sally could see this bit of information had particularly disturbed him.

'Is this co-incidence, Jack, or do you think it might somehow be connected to Granddad's death?'

'I'm not sure, but these waters seem to be getting ever murkier,' he commented without expanding further.

'How about your contact at the MoD? Any word back from him yet on Granddad's war record?'

'Not yet,' answered Jack, 'but I'm hoping there might be an e-mail waiting for me when I get home tonight.'

'Oh, please give me a ring if you find out something,' urged Sally. 'I'm longing to know more about the grandfather I never knew.' She nodded over towards the sheds of Full-deck Marine. 'Must go, as I'm meeting Jayne Howlett to peruse the yard accounts.'

'Should be interesting,' commented Jack before concluding, 'Time to be off myself. I'll ring tonight if I've found out something.'

Sally thanked him and then set off for the yard. How she hoped that some light might soon pierce the darkness of this whole mysterious business. She loved the Broads, but wanted so much to know why she actually came to be amongst them.

* * *

'So, on paper, we made a respectable profit last year?' Sally worked her pencil down the lines on the computer printout and underlined the magic figure.

Jayne nodded. 'It only represented eight per cent of turnover, but that was reasonable in the present economic climate.'

'Then why,' asked Sally, pulling the balance sheet towards her and ringing the relevant figure, 'have we so little cash in the bank?' In the short while she had spent with Jayne Howlett, she had formed a liking for the girl, but had reservations as to her grip on Full-deck's finances.

'The electrification programme soaked up most of the yard's cash,' explained the young bookkeeper. 'All those batteries and electric propulsion motors cost a fortune.'

'Buying components simply means exchanging one asset for another.' Sally ringed another figure on the sheet. 'We should consequently be showing a high "Stock" figure but we aren't.'

'That's because the equipment was installed in the boats so it's the "fleet" figure that will reflect the new equipment,' explained Jayne, leaning across the table and pointing out that figure on the balance sheet.

'But, from what I understand, the electrification programme has been reversed,' queried Sally, determined to get to the bottom of Full-deck's apparent cash crisis. 'If those motors have now been removed from the boats and returned to store, they should show in that section of the accounts. From what I can see,' Sally pulled another computer listing from the selection spread before her, 'our stores comprise a couple of fenders and half a dozen nuts and bolts.'

'Well, over three thousand pound's worth of items, actually,' Jayne replied, defensively.

'Peanuts!' Sally shook her head in bewilderment. 'This yard's been indulging in a major re-engining project with, it seems to me, very little accountability of assets.'

'What are you insinuating then?'

Sally turned round to find the stocky figure of Henry Higgs filling the doorway.

'Seeing as you've blessed us with your presence, Mr Higgs,' retorted Sally with as much sarcasm as she could generate, 'I'll make it plain what my thoughts are. Money has been going out for electrification components which, thanks to your reversing the programme, have never been used. There is, however, no record of what has happened to those components. If they are "in store", show them to me. If they've been sold, show me the entry.'

'Boatyards don't do business like that,' explained Higgs, patronisingly. 'A lot of what we do is in cash…' he gave a sneering nod towards the accounts sheets, 'and it doesn't always go through your precious computer system.'

'Well, it should do!' exclaimed Sally with an equally meaning look at Jayne Howlett, who seemed to have shrunken away from this rancid discussion. 'I'm going to need some answers as to where that cash has gone but, in the meantime I'd like an explanation of these entries.' Sally pulled another spreadsheet from the pile. 'The "payments" journal shows a monthly "rent" of over fifteen hundred pounds. The balance sheet,' she stubbed her pencil towards the "credit" side of the statement, 'shows no property assets whatsoever.' Sally sat back and looked from one to the other. 'Can either of you explain why Full-deck Marine no longer appears to own the freehold of its own yard?'

'Because it was sold off to generate more cash,' explained Higgs.

'When?'

'A few months ago.'

'When, I understand, Granddad was quite ill and, in your own words, "making quite a few screwball decisions". Was he aware of the transaction?'

'Of course he was. He had to sign the papers, didn't he,' came Higgs' surly answer.

'So, how much did it make?'

'About half a million.'

'Good heavens!' Sally shook her head. 'So, where is that money now?'

'Some was spent on that useless electrification project,' grumbled Higgs.

'… but the bulk went into your grandfather's personal account,' added Jayne, obviously anxious to assure accountability.

'… a third of which *you* have just inherited,' added Higgs, bitterly.

'And our new landlords, this "Marine Development Holdings",' Sally, jabbed her pencil against the name on the spreadsheet, 'who are *they* exactly?'

She was directing the question towards Jayne Howlett, but the bookkeeper simply lowered her eyes. Sally transferred her questioning look to Higgs who answered cagily, 'Just a group of local businessmen who got together and bought the yard as an investment.'

'I see.' Sally gathered up the printouts and jammed them into her rucksack. 'Right, you two…' she looked at both Higgs and Jayne, '… I want a summary of cash received for selling off that electrical equipment and also,' she looked this time only at Higgs, 'the names of the so-called investors who've bought this yard from under my grandfather's nose.'

And with that Sally stormed out, leaving her staff staring at each other in bemused silence and herself wondering why she'd had the distinct impression that her late grandfather had been hovering around them throughout the complete discussion.

* * *

'Dinner smells good, Audrey. Casserole isn't it?'

Walking into the cottage kitchen at the end of his day's duty, Jack sniffed the evening meal cooking in the oven with an appreciative sigh.

Audrey came out from the lounge where she had settled down just minutes before to watch the evening news. 'Right first time, Jack Fellows. Be about another ten minutes. Come and watch the news and have a gin and tonic while you're waiting.'

'Perfect.' Jack kicked off his shoes. 'Done anything special yourself today, love?'

'Oh, just the church accounts on the computer,' she answered, pouring a measure of gin into her husband's favourite glass. 'By the way, I noticed there was an e-mail for you.'

'Who from?' asked Jack, over his shoulder as he washed his hands in the sink.

'Not sure, but I think it's from your friend at the MoD.' Audrey added tonic to the gin. 'Do you want ice in this, Jack?' But she got no answer. Already her husband had left the kitchen and was running up the stairs.

In his study, Jack's laptop seemed to take an eternity to bring up the e-mails. He clicked open the only message in his inbox. It was indeed from his friend answering his request for details of Captain Charles' naval service. Perhaps now he would have something definite to pass on to Sally Beckett.

Jack scanned through the information his friend had sent him. He blinked twice and read right through the contents again, more slowly and carefully. Then he sat back and rubbed his forehead, trying to bring some sort of logic to its disclosures.

'Do you want your drink up there or down here?' called Audrey from below.

'Down there, love,' answered Jack, before adding, 'and make it a double.'

*　　*　　*

Chapter Thirteen

After last night's good food, wine and company, Sally was finding this evening alone at *Marsh Haven* rather an anticlimax.

The revelation that her boatyard's finances were far from healthy was yet another worry to be mulled over. The present economic climate was causing many businesses to face cash crises, but Full-deck's problem was patently self-induced. Sally's years in The City had not been ones she had particularly enjoyed, but they had given her a certain nose for sharp practice and what she smelled at that boatyard was downright fraud. Plainly, Henry Higgs had been selling off unwanted electrical components and pocketing the cash.

What was harder to take was that young Jayne Howlett, the bookkeeper, had obviously been part of the cover-up. Sally found it difficult to imagine any woman being emotionally involved with a bully like Higgs, but Jayne Howlett certainly seemed to be dominated by the man.

Lack of cash, however, seemed only to be the tip of this venal iceberg. Selling off components was serious enough, but someone had even sold the freehold of the yard. She made a mental note to call Landers, Simpson & Hedges first thing in the morning. Her grandfather's solicitor, Herbert Blenkinsop, would surely have handled this dubious transaction. Then, perhaps, she'd find out who the new owners of the freehold really were.

Sally felt the need to talk all this over with someone and badly missed Ian Haverson's company, but the young engineer was off fixing a problem on someone's electric boat and wasn't sure when he'd be back. It was a great relief therefore, when her mobile phone rang.

'Sally?'

'Jack, lovely to hear from you.' She felt a sense of nervousness as she asked, 'Have you heard anything?'

'Yes.' Jack's tone was unusually subdued. 'I've had a mail back from my contact at the MoD. He did a full check on the naval record of Charles McKenna-Hynes.'

'Wonderful. And...?'

'And... nothing.'

'Nothing?' Sally couldn't believe what she was hearing. 'But, Jack, everyone around here seemed sure that Granddad had been in the navy.

You were yourself.'

'I know,' admitted Jack. 'The fact that he'd mentioned being on small boats made me think he was probably RNVR Coastal Forces, but my contact checked those records, with a negative result. He then went through Royal Navy, Royal Naval Reserve, Royal Marines and even the marine branches of the RAF and army but, the fact is, Captain Charles has never served in any branch of the armed services.'

'My goodness.' Sally rubbed her forehead as she took in this unexpected information. 'So what are your conclusions, Jack?'

'Well, he wouldn't be the first man to claim he'd done his bit in the war and never served at all,' said Jack, regretfully.

'But, surely he wasn't that sort of man, Jack!' exclaimed Sally. 'Everyone says what high principles Granddad had and even Doctor Newson told me he had scars which were from war wounds.'

'But that was only what *he* said,' responded Jack. 'They could, just as easily, have been from some industrial accident or the like.'

'I suppose so,' admitted Sally, painfully accepting that her grandfather might well have not been all that people thought. 'It could explain why he was always, apparently, so reticent about giving any details of his war service.' She gave a little sigh of regret. 'I'm sorry you've had such a wasted effort, Jack.'

'Oh, it wasn't wasted. Remember, I said I'd also get them to do a check on your other grandfather, Sub-Lieutenant Halard RN, while they were about it. Well, they certainly had a full record on him.'

'Go on…'

'Like we surmised,' said Jack. 'A regular General List officer who'd been through Dartmouth, married Emily in 1939, gained excellent performance reports but, sadly, been killed on war service.'

'Yes, we knew that. He was killed on D-day.'

'No, he wasn't,' Jack replied.

'But, I was sure… Granny Emily always said…'

'Sally,' interrupted Jack, firmly, 'finding Captain Charles hadn't been in the navy was a bit of a shock but, believe me, your Grandfather Halard's record was the real stunner.'

'Why… what had he done… or *not* done?' asked Sally, wondering what new revelation she was going to have to face.

'Oh, don't worry,' reassured Jack, 'he died a hero's death just like your granny said, but not in 1944.'

'When then?'

'1941. You see, Edward Halard's last ship was H.M.S. *Hood*, and she was lost that year with virtually all hands.'

* * *

Sally sat back with the rum and coke she had just poured herself, all the financial worries of the yard now forgotten in the face of this last bombshell.

Jack had given her more details of *Hood*, which Sally thought had been a battleship.

'The largest warship in the world but a *battlecruiser*, actually,' Jack had corrected, before going on to explain how *Hood* and *Prince of Wales* had intercepted the German battleship *Bismark* in the Denmark Strait, during which the battlecruiser had taken a direct hit in a magazine and blown up. There had only been three survivors, 'and they didn't include Sub-Lieutenant Edward Halard,' he'd concluded.

So much for the technical details, thought Sally, as she sipped her drink and wondered why her grandmother had never told the truth about her husband's death. Dying in such dramatic action had surely been a noble enough end for a naval officer, so why had Gran thought fit to change the facts? She had always been so adamant that husband Edward had been killed on D-day. 'Are you absolutely sure about this, Jack?' she'd asked. The Ranger had expressed total faith in his contact but, nevertheless, promised to delve deeper into all the facts surrounding the tragedy.

Perhaps I ought to do a little fact-finding myself, thought Sally, bringing her mind back to the present. In the bookshelves behind her were dozens of books on nautical subjects. Surely there would be something on the loss of *Hood* in one of these. She didn't expect to find anything directly linked to her own mystery, but if Grandfather Halard really had died in that historic engagement, then family history, at least, dictated she should know more about it.

Sally went to the bookcases and started scanning the volumes. They were not in any specific order so it was a case of fingering her way along the rows, removing, checking and putting back when they proved irrelevant. Finally though, she came to one which seemed hopeful: *Decisive Naval Engagements of World War Two*. She took it out and soon found the chapter she needed.

Apart from her own personal interest, it was a story which soon had her enthralled. Snuggling down before the log fire, she read of how the brand-new *Bismark* had escaped into the Atlantic on her first foray against convoys. Cruisers of the British Home Fleet had located and shadowed the German battleship, but it needed heavy units to deliver the firepower to destroy her and that was left, initially, to *Hood* and *Prince of Wales*.

Hood was a fine and much-loved ship, but she had been designed before Jutland and suffered the weakness of light deck armour. That had probably been the reason Vice-Admiral Holland intercepted at such an extreme angle, in order to close the range and avoid plummeting shells. He went into battle, therefore, with only his for'ard turrets able to bear and the irony was that when he did ultimately alter course to open up their full broadsides, *Hood* received her deathblow.

What specifically happened was never known for sure, but all indications were that one of *Bismark*'s rounds had struck a main fifteen-inch magazine, causing *Hood* to break in two and sink within two minutes. There were only three survivors: a Midshipman Dundas, Ordinary Signalman Briggs and Able Seaman Tilburn. They had been found, clinging to liferafts within a sea of oil and wreckage, by a destroyer sent to search the scene. One thousand, four hundred and fifteen men had gone down with *Hood*... 'including my Granddad Halard, apparently,' thought Sally, as she turned the page. As she did so, some notes slipped from between the leaves and fell to the floor. Sally bent down and picked them up.

They were *Bank of England* five pound notes, but much larger and of a much thicker material than Sally had ever seen before. The figure of Britannia stood proudly in the upper left corner and, halfway down, the date of *16th March 1936*. The notes were crisp and clean, as though they had never been used.

Presumably, they held some sort of sentimental meaning for Charles. Possibly they were somehow connected to his wartime romance with Emily. When, she wondered, had that romance taken place? She preferred to think it was *after* Edward's death in 1941. Charles, it seemed, had not been in the service, so he and Emily could have met at any time. If Emily had not become pregnant with Sally's mum until 1944, then the odds were that their romance had been late in the war and, probably, the reason she had lied about poor Edward's death. Working in Suffolk throughout the war, it was possible friends in London knew nothing of her husband's loss in *Hood*. Returning home pregnant with the story that the baby's father had died just weeks before on D-day would have been far more acceptable to post-war society.

Why, though, had she not married Charles? War-widows remarrying must have been a very common occurrence at that time and carried little stigma. Perhaps it was connected to Charles having spent his war safely in England. In the heady period of post-war hero-worship, Emily's feelings may well have changed. Sally, herself, knew all too well that you could fall out of love as easily as in, but Gran had never given the impression of being fickle and Charles had obviously carried a flame for his wartime love for the rest of his life. Another explanation might simply be that Charles was already married and unable to get a divorce.

It was a mystery now put on one side as Sally saw the navigation lights of a boat silently entering the basin. She recognised it immediately as *Electrifier* and felt her heart miss a beat at the thought of Ian being back.

It would be good to talk things over with him. She slipped on her fleece and went out to help him moor up.

* * *

Sally's weren't the only eyes watching *Electrifier* glide into *Marsh Haven*'s moorings. Hidden in the reedbeds, on the other side of the channel, was the black dinghy and watching from it with binoculars, the figure who had spent each night in lone vigil. Ian Haverson returning to *Marsh Haven* for another night was bad news indeed. Would he be there until dawn? The figure gave a frustrated sigh and settled down for what might be another long cold night.

* * *

The next morning was sunny, dry and windy. Gusty enough to cause *Joker* to heel alarmingly, but Sally, remembering what she'd been told, eased the mainsheet and allowed the dinghy to accelerate even faster.

How glorious it was to be speeding towards the village staithe in this little boat. To feel *Joker* responding to her every little input, see the wash creaming away on each side and hear that wonderful chuckling sound of clinker planks on water, was heaven indeed.

Perhaps her decision to collect Mrs Jenkins by sailing dinghy rather than the dory was a little cavalier, but Sally wanted to practise her new-found skill and using free wind rather than fossil fuels seemed ecologically friendly and financially cheaper. Whether Mollie Jenkins would share those sentiments remained to be seen.

It surely wasn't the best of mornings to be indulging in alternative transport. The broad had a slightly choppier look today, with little wavelets dancing before the fresh wind. Even the waterbirds were shunning their usual early morning excursions, except for a little family of coots, which went scurrying out of her way in that funny half-running, half-flying way they had. She'd always thought that the white on the tops of their heads were feathers, but Ian had explained it was bare bone, a sort of protection plate that inspired the expression, "Bald as a Coot".

She'd left him working on *Ace of Hearts*, checking the rigging, getting the sails from the shed and tying them on the spars. "Bending them on" was the odd way he described it. How strange were all these funny nautical expressions, but part of the learning process and all good fun. She hoped the boat would be ready for the proposed expedition tomorrow; it would be good to get her hands on the helm of that big cruiser, be it under strict supervision.

But, was she ready for that? The next few minutes might decide because the staithe was coming up and she could see Mrs Jenkins on the jetty talking to a slim girl she recognised as Jayne Howlett. What was her bookkeeper doing there? It was a question that would have to wait as Sally concentrated once more on planning her approach in the knowledge that this time, there would be no going astern on an engine to stop. Coming alongside in *Joker* meant judging her speed and angle just right so that when she "brought up", the wind would be the brake that stopped them… she hoped!

One problem was already presenting itself. Sally had hoped to arrive with just a ninety-degree turn at the jetty's end. Unfortunately, a check of wind direction relative to the landing, showed it to be blowing straight on to the staithe. That would mean coming in parallel to the jetty and then swinging round a full half-circle to stop alongside. Would *Joker* be able to make a complete u-turn in that confined area? She'd soon find out.

At what seemed an alarming rate of knots, Sally brought the little dinghy steaming in. Mollie Jenkins had stopped talking to Jayne Howlett and recognised her employer sailing towards her. Sally couldn't decide whether the look of consternation on the housekeeper's face was horror at the prospect of sailing to work in that tippy little boat, or the thought that *Joker* might soon be matchwood anyway. It didn't matter; what did was the timing of putting the helm over at just the right moment and hoping it would all work out. With *Joker* just a boat's-length from destruction and Sally wondering again if she'd left it all a bit late, she pushed the tiller hard over and held her breath.

With a shaking and slapping of the luffing sail and a clattering of her small blocks, *Joker* spun round, her speed falling off dramatically as she came into the wind. Sally stopped the turn a little short of parallel to the jetty so that the little boat crept in the last remaining inches from its edge. Jayne Howlett grabbed the mast, Mrs Jenkins knelt down and took a rope and Sally breathed again.

'Good grief, girl, I thought you was going to demolish us an' the jetty all in one go!' exclaimed the housekeeper.

'But thankfully, I didn't.' Sally breathed a sigh of relief as she dropped the sail, clambered out, secured the dinghy's painter to a ring and then turned to face her bookkeeper. 'Hello, Jayne, I didn't expect to see you here this morning.'

'I just wanted to talk to you…' Jayne seemed to instinctively glance over her shoulder towards the Full-deck yard and Sally guessed this impromptu meeting was without the knowledge of the ever-watchful Henry Higgs. '… alone,' she completed with a nervous glance towards Mrs Jenkins as well.

'Right.' Sally walked down the jetty and, when they were hopefully out of earshot, turned and said, 'What do you want to talk to me about, Jayne?'

'First, I just want to say how sorry I am for being so unhelpful at our meeting yesterday.' Jayne bit her lip. 'I wanted to tell you the truth but…'

'I know… Henry Higgs was hanging around listening and you felt you couldn't.' Sally looked the young bookkeeper straight in the eyes. 'He works for *me*, Jayne, so don't let him intimidate *you*. What would you have told me if he hadn't been there?'

'A lot of things, Miss Beckett. I let my heart overrule my good sense and I've been tearing myself apart wondering what to do.' She wiped a tear from her cheek. 'I know I'll feel better if I tell the truth so, can I meet you again…' she glanced around again, nervously, '… but not here?'

'Well, you could come out to *Marsh Haven*…' began Sally before Jayne burst in…

'No, not there.' Even Jayne seemed to recognise the almost-irrational panic in her voice and quickly moderated her tone to explain, 'There's no way I could boat out to the house without Henry knowing.'

'So where and when, then?' asked Sally, becoming just a little weary of all the intrigues surrounding Full-deck Marine.

'I'm not sure yet,' said Jayne apologetically. 'I'll have to check, so could you call me later and I'll let you know then.' She gulped back a tear. 'I don't know which way to turn. There's more than one thing I need to talk to you about, Miss Beckett but…'

'I'm a good listener, Jayne.' Sally put a reassuring hand on the girl's heaving shoulders. 'I'll call you later this morning.'

'Thanks,' said Jayne, gratefully, before another flood of tears welled up in her washed-out face. She handed Sally a scrap of paper with her mobile number. 'Call me about elevenish when I should be alone,' she said between sniffs before adding, 'but *please* don't tell anyone that we're meeting.'

'I won't,' promised Sally. She watched the young bookkeeper walk along the jetty before examining more closely, the hastily scribbled note. Were those numbers the same handwriting as on the wreath at the cemetery? Just a glance at the small neat figures showed they definitely weren't. One mystery still unresolved, Sally returned to the end of the jetty and Mrs Jenkins who, surprisingly, had climbed by herself into *Joker*.

'She's real upset about somethin'.' The housekeeper nodded towards Jayne's round-shouldered figure scurrying off in the direction of the yard. 'No wonder she wants a chat with you.'

'Yes, things are getting on top of her,' answered Sally, thoughtfully.

'Including that Henry Higgs, probably,' commented Mrs Jenkins.

Sally wasn't sure whether Mollie's remark was clever sarcasm or just plain comment, but either way, she was probably right. She had no intention, however, of discussing Jayne Howlett with the well-meaning, but ever-gossiping housekeeper. Instead, she climbed down into *Joker* where Mrs Jenkins had already seated herself on the centre thwart.

'I'm impressed, Mollie,' said Sally sincerely as she squeezed past and again hoisted the tiny lugsail. 'I didn't realise you were quite such a mariner.'

'Oh, all us children round here were born with webbed feet,' laughed the housekeeper, 'and your granddad taught me a few things about sailing as well over the years.'

'Am I the only one around here who didn't grow up with boats,' thought Sally as she slipped her lines, sheeted in the sail and helmed *Joker* away from the jetty and out into the broad.

Mollie Jenkins seemed to have overcome her initial fears, realising her employer/skipper, though inexperienced, was careful and competent. 'Wonderful to be actually sailing again,' she laughed, as she lowered the centreboard on Sally's orders.

It was indeed magical, but Sally's thoughts couldn't help returning to the conversation she'd just had with Jayne Howlett. Not only was the girl emotionally distraught, but obviously very frightened as well.

One man had already died in mysterious circumstances so, perhaps, Jayne had good reason to be fearful. Of what, Sally hoped to find out when they met that evening.

*   *   *

Chapter Fourteen

When Sally and Mrs Jenkins arrived at *Marsh Haven* after their bracing sail, it was to find *Ace of Hearts* with her tan mainsail flapping in the wind.

'Giving it an airing,' Ian explained, as he spliced an eye into a new shroud lanyard. He'd obviously done far more than that because the old boat's varnished woodwork now shone brightly, the decks glistened from a recent mopping and even the few bronze fittings gleamed with polish.

'She looks wonderful!' enthused Sally, thrilled at the transformation worked on the old boat in so short a time. 'Granddad would be so pleased.'

'It wasn't a big job,' explained Ian. 'A bucket of hot water and vinegar soon brought the varnish back, and polishing the bronze didn't take long.' He leapt aboard and lowered the large luffing sail to form an equally huge pyramid of canvas on the cabin roof. Now, the only sound was the creak of the mill's sails as they perpetually turned the fresh westerly wind into ever-needed amperes. 'Just a few bits of rigging to renew,' he said, checking the tension on the starboard backstay, 'and then I'll wash the hull and she'll be all ready for tomorrow. We'll make an early start,' he added, 'and have a fair tide both ways.'

'How early?' asked Sally, wondering just what she'd let herself in for.

'About six.' Ian glanced up at the burgee now flying from the masthead. 'If this wind backs southerly as forecast, we should be able to reach both ways.'

'You seem to have the deck department well and truly sorted, so I'd better start getting my catering organised, or we'll have a mutiny on board.'

'Starting this very morning, if I don't get a coffee soon.' Ian gave her a wink and a quick kiss before jumping into the cockpit and hauling yet more cordage from the portside locker.

Sally went off to put the kettle on. In spite of all the complications of her new life, she realised she was happier now than she'd been for a long long time.

*   *   *

The same could not be said for Doctor Helen Newson. The very nature of General Practice meant she was not a woman to worry unnecessarily, but now she had a situation that was generating anxiety to the point of distraction. She needed to talk to someone and, with a few minutes between patients, she dialled the number of a mobile phone.

'Can you talk?' she asked, when her call was answered, 'I'm worried sick.' Then, with an increasingly emotional edge to her voice she continued, ' ... those records ... Charles' was amongst them ... if they get into the wrong hands, I'm finished ... just as things were working out, this has to happen... I don't think the granddaughter suspects, but this could ruin everything... I wish I'd destroyed those records while I had the chance... I *know* they're going to be used against us.'

Pleading was not a tool Doctor Newson used very often, but there was a slight tremble in her voice now as she choked back a tear and asked, 'Can't *you* get them back?'

*   *   *

Everyone at *Marsh Haven* was busy: Ian, on *Ace of Hearts*, Mrs Jenkins with her domestics, Sally, listing which provisions she needed to buy for tomorrow's expedition, and then the Ranger's launch arrived in the basin. Sally willingly dropped her notebook and went out to meet him.

'Good to see you, Jack. Coffee?'

Jack never turned down a hot drink and it wasn't long before he was sitting opposite Sally at *Marsh Haven*'s big kitchen table. The coffee tasted good, but the purpose of his visit might be a little harder to swallow.

'Sally, you asked me to check further and confirm that your other grandfather, Edward Halard, really was in *Hood*.'

Sally nodded, wondering what the Ranger's subdued tone portended.

'Well, after calling you, I did some further research of my own.' He took another appreciative sip of his coffee. 'Through the internet, I managed to bring up a complete listing of the men lost on *Hood* on May 24th 1941.' Jack raised his eyebrows. 'They confirmed Sub-Lieutenant Edward Halard RN as being amongst those lost on that day. It even gave his record,' said Jack, sliding across a printout of his findings. 'It's all there: entered Dartmouth 1937, commissioned 1939, joined *Hood* 1941. The file even includes his photo.' Jack took another printout from his case and handed it across to Sally. 'Is this the man you thought was your grandfather?'

Sally studied the photo and nodded immediately. 'Yes, this is the same photo Gran kept framed on the sideboard at home.'

'I even cross-checked against the Navy Lists for that month,' continued Jack, 'and they confirm Sub-Lieutenant Halard was on *Hood*'s establishment from the 12th of March 1941.'

'Just two months before the ship was lost,' mused Sally, sadly. She handed the printout back to Jack. 'That seems to be pretty conclusive then.'

'Probably,' conceded Jack. 'What I need is something… anything… that relates to Charles' early background.' He looked around. 'Have you found *anything* here that might give us a lead?'

Sally shook her head. 'Nothing really. Only some old banknotes that slipped from a book here last night.' She went and collected the notes and brought them back.

'Very interesting,' said Jack, slowly turning the two five-pound notes over in his hand, 'but why would Charles have these?'

'As mementoes of something, possibly?' offered Sally. 'I don't see how they can help us any.'

'Probably not,' agreed Jack, but he held up the notes anyway. 'Okay if I keep these for the time being?'

'Of course, if you think they might help.'

Jack slipped the notes into his pocketbook. 'What I need, though, is something relating to even *earlier* life, something that will tell me where he's from, where he grew up. Did you find anything that would help us with that?'

Sally shook her head again. 'Absolutely nothing. Here I am, heir to his estate and the poor man's still a virtual stranger.'

'In my experience, people always inadvertently retain some clues to their past,' said Jack. He finished his coffee. 'I know it's an intrusion, but would you let me have a snoop through his things?'

'I'd be delighted if you would, but I'm afraid you'll be wasting your time. I've been right through his desk and not found as much as a driving licence or a passport.'

'Because he never had either,' responded Jack. 'He told me so himself.' The Ranger thought for a second. 'What about his clothes; what happened to them?'

'I got Mrs Jenkins to box them up to go to a charity shop. They're still upstairs waiting to be taken. You're welcome to go through them.'

'Clothes are very personal things, so I might pick up something,' explained Jack as he followed Sally upstairs to where Mrs Jenkins was busy dusting. The housekeeper was only too happy to break off and show them where she'd put the cardboard boxes in the spare bedroom.

'All his things are here, bless him,' she said with a catch in her voice.

'He had no interest in clothes, hated buying them an' always wore everything 'til it fell apart. So, you won't find much of value.'

'All the better,' said Jack, opening the lid of the first box and removing the contents. 'All I'm trying to do is get some *feel* of the man.'

With the two women watching, he went through the plaid working shirts, heavy woollen jumpers and serge trousers that seemed to comprise Charles McKenna-Hynes' complete wardrobe. The second box was filled with much of the same.

'Not Saville Row's best customer, was he?' said Jack with a chuckle before suddenly exclaiming, 'Hello, what's this!'

Very near the bottom of the second pile lay a tie. Jack held it up. It was obviously very old, frayed at the edges and faded in colour.

'That's the only tie he possessed,' said Mollie Jenkins with a little roll of the eyes. 'Only wore a tie when he had to an' said this would do him out. An' so it did,' she added, taking a tissue to her eye.

'Did he say what it represented?' asked Jack, noting the diagonal yellow, green and black stripes. 'It could be a school or a club or something like that.'

'Well, he did go to school in Norfolk.' Mollie brightened at the thought she was helping. 'Perhaps it's that.'

'It might be,' muttered Jack, almost to himself, before turning back to Mrs Jenkins. 'Did he say *which* school he attended?'

'No, but I know he loved it.' Mollie Jenkins turned to her employer. 'Like I told you, Miss Sally, he did tell me his nickname once...' she rubbed her hand over her face as though to stimulate thought, '...oh goodness... what was it... Ca... Cal...'

'Caloy,' completed Sally, glad she had made a mental note at the time.

'Caloy?' repeated Jack. 'A strange name. Why was he called that?'

'He never said,' answered Mrs Jenkins, 'but I thought it might be somethin' to do with his Scottish background.'

'Maybe.' Jack held up the old tie to Sally. 'Would you mind if I borrowed this as well? I might be able to find out something.'

'Please do,' responded Sally, before suddenly remembering something else and hurrying off to the master bedroom. She returned seconds later, with the small photo of Captain Charles with Aunt Emily. 'This is the only one I found of Granddad when he was young,' she explained, handing it across to Jack.

The Ranger studied the old snap carefully. 'Had a beard even in those days,' he commented, before handing it back.

Sally gave a sad smile. 'I'm sorry I can't help more, Jack. On a personal level, Granddad really didn't leave much to show for his life.'

'No, but it's given a few leads, and I'm hoping I'll find out more in Suffolk tomorrow,' replied Jack, cocking his head in a southerly direction. 'The wife and I are giving ourselves a day out. If I can find where your gran spent the war, we might learn something. I'm convinced the answer to much of all that's happened started there.' He gave Sally a frown. 'Now, before we go, are you *sure* she never told you specifically where she worked?'

'No. All I know is that it was some sort of estate by the sea,' answered Sally apologetically. It was her turn to frown. 'How on earth will you know where to start looking, Jack?'

The Ranger gave a reassuring smile. 'In the police, we got used to looking for needles in haystacks and Suffolk's quite a small county, actually. Surprisingly, there aren't too many such estates that border the North Sea and I have a hunch already which one it might be.'

'Well, good luck!' Sally led them back downstairs but, as they went through the hall, Jack stopped to study some of the watercolours hanging there.

'Are these some of Emily's works?'

'Yes.' Sally was always pleased to show off her grandmother's abundant talent. 'These are ones she obviously painted for Charles.'

Jack nodded. 'Her skies are wonderful,' he commented, studying one of the seascapes.

'Mmm, but waterbirds were her speciality.' Sally pointed out the minute detail in the many depictions of ducks and geese.

Back outside on the jetty she said, 'You will call me won't you if you find something, Jack. I'm getting a bit desperate and *anything* will be *something* in solving this mystery.'

As she waved the launch on its way, she doubted two old five pound notes, an old tie and some unknown location in Suffolk could provide any answers. Or did Jack know facts he still hadn't disclosed? Somehow, she felt he was holding something back about Grandfather Halard. But what?

There were still so many questions and the thought of finding *some* answers reminded her she still had to phone Jayne Howlett about tonight's mysterious meeting. At least then she might discover what was going on at Full-deck Marine.

* * *

'Jayne? Is it okay to talk?'

She'd called the bookkeeper's mobile number, but Jayne's hushed response made Sally wonder if the Svengali-like Henry Higgs was hovering somewhere in the background.

'Yes, but not for long.'

'Right,' Sally was happy to keep things brief, 'have you thought of somewhere to meet tonight?'

'Yes, could you meet me at the church?'

'All Saints!' exclaimed Sally, somewhat taken aback.

'Yes,' whispered Jayne. 'I live with my auntie who's a key-holder, and she's agreed to let me borrow it. I told her some tourist customers at the yard wanted to see inside.'

'Well, if that's what you want.' Sally made a mental note that Jayne Howlett could certainly be imaginative with her lies when she needed to be. A place of worship wouldn't have been Sally's own choice for clandestine assignations, but she was anxious to learn how she was being defrauded, so she simply asked, 'What time?'

'Six-thirty?'

'It won't be dark until nearer seven,' said Sally, 'so, later would be better if we don't want to be seen together.'

'Okay, seven then,' agreed Jayne, before adding, 'but I'll be around from six-thirty, as that's the time Aunt Agatha thinks I'm meeting the tourists. I'm sure I can find some jobs to do in the church while I'm waiting.' In the background there was the sound of a door opening accompanied by the bookkeeper's slight intake of breath. Then Jayne continued, in a slightly louder tone. 'Yes, that's right, *seven* new life-rings.'

'I'll be there,' whispered Sally and rang off.

Obviously the odious Henry Higgs had come in as feared. She just hoped he hadn't heard more than he should.

Perhaps it was this worry that prevented Sally being aware of Mollie Jenkins on the landing above, listening to all that had just been said.

* * *

'So, what time are we leaving, Jack?'

Another kitchen table, but this time it was his own and Jack was facing his wife with an Ordnance Survey map of the Suffolk coast spread between them.

'We'll make it early if that's okay with you?'

'Great. I'll do us a packed lunch.'

'Nope, we'll get something in the pub, love. My treat.'

'Fine by me, Jack Fellows.' Audrey looked again at the remote section of Suffolk coastline that her husband had ringed on the map. 'What makes you so sure that this is where Emily Halard spent the war?'

'There aren't too many coastal estates it could have been, but I'm sure it's this one.' Jack fingered a location on the map. 'Emily spoke of the wonderful wildlife habitat she found there so it's logical it's the one which became the nature reserve after the war. Just to confirm it, though, I looked up that reserve's website on the internet.' He passed some coloured printouts across to his wife. 'These are coastal scenes of the reserve today.' Jack sat back. 'This morning I saw those same locations, painted by Emily during the war, hanging on the walls of *Marsh Haven*.' Jack stubbed the ringed area with his finger. 'It *has* to be that one.'

'I'm sure you're right,' agreed Audrey, 'but, even if it is the place Emily spent her war, what's it going to tell us?'

'*It* won't tell us anything,' Jack answered, 'but, hopefully, *someone* will.'

'Who?'

'I don't know until we get there.'

'This all seems an awfully long shot, Jack. If nobody around here has the foggiest about Charles' past, what chance is there that some yet unknown person in Suffolk will know anything?'

'Because I'm sure it's at that Suffolk estate where Emily and her partner were together in 1944.' Jack tapped the table with his forefinger. 'All I need is just *one* person who met him and can identify him from a photo.'

'But you don't have one of Captain Charles from that time.'

'No, but I have one of Edward.' Jack slid the photo of the young Sub-Lieutenant in front of his wife.

'But…' Audrey looked at the photo and shook her head, '… you told me poor Edward Halard was killed in *Hood* in 1941, Jack. How could he be in Suffolk in 1944?'

Jack sat back. 'Audrey, during all that research I did on *Hood*, I did uncover one interesting fact, something I haven't even told Sally.'

Audrey's eyes narrowed. 'What?'

'That there may have been a fourth survivor off *Hood*.'

'But, surely, that was impossible.'

'Not according to the papers at the time.' Jack tapped some more printouts. 'Not long after *Hood*'s loss, the police picked up a chap in civvies. When questioned, he disclosed he'd been a stoker in *Hood*, miraculously survived the explosion and sinking, but been missed by the destroyer that picked up the other three. According to him, he'd continued clinging to a liferaft until found by a trawler days later. He eventually landed at Liverpool and, pretty traumatised, decided not to report back to the navy.'

Audrey leaned forward. 'Jack… are you saying…?'

'No I'm not,' said Jack quickly. 'That man turned out to be an impostor, an army deserter whose brother had been the stoker lost in *Hood*. Deciding to use his brother's identity, he thought it would get him some sympathy but, instead, it got him three months.'

Audrey sat back, slightly deflated. 'So, what has this got to do with Edward or Charles?'

'Perhaps nothing,' admitted Jack, 'but it does open up the fact that even the Admiralty considered the *possibility* of other survivors.'

'You're saying that Edward Halard might have actually survived and that Charles McKenna-Hynes might be…?'

'I'm not saying *anything* until I've more facts myself, which is why I haven't even told Sally about this angle yet. I need something more concrete than suspicion, Audrey.'

'But Sally showed you a photo of Captain Charles when he was young. Did he look the same as this?' asked Audrey, tapping Edwards' studio photograph.

'Difficult to say,' frowned Jack. 'Their hair could have been about the same colour, but even then Charles had a beard which prevented any direct comparison of facial features.'

'And so, tomorrow, you hope someone can identify Edward's photo and confirm him alive in 1944?'

'Something like that,' agreed Jack.

'And how do you propose to find this most-convenient person who will have known Emily Halard during the war?'

'By asking at the place where everything about a village and its inhabitants, is talked about,' answered Jack, re-folding the map and standing up. 'The pub, Audrey. That's where we'll get the name we want.'

Seeing Jack rise, Spike went and nuzzled his master's leg.

'Are we taking him?' asked Audrey.

Jack shook his head. 'These nature reserves don't usually allow dogs, love.' He gave the collie a scratch on his head. 'Sorry, old chap, but it's a day guarding the family home for you.'

'Never mind, Spike,' sympathised Audrey, as her husband disappeared up the stairs for his bath, '*I'm* only getting a meal in the pub because he needs to suss out the locals.'

Audrey looked forward to her day on the Suffolk coast. She only hoped it would produce the results Jack so desperately wanted.

* * *

At Full-deck Marine, the workforce had finished their day's labours and gone. Now empty, the corrugated workshops seemingly rattled and whistled at twice the volume, but only one employee still remained to hear it and he was too preoccupied to bother. In his small office, Henry Higgs sat nervously tapping his desktop with an ebony rule, a deeply troubled man.

Higgs cast his mind back to those days when all had been panning out so well. Okay, he'd been struck out of the will but, with the old man confused and Full-deck almost devoid of cash, it hadn't been difficult to talk him into selling the freehold of the yard. It had been at the same time his wife had sussed the other woman and kicked him out. That had left him virtually homeless, but it didn't matter because his new love had made the sale of the yard possible, leaving little doubt that he'd be elevated to Managing Director when the time came. That "time" had come even sooner than expected with the old man's death, but then, like it always did, everything went to hell.

First, that Ranger, Jack Fellows, had stirred up the coroner and he'd had the police to deal with. Then some previously unknown granddaughter had appeared on the scene, building herself a new life at *Marsh Haven* and taking an unhealthy interest in the yard. If she'd been some naive little bimbo, he could have handled her. Instead, this Sally Beckett was a savvy businesswoman who'd soon sussed that Full-deck Marine's finances were not all they should be.

The result was that he couldn't even trust Jayne anymore. He'd heard her through the wall this morning, arranging that meeting with the Beckett woman. Higgs had little doubt there'd be more confessions in All Saints tonight than the old church had heard in years.

Well, not if he could help it. Six-thirty, Jayne had said. Henry Higgs glanced at his watch: only half an hour to go. He stood up, put on his coat and strode out of the yard.

This time there would be no mistakes.

* * *

In her everyday routines, Mollie Jenkins was a very predictable creature. When she arrived home from her domestics at *Marsh Haven* at about two o'clock, she would always make a cup of tea, settle down in her favourite chair and read the local paper. She liked to keep abreast of rural affairs and, in particular, any juicy scandals that were brewing close to home.

Another very important section of the paper that Molly scanned every day, was the evening's television guide. It would have been easy to assume her viewing was restricted to soaps. Actually, she did like to follow most of them, but it was the documentaries that really interested her and one type in particular. She watched anything on the subject that was also written about in the piles of books hidden behind the closed door of the cupboard under her stairs.

After checking the "What's On" and deciding her viewing times, Mollie would invariably finish her tea reading one of those books. It was probably one she had read many times before, but that didn't matter; the subject itself was always exciting, no matter how many times she had scoured its depths. And, anyway, these days she seemed too tired to read many pages before she dropped off into one of those naps that now seemed to stretch the rest of the afternoon. For that reason, Mollie always locked her door. If someone ever sneaked in and found one of *those* books on her lap, she would never be able to show her face in the village again.

She normally woke at around four o'clock and then prepared a simple meal to have while watching the news, as a prelude to the rest of the evening's viewing.

Today, though, Mollie Jenkins' routine was seriously different.

After arriving home from M*arsh Haven*, she'd made her cup of tea as normal, but there had been no reading the paper or checking the television times. Instead, she had read the note found on *Lichens'* doormat and the content of that note meant she would not be watching TV at all this evening. This cold dark night, she would be going out.

That alone, was not something she relished doing. The village had no street lighting and you heard so much about elderly people getting mugged, that your own fireside seemed the safest place to be. But the proposal in the note, pushed urgently through her door, was enough to make Mollie forget any inhibitions she may have had about nocturnal wanderings. This night she would have a very specific programme, and it wouldn't be one on television.

She did still dip into one of her books, because she needed to be well informed for the night ahead. She didn't fall asleep afterwards, though, because her mind was too active working out how she would reach her destination without others seeing. The person who had put that note through her door was the only other villager who shared her secret. If she left just before six-thirty, dusk would help cover her movements.

She was so excited, she made herself another cup of tea.

* * *

At the Health Centre, there was much agitation amongst the patients. With still an hour to run until the end of evening surgery, Doctor Newson had cancelled all further appointments.

Earlier that afternoon she'd received a call that changed her earlier misgivings into full-blown despair. With the situation rapidly running out of control, clearly the time had come to take charge again. Desperate measures were now called for and Helen Newson looked deep into her soul and drew upon the reserves of clinical objectivity that had seen her through a career full of crises.

Until now, those crises had always been someone else's, to be treated with the detachment that medical practice demanded. This one was of her own making, but she still tried to remain level-headed despite her own personal involvement. The professional and financial ruin that could ensue if that girl shot her mouth off made it all the more imperative that this particular malignancy be removed with all the precision of invasive surgery.

Helen Newson stood up, clicked shut her medical-bag, put on her coat and walked out to reception.

The girls at the desk were still dealing with irate patients. The doctor ignored them all, continued out to her car and drove out of the centre.

Swinging right, towards the church, she knew exactly how this particular operation would be performed.

* * *

All Saints Church had an altogether more sinister feel this night as Sally walked through the lych-gate and up the pathway towards the porch. She remembered the sense of peace and tranquillity she'd felt the last time she'd been in this hallowed place. Now, those trees which had rejoiced to the lilt of birdsong were creaking and bending before the gusting wind, while from the round tower came the moan of cold night air passing through its open portals. More than ever, Sally wished that Jayne Howlett could have chosen a warmer and more amiable location for this assignation.

Already, she'd had a wild ride from *Marsh Haven* in the dory. This storm-laden night was definitely not one for sailing the dinghy, and handling the dory in the choppy waters, with the spray continually breaking over its bluff bows, had been scary enough in the darkness. She would have welcomed Ian's company, but she'd promised Jayne secrecy and, anyway, he'd been called back to teething problems on the electric boat he'd been working on. So, she had set off alone.

As dusk turned to night, the gathering darkness had been a challenge she faced with some trepidation. As it was, the lights of the village had guided her, together with a single toll of the church bell.

That had surprised her. Did it always ring at this time, she'd wondered, glancing at her watch and noting it was six-fifty. Whatever, its deep sonorous note was another beacon to guide her to the staithe where she arrived, cold and wet, but otherwise safe.

Safer, in fact, than she now felt in the eerie shadow of All Saints as her torch lit the way up the pebbled path. Sally had always prided herself on being rational and pragmatic, but there was no denying that walking here, between century-old tombstones, was causing icy fingers of unease to stroke her already-shivering backbone.

One concern was that not a glimmer of light came from the stained glass windows above her. She'd expected Jayne to be already here and waiting. Sally glanced again at her watch: she was a little late, so perhaps the bookkeeper had already given her up and left. Another explanation might be that Jayne had left the lights off to keep their meeting secret. That made sense, but Jayne Howlett was surely not the sort of girl to sit alone in the darkness of an unlit church. Reaching the stone-floored shelter of the porch, Sally's enthusiasm for this seemingly futile excursion was cooling as rapidly as her body.

She turned and looked out over the expanse of All Saints' graveyard, its rows of tombstones lit by the spasmodic light of a moon dodging in and out of the scudding overcast. She gave a little shudder, not because of the cold, but because of something she'd seen.

It was only fleeting, a movement between the tombstones, right by where her grandfather lay at the edge of the graveyard. She strained her eyes to confirm that what she had seen was real, but could see nothing more. Switching on her torch, she aimed it towards the spot. The sudden shaft of light brought the new grave into vivid detail but all else to total blackness. It revealed no other movement, save the bushes at the graveyard's edge leaning to the ever-more gusting wind.

Had she imagined things? Surely Jayne Howlett wouldn't have chosen to wait for her in such a spooky part of the churchyard. Just the same, she shouted, 'Jayne…is that you?' but no voice answered except the moan of the wind in the trees. 'I must be getting twitchy,' Sally scolded herself as she turned around and faced the solid wood door that stood between her and the church's interior. Part of her just wanted to turn again and run, but instead she took hold of the massive ornamental ring-handle and gave it a try.

To her great surprise, it turned and the door moved, proving Jayne had already been and unlocked. So, where was the bookkeeper? Summoning reserves of mettle, Sally pushed the heavy door further and felt it swing inwards with a nerve-grinding creak. With every instinct telling her not to, she went slowly and quietly inside.

Stillness and silence filled the mighty nave. Immediately, the long-forgotten odour of old wood and stone, of fusty hymnbooks and… something else, filled her nostrils. As in any place of worship, the slightest sound seemed intrusive, but in this atmosphere of black unearthly stillness, even the soft footfall of Sally's trainers sounded like the thump of a marching sentry. She stood still and almost whispered, 'Jayne?' at the same time again switching on her torch.

Piercing the almost-tangible blackness, its searching beam picked out piles of hymnbooks, the organ, a faded banner and… Sally felt a gasp of sheer terror erupting from her throat, only to be paralysed into non-action along with the rest of her body, as she slumped against a pew. The torch beam flashed up into the church rafters before clattering to extinction on the stone floor and rolling away.

Sally was left gasping, the church in total darkness and the scene she had just witnessed, only feet away.

In that horrifying second, the torch's beam had revealed the ashen faces of two people lying lifeless in the aisle.

*   *   *

Chapter Fifteen

For what seemed a lifetime, Sally just remained there, breathing deeply to calm her palpitating heart, and stabilise the terrifying images that swirled through her brain. Gradually, reason began reasserting its calming influence and her grip on the pew-end eased just a little as she straightened up.

'They're dead and can't harm you,' she told herself, in far from convincing tones. Hopefully, no-one else was going to harm her either, for the cavern-like emptiness of the church remained in deathly silence, but for the thumping within her chest.

Her overriding desire now was to get out of the building as soon as possible and feel fresh air on her face once more. But how? She was without light, in a church containing two corpses, and not the faintest idea of where the main door now lay. Her disorientation was complete. It was a realisation that came with the bitter taste of panic welling again in her throat. She fought it down and quelled her spinning thoughts into rational action.

The torch… if she could find the torch and get it working again, seconds would see her through that door and making her break. But where was the wretched thing? It couldn't have rolled far. Sally lowered herself to her knees and, with outstretched fingers, felt around, the stone floor cold to her touch and the hard wood of the pews blocking her every move. Finally, she felt something slide into her hand and, just as quickly, realised it was warm and alive and… there was a small squeak and movement, causing Sally to spring back in horror. 'A mouse…' she said to herself, '… a bloody church mouse.'

She'd leapt so far that she wondered now if she was anywhere near that infernal torch. She leaned again on a pew-end and felt something hard in her fleece pocket press into her side. Her mobile phone!

'Start thinking Beckett,' she said to herself, taking out the phone, furious that fear had so stymied her thought processes. She unlocked the keypad and had put two nines onto the phone's screen and about to finger a third, when the realisation hit her.

Light! Of course, with the illuminated screen of the mobile, she had this minuscule but oh-so-welcome glimmer. With calls temporarily forgotten, Sally went back onto her knees and scanned the phone's small circular glow over the floor and under the pews. Just when she was thinking the torch had rolled well out of her search area, she saw an object, darker than the darkness, lurking beneath the next pew. Placing the mobile on a hassock and lying flat on the floor, she stretched out her arm and hand and felt her fingers close around the welcome hard rubber of her torch. 'Glory be,' she said out loud, as she scrambled to her feet and switched it back on. Nothing.

'Oh, no!' She gave the instrument a hard thump on the pew-end and a column of heavenly light beamed up once more into the lofty rafters of the nave. Sally swung the beam along the wall and saw the blessed doorway only feet from where she'd been standing.

Relief drained from her and, with it, all urgency to make the desperate flight she'd longed for these last horrifying minutes. Soon she'd be outside and calling the police, but first she must summon up the courage to look once more at the bodies.

Holding the torch like a gun, Sally slowly swung its beam back towards the area where those two lifeless forms had lain. Hymnbooks, organ, banner and… there they were, lying side-by-side just as she'd first seen them.

Sally stood, stock still, and, for the first time that night, was infinitely glad she was alone. She didn't know whether to laugh or cry, only that she was feeling foolish beyond words.

The two bodies lay as before, on a small plinth, just inches above ground level, hands clasped together in prayer, gazing heavenwards as they had for probably nigh on five centuries. A tomb… the alabaster tomb of some local nobleman and his wife that, in that second of torchlight, had… Sally sank down onto a pew and ran a weary hand through her hair. 'How stupid can you get?' she asked herself but, at the same time, feeling so utterly grateful that she'd spared herself the even-greater embarrassment of calling the police and giving DCI Hengrove and the rest of the CID, something to laugh about for the rest of their careers.

Sally made her way out of the church, down the path, through the lych-gate and back along the village street to the staithe.

She walked in deep thought. In spite of her own stupidity, there were some unanswered questions posed by tonight's venture. Why had Jayne not been there to meet her? Why then, was the church unlocked?

Most disturbing of all, why, the whole time she'd been in that church, had she sensed the presence of her dead grandfather in there with her?

*   *   *

'But, your grandfather's dead.' Ian took Sally's hands between his and looked her straight in the eyes. 'Believe me, we all attended his funeral.'

They were sitting in *Marsh Haven*'s kitchen, the table and a half-drunk bottle of Beaujolais between them. Ian had arrived back in *Electrifier* as Sally was mooring the dory. She'd poured out her experiences at All Saints in all their horrifying and farcical detail. Ian had laughed but, more surprisingly, had also been totally aware of her mission.

'How on earth did you know about it?' Sally asked in consternation. 'It was supposed to be a complete secret.'

Ian laughed again. 'Believe me, you won't have many secrets with Mollie Jenkins around. She overheard your conversation with Jayne and told me about it later.'

'The nosy devil!' exclaimed Sally.

'Don't be too hard on her, Sal.' Ian poured himself another half-glass. 'She was worried for you and felt someone else should know of your movements, especially as you were crossing the broad in darkness. At least, if you hadn't returned at all, I'd have known where to come looking for you.'

Which was a good thought, Sally mentally conceded. Ian's reassurance about her grandfather's death was less so. 'Yes, but did you *see* his body? Who identified him?'

Funny as the debacle of the tomb was, Ian could tell she was still shaken from the experience, especially her recurring feeling that Charles McKenna-Hynes was still lingering in his earthly realm. To her last question, though, he could be totally reassuring.

'Jack Fellows identified him, Sally. There was absolutely no doubt about it.'

'So, why do I keep sensing his presence?' she asked, taking another welcome gulp of her wine.

'Probably a combination of factors,' reasoned Ian. 'Your whole life has changed in just the last week and you're now living in a house and village that are totally unfamiliar to you, but where the past life of your grandfather is always present.'

'But the church?' Sally was still not wholly convinced by Ian's rationalisation. 'From what I know of him, Granddad wasn't a staunch worshipper, so why would his personality be lingering there?'

'It wasn't...' Ian refilled Sally's empty glass and topped up his own at the same time, '... but you were in a scary situation with your imagination running wild. No wonder you were fantasising.'

'I suppose you're right,' conceded Sally, taking a smaller sip of her drink and forcing her thoughts into more pleasant channels. She looked up with a smile. 'How about *Ace of Hearts,* is she ready for our expedition tomorrow?'

'Absolutely,' said Ian, glad of the change of mood and a return to things he had a practical knowledge of. 'We'll start off early as planned and take full advantage of the fair tide. With a bit of luck we should make Saint Benet's well before midday, have our lunch there and still be back here for early evening.'

'Sounds wonderful. I could do with a day away from here and all the worries it's producing.' But just the thought of those worries brought Sally's mind back to the evening's earlier events. As she topped her own glass, she said, 'I wonder why Jayne never turned up?'

'No doubt she had a good reason. I wouldn't let it worry you.' Ian sounded dismissive.

'Yes, but she was so anxious to talk and she didn't give the impression of being unreliable. I was a little late so, perhaps she just bottled out. Anyway, I'm going to call her and find out,' decided Sally, plonking down her wineglass. '… oh no…'

'What's the matter?' asked Ian, seeing her feeling in all her pockets.

'My mobile phone… after using it to find the torch, I put it down on a hassock and that's where it must still be.'

'No problem,' smiled Ian. 'There'll be a service there on Sunday and someone's sure to hand it in to the churchwarden. We'll go along and get it back together. If you need to call Jayne though, you can use my…'

'No, it's okay thanks.' Sally finished her wine and stood up. 'I don't need my phone and I'll talk to Jayne in person on Monday when I go to collect Mrs Jenkins. For the moment, I'm going to forget all about this night's adventures and start preparing the food for tomorrow.'

'Good idea,' agreed Ian, but, as he went to help her, he said, 'Talking of Mrs Jenkins, have you told her about these feeling you have about your granddad's spirit still lingering?'

'No, I didn't want her to think she'd got some neurotic woman as her new employer.' Sally paused at the larder door. 'Why do you ask?'

'Oh, only that she's very into all things spooky,' said Ian with a smile. 'She'd love to think this place was haunted.'

'Well, yes, she did give me a good lecture about the corpse-candles,' remembered Sally. 'I thought that was just human interest, though. I didn't know she actually made a *study* of the paranormal.'

'More than just a study, according to village gossip,' said Ian, placing some of tomorrow's rations on the kitchen table. 'Word is that our dear little Mollie Jenkins was something of a witch in her time.'

'*A witch…* Mrs Jenkins!' exclaimed Sally, unable to believe her inoffensive little housekeeper capable of such dark activities.

'Oh, yes, and not just her. Apparently there was a whole little coven going at one time…' Ian nodded in the direction of the village, '…

including Agatha Howlett, your bookkeeper Jayne's strange aunt.'

'Good heavens,' said Sally, shaking her head and wondering how this little community could produce such an unerring string of revelations.

As she prepared the food for the morrow, she wondered at other things also. She knew that DCI Hengrove still regarded the beneficiaries of her granddad's will as the most likely suspects for his murder. Even little Mrs Jenkins had a darker side, it seemed, and inheriting the money to buy her own house was certainly motive enough to call up the powers of evil.

* * *

At a lonely cottage, just outside the main body of the village, Mollie Jenkins took her leave and set off homewards to *Lichens*. Midnight had passed and it was very cold, but Mollie's step was light as she walked along the darkened main street. This evening had been more like the old days, a chance to share stories with a like-minded friend and feel the companionship of someone who didn't regard her as some sort of oddity.

As she passed All Saints, Mollie paused to see if any light shone within, but a glance told her the church was as quiet as… the grave. She gave a little shudder at the thought of Captain Charles' funeral being so recent. Should she go and have a look at the grave? Mollie checked the time and decided that the early hours of this Saturday morning were perhaps a little late for paying respects. And, anyway, she had only been talking to the man himself just an hour ago.

* * *

In another village, not far away, Audrey Fellows felt her husband turn over for what seemed like the hundredth time that night.

'Jack, you're not sleeping are you?'

'Not really.' Jack rolled over to face his wife. 'Sorry, Audrey, but my head's buzzing with all the strange aspects of this case. So many pieces but none that seem to be gelling together.'

'It's always the same, Jack Fellows,' Audrey complained with mock admonishment, 'you get your head into yet another mystery and it takes over your life.'

'I know, but I can't help it, love,' admitted her husband, 'it's just the way I am.'

'After thirty-two years marriage, do you think I don't know that,' Audrey sighed. 'Just for once, why not let that brain of yours do a little less "buzzing" and find a little peace instead. It'll do you far more good and allow us both to get *some* sleep before we make that early start for Suffolk tomorrow… today,' she corrected on checking the illuminated figures on the radio alarm. She gave Jack a loving pat on the shoulder. 'Perhaps things might "gel" a little better after you've talked to someone down there.'

'Hopefully,' muttered Jack and turned over again.

'Not as "hopefully" as me,' thought Audrey. She'd thought that retirement from The Met and this wonderful new job as a Broads Ranger might have spelled an end to Jack's vocational insomnia. Generally it had but, at times like this, Audrey knew only too well what this restless sort of night foretold. That sixth sense, which had brought success to so many investigations, was tuning in once more to her husband's subconscious.

It invariably meant that something bad was happening.

* * *

Chapter Sixteen

Only hours later, at the same time as the Fellow's alarm clock was sounding its unwelcome buzz, Sally and Ian were loading the last of their kit onto *Ace of Hearts* and preparing to cast off.

'Brrr.' Sally was shivering in the first light of a beautifully clear, but somewhat frosty morn. Even the ropes holding the cruiser to the jetty were hard and unyielding and Sally cursed as she tore a fingernail trying to loosen a knot.

'Here, I'll do that,' volunteered Ian, seeing her struggle. 'You jump on board and get some coffee going on the stove.'

In the stillness of the dawn, the putt-putt of *Ace of Hearts'* single-cylinder diesel seemed almost irreverent. 'An electric motor will be the next job,' promised Ian.

'Well, noisy or not, we're going to need it to start with,' reasoned Sally, glancing aloft to the limply hanging burgee, 'but I hope we get some breeze soon so we can get sailing,' she added as she slid down the companionway.

'We will,' promised Ian, throwing the headwarp on board, casting off the stern and taking that warp with him into the cockpit. With the tiller to midships, he eased ahead the throttle, producing a froth of propwash at *Ace of Hearts'* stern. 'We're off.' Soon, the big sailing cruiser was chugging ahead, an arrowhead of wash spreading back to the mooring she was leaving for the first time in a month.

'Wonderful!' exclaimed Sally, standing in the hatchway, her head just above the cabin top, watching now-familiar surroundings slip by. 'So nice to think we're actually *going* somewhere.'

'Yes, you can't beat making a passage,' agreed Ian. They were out on the broad now but, instead of continuing on to the village, he put the helm down and swung the boat through an almost-half circle until they were heading downstream through the reed-lined sound that led to the main river. 'I've seen all this before,' he said, moving for'ard and indicating the tiller to Sally, 'so here, you take it and I'll get the coffee.'

Making a few nervous adjustments, Sally thrilled at seeing *Ace of Hearts'* long bowsprit curve this way and that. This big cruiser was heavier on the helm than little *Joker*, but the positive way she handled was a delight in itself. The dawn had broken completely now, the mast and rigging pointing to the cloudless sky where the white moon still lingered, as though reluctant to leave its night abode. Like a new arrival edging it out, the sun rose steadily from the eastern horizon, revealing mist-laden marshes on either bank, pearl-like in the first light. From the galley came the delicious aroma of freshly made coffee. Could there really be anything more perfect than this, wondered Sally. She looked astern to where their wake stretched back like a well-travelled road and felt she was leaving all her worries behind in that trail of agitated water.

'One coffee for the First Mate.' Ian emerged from below and placed a steaming mug by the coaming. Taking a seat on the locker top beside her, he glanced around with obvious pleasure of his own. 'This has to be the most magic place in the world,' he declared contentedly.

Working the tiller with one hand and feeling Ian gently take her other in his, Sally was helpless to do anything but agree with all her heart.

Just ahead, a heron lifted off in lazy flight across the cut where a cat's paw of dappled water gave the first hint of shifting air mass. Ian looked aloft to where the burgee momentarily began to flutter.

'Let's get the sails up,' he said with a grin.

* * *

The Fellows were also on the move by now, motoring at a rather faster pace towards Norfolk's smaller neighbouring county. Halfway down the A12, Jack pulled into a small roadside café. He always preferred to put a few miles behind before stopping for breakfast and, while the waitress went to organise their eggs and bacon, he and Audrey sipped a welcome coffee and generally relaxed.

'Always good to get away,' Audrey commented, looking around, but seeing no other travellers joining them for early breakfast. It seemed safe to talk but she leaned closer anyway. 'Jack, what you were telling me about *Hood* and her survivors; are you seriously thinking Edward Halard survived and started a new life as Captain Charles?'

'It's a pretty wild theory, I admit,' conceded Jack, enjoying another sip of his coffee, 'but Doctor Newson told Sally that Charles had bad scarring from what, he said, were wounds sustained in the war. He wouldn't be more specific about that anymore than the rest of his service, but it would further explain why Emily told the lie about Edward dying on D-day.'

'And you think this could have some sort of bearing on his death?'

'When a man dies a mysterious death and you find mystery in his life, the chances are, the two are connected. But the murder investigation is Phil Hengrove's problem,' Jack quickly added. 'Mine is to just sort out the family conundrum for Sally.'

'Yes, but what I don't understand,' queried Audrey, 'is why she and her husband, if that's who Charles was, then lived separate lives *after* the war? Surely, they would have stayed together?'

'I know, that worried me at first,' admitted Jack, 'but I've been giving it some thought.' The waitress was gathering their breakfast things together and would soon be at the table again. Jack lowered his voice. 'On a purely monetary level, Emily would have been receiving a widow's pension for husband Edward. If she'd remarried Edward under his new name that would have stopped, but the bigger problem would have been the formalities necessary to get another marriage certificate.' Jack lowered his voice still more and leaned a little closer. 'That would have entailed producing birth certificates and the like which would have been impossible for Charles. Remember, if Edward really did fail to report back to the navy, we're talking desertion and probably a good spell in prison, possibly for Emily too, if she'd been fraudulently drawing his pension. It wouldn't have been worth the risk.'

'But why bother if they were man and wife already,' argued Audrey. 'Surely no-one would have been any the wiser if they'd just lived together.'

'Perhaps they'd grown apart anyway by the end of the war.' Jack shrugged. 'In the aftermath of victory, Emily may have reconsidered spending the rest of her life with a deserter and having to start again somewhere no-one would know them…'

'… like a remote Broadland village,' reasoned Audrey. 'Certainly a perfect place to take on a new identity.' She paused, trying to place herself in the other woman's shoes. 'For Emily, that would mean not only leaving her home and friends in London, but living the rest of her life as a sham. I can understand any woman being reluctant to do that, however much she loved a man.'

The waitress had arrived with their breakfasts now, effectively ending the conversation. There were good platefuls and Jack set to with a will.

His thoughts, though, were on what Audrey had just said. Whoever Charles was, the war had altered his life forever. Perhaps today's investigation would reveal more about Emily Halard's.

* * *

Late-morning found *Ace of Hearts* well down river, the breeze now fresh and the boat bowling along "with a bone in her teeth", as Ian described it.

'Just ease it out a little more,' he shouted from his place at the tiller.

Sally allowed yet more mainsheet to slide through the blocks and the big boom to swing ever-further out. The wind was from the left and behind or "port-quarter", to use the correct expression, Sally reminded herself. Would she ever learn these funny terms?

'This is broad-reaching, the fastest point of sailing,' Ian explained, giving her yet another one to learn as they surged along the river, the gladsome sound of water at *Ace of Hearts'* stem now an exciting gurgle and her quarter-wave, rolling outwards into the protesting reedbeds. There was a motor cruiser ahead of them, correctly keeping to the five miles-per-hour speed limit. Not using her engine, *Ace of Hearts* had no such restriction and soon overhauled it.

'Ian, I love this,' shouted Sally, hardening the mainsheet in just a little as the river curved round and the sail started to flap… or luff, as Ian called it.

After raising the sails, he'd let her continue her trick at the helm. Then he'd taken over tiller and mainsheet and put Sally on the jib-sheets, the ropes controlling the small triangular sail "up for'ard". This was a new experience as *Joker*, being a lugsail dinghy, had no jib at all. Sally soon had the hang of working those sheets and, as they were reaching with no tacking, it wasn't long before Ian handed her the mainsheets also.

These, she found, needed constant adjustment. The wind was steady but the river wasn't. Like any river anywhere in the world, it twisted and turned in a series of loops, which meant she was constantly easing or hardening the sheets to keep the big tan gaffsail drawing at its most efficient.

Huge as that sail was, Sally was to relieved to find the work didn't need a great deal of strength, as the sheet had the mechanical advantage of running through a series of blocks. Just as well as the river was once more turning back to starboard.

In fact, it was turning so much that Sally soon had the boom sheeted right out until *Ace of Hearts'* sail was actually touching the shrouds.

'Now we're really "running",' said Ian. He glanced again at the relative wind direction as the river continued to bend to starboard. 'Stand by to jibe…' he warned with enough urgency in his voice to have Sally nervously wondering what to do. '…right, start sheeting in… lively now!'

Sally hauled in the thick halyard as quickly as she could and just as the boom came almost amidships, *Ace of Hearts'* stern went through the wind and the big sail and spars came flying across to settle on the starboard tack. 'Wow!' gasped Sally, somewhat startled. 'That seemed a bit sudden.'

'It always is,' explained Ian with a smile. 'That's why you have to avoid a jibe all-standing… an accidental jibe. Imagine that boom flying right across from one side of the boat to the other. Get your head in the way of that and you wouldn't wake up for a long time… start easing that sheet now we're broad-reaching again.'

'Right.' Sally did as ordered but her mind was on her grandfather. Her short exposure to sailing had revealed a host of ways the unwary could come unstuck. Granddad had been an experienced skipper, but was nearly ninety with, doubtless, slower reactions. Handling this boat alone, it would have been all too easy to be caught out and knocked overboard.

She was about to question Ian on the subject when the curve of the river opened out to a whole new vista. On the north bank, the ground was rising and she could already see the stone ruins of some ancient structure. Within these first low walls there rose a large wooden cross, while much further away sat the remains of a mediaeval gateway. Built into this were the remains of an old brick mill, strangely out of place in what must have once been an extensive religious site.

'St Benet's Abbey,' said Ian, moving for'ard to the halyards in preparation for lowering the sails. He glanced at his watch. 'We've made good time. We'll have a walk and look round before lunch.'

*   *   *

At this same time, Jack and Audrey were driving into the small Suffolk village where clear sign-posting directed visitors to the nearby nature reserve.

The term "village" might be a little ambitious, Jack decided, for only a few cottages clustered around the small pub that served this pretty hamlet. With so few people living here, finding someone who had known Emily Halard in the war years might be a little more difficult than he'd hoped, assuming that this really was the remote spot where Sally's grandmother had spent her war. 'Let's make contact with the local intelligence centre,' he said with a grin as he swung straight into the pub car-park.

Inside the *Boot and Oyster*, a log fire burned in the grate while soft music played over a small saloon bar. The young barmaid smiled warmly as they entered. There were several drinkers already seated at the scattered round tables, older couples mostly, chatting cheerfully and sporting sensible outdoor clothes and walking boots. Expensive binoculars and telescopes hung from chairbacks, confirming Jack's suspicion that most of the pub's clientele were visitors to the reserve.

The few locals sharing this friendly atmosphere were seated at the bar itself where Jack now ordered drinks. 'How about yourself?' he asked the older gentleman seated nearest.

'Very kind of you. I'll have a half of Adnams if I may,' he accepted with a smile.

'Nice little place,' said Jack, nodding outside.

'Yeah, we don't get bothered by many unwelcome visitors here. Just birdwatchers and the like.' He was probably in his late seventies, with the weathered face of one who had spent little of his working life inside. 'Good health to you, sir,' he said as he took an appreciative sip of his ale.

'Are you from these parts?' asked Jack, after taking Audrey her drink and re-joining this character at the bar.

'Nope, born twenty miles from here.' He took another good swig. 'After National Service, though, got a job here in 1950 and stayed ever since.'

'On the estate?' asked Jack, taking a sip of his lager.

'How'd you know that?' There was just a glint of suspicion in the old man's eye.

'A good guess,' said Jack, giving himself a mental pat on the back that his policeman's instinct had zeroed straight in on this local gem, but disappointed the old chap probably wouldn't be able to help directly. 'So, you weren't here during the war?'

The pensioner shook his head without slowing his drinking.

'You might still be able to help me with some information, though,' continued Jack, keen to keep the dialogue rolling. 'I'm researching the experiences of people living in coastal communities during the war.' He smiled knowingly at his drinking companion. 'I bet you'd know someone still around here who'd remember those times?'

'Hmm, might do.' The old man put down his empty glass with, perhaps, slight deliberation. Jack caught the barmaid's eye and soon another glass of ale was stimulating recall. After a slow, discerning imbibe that would have done credit to a wine-taster, the old man smacked his lips and said, 'Person you need to speak to is Gladys Evens.' He nodded down the road. 'Third cottage on the left. She's a friendly soul and'll be glad to help you all she can.'

Jack hoped he hadn't shown indecent haste in wishing this helpful man swift thanks and farewells. Extracting Audrey from conversation with a pair of ramblers, he led her out of the pub and down the road towards the indicated cottage.

'How about that lunch you promised me, Jack?' she protested.

'Later, love. We might even treat this old girl as well.'

He wasn't normally impatient, but he wanted so much to clear at least some of the mist from this most-obscure of riddles.

*   *   *

'This was called Cowholm Island in mediaeval times,' explained Ian, with something like the tone of a tour guide. 'You can see that it's slightly higher than the surrounding marshes, which made it an ideal place for a religious settlement when Suneman came here in 800 AD. Unfortunately, that was destroyed by Viking raiders in 870, as was the next settlement founded by a chap called Wolfric a hundred years later.'

They had tied *Ace of Hearts* alongside the public moorings, just upriver of the imposing gateway. Even this early in the season, there were a few boats already moored enjoying the crisp spring sunshine. After another quick coffee in the cockpit, Ian had taken Sally off to explore the rest of this huge open area with its wonderful vistas of surrounding Broadland. Not so very far away, just over the marshes, Sally could identify two windmills that they had passed, seemingly, hours ago. Now she and Ian stood close by the huge wooden cross she had first seen as they approached Saint Benet's. Ian said it marked the position of the old High Altar.

'Was this destroyed by the Vikings too?' asked Sally, her eyes on the remains of the old chapel wall.

'No, it was built *by* the Vikings, actually,' replied Ian with a grin. Seeing Sally's quizzical expression he quickly went on to explain, 'The Viking king, Canute, was eventually converted to Christianity and had a stab of conscience at all the havoc his Danes had caused. So, in 1020, he paid for the rebuilding of the abbey and endowed it with the income of several local manors, making it the wealthiest in the kingdom. It was Henry VIII who finally led to its downfall.'

'... by closing it during the Dissolution of the Monasteries, no doubt.' Sally had always enjoyed her history.

'Wrong again,' grinned Ian. 'Saint Benet's was the only abbey he *didn't* dissolve, but only because it was so wealthy and he needed the money. Instead, he installed the Bishop of Norwich as its Abbot and took all its income, which, in the end, was equally destructive. Without funds to support itself, Saint Benet's closed its gates for good about 1545 and was soon dismantled by locals for its stone.'

'What a shame,' said Sally with feeling, thinking what a truly imposing sight this great place of worship must have been, seemingly rising out of the desolate marshes.

'Yep, it must have been quite something.' Ian glanced at his watch. 'I reckon by the time we get back to the boat we'll be ready for that lunch of yours.'

As they returned to the moorings, he swept the expanse of the thirty-five acre site theatrically with his hand and said grandly, 'Somewhere here lieth the remains of Lord Falstaff and his wife.'

'My goodness, Shakespeare come to life,' remarked Sally, as they made their way through the gatehouse. It was an interesting fact but, somehow, it seemed to emphasise each individual's microscopic place in the scheme of things. Death came to us all, she surmised grimly, and her grandfather's was just another blip in an unending line that made up the mighty pageant we called "life".

They were at the boat now.

'What's for lunch?' asked Ian.

* * *

'It must be years since I last sat here,' reminisced Gladys Evans.

She had welcomed Jack and Audrey into her cottage with the delight of someone who loves human company, but enjoys little enough of it. When Jack had explained his supposed research on the war years, Gladys had been only too happy to sit down and pour out her memories. It was Audrey though who had suggested that, in the lovely spring sunshine, this sprightly lady might well enjoy a drive through the reserve. Gladys had accepted with alacrity, but with the further suggestion that they drive only as far as the car park and then walk from there out over the marshes.

And so, the next hour found them a good mile from the car, at the far end of the reserve with the gentle sound of waves breaking on the other side of the dunes.

'I used to walk here daily when I was younger,' Gladys explained as they all took a break on a low grassy bank, 'but it's beyond me now, all the way from the cottage.'

'Did you come here during the war?' asked Jack, easing the subject his way. So far, he and Audrey had just enjoyed the rambling company of this dear old lady and avoided direct questions too early in the meeting.

'Oh yes, indeed.' Gladys nodded enthusiastically. 'We weren't supposed to, of course, with all the invasion defences, but Emily knew the sentries and they used to turn a blind eye to our wanderings.'

'Emily?' Jack couldn't believe his ears. The subject of this visit had been brought up without his even mentioning the name himself.

'Yes, Emily Halard,' answered Gladys with disarming frankness. 'She was the estate warden here during the war and really, my best friend for most of it.'

'And she is the grandmother of a good friend of ours and the real reason we are here,' admitted Jack, deciding he couldn't continue this conversation under false colours. 'You probably don't know, Gladys, but Emily passed on some time ago.'

'Oh bless her. I wish I'd known and sent some flowers.' The old lady wiped a tear from the side of her eye. 'She was a little older than me, of course, but such an able girl. I idolised her. A clever artist too.'

Jack nodded. 'Yes, I was only admiring one of her paintings the other day...' he indicated the landscape in front of them, '... this very scene, in fact.'

'Yes, this was one of her favourite spots. She didn't paint many landscapes though. Birds were her real speciality. She'd sketch them first then paint the watercolours later in her cabin.'

'Cabin?' queried Jack.

'Well, a sort of hut really, but we used to call it "The Cabin". It was Emily's accommodation, pretty small, but so snug and cosy. I used to spend hours in there with her, talking about birds and wildlife and, when she was feeling a bit low, about her dear husband, Edward.'

'Ah yes, Edward.' Jack, sounded suitably vague. 'He was killed during the war, wasn't he?'

'Mmm, just a year after Emily came here.' Gladys ran a hand through her white hair. 'She took this job because he was at sea with the navy and she wanted to do her bit and keep herself occupied while he was away. She used to say she wasn't as worried as she might have been because he was on the biggest warship in the world and as safe as he could be.'

'Can you remember the name of that ship, Gladys?' asked Jack.

'My memory isn't quite what it was, but it was that one that blew up fighting that big German one.'

'The *Hood*, sunk by the *Bismark*?'

'That's it... *Hood*.' Gladys shook her head again. 'I remember them reporting it on the radio and them saying they feared there would be few survivors. I went straight to see Emily and, of course, she was frantic with worry. A few days later she got the telegram confirming Edward was "lost in action".'

'How did she take it?' asked Audrey.

'Oh, devastated,' said Gladys without hesitation, 'inconsolable for a while. The squire wanted her to take some compassionate leave, but she wouldn't, saying she preferred to work her way through it.' Gladys shook her head sadly. 'Poor girl, she'd only been married two years and said they were so perfect for each other in every way.'

Jack placed a comforting hand on the old lady's shoulder. 'I'm sure you were a great comfort to her, Gladys.'

'I like to think so. I used to cycle straight to the cabin after school every day and we'd chat while walking over the marshes, or while Emily painted. I know she also spent hours walking alone by the sea where, she said, she felt closest to Edward.'

'So much sadness,' said Audrey who felt for any soul suffering bereavement. 'How do you get over something like that?'

'I don't think she ever did,' sighed Gladys. 'She was never again the happy-go-lucky girl that I'd first known... or at least not until the end of the war.'

'Why, what happened then?' enquired Jack, trying not to sound too inquisitive.

Gladys's features clouded slightly. 'I'm not sure really but, almost overnight, a change came over Emily.'

'What sort of change?'

'A sort of excitement, I suppose,' explained Gladys, trying to find the correct words, 'like something really special had happened.'

'Well, that was good wasn't it?' asked Jack, sensing the old lady's lack of enthusiasm for what had happened.

'I suppose,' she admitted, 'but for me, it meant the end of our wonderful friendship.'

'In what way?' enquired Audrey.

'Simply that Emily told me she didn't want me coming to the cabin anymore.' Gladys had enough catch in her voice to show that the hurt still rankled.

'Did she give a reason?' asked Jack.

Gladys shrugged. 'Oh well, she made some sort of excuse about having to work longer hours and not having time to walk any more, but I knew that wasn't true.'

'When was this?'

She thought for a few seconds. '1944, it would have been... yes, the spring of 44.'

'And what do *you* think was the real reason for this sudden change of attitude?' probed Jack.

'I was just a schoolgirl at the time, and had no idea except to feel horribly abandoned,' replied the old lady. 'It was only later, when I started having boyfriends of my own, that I realised Emily must have got herself a man at the cabin and wanted me well out of the way.'

'All a bit sudden though,' observed Jack, frowning. 'Had she given no previous indication of any romance, Gladys?'

'None at all. She didn't go to any of the local dances where she might have met someone, and the cabin was so isolated in the woods that not a soul ever went there, except me. In the end, I came to the conclusion she must have met someone on a shopping visit to the village.' The old lady shook her head again. 'After all the grief of losing her husband it seemed so out of character that she should immediately live in sin with someone she had just met, but there you are, people are always full of surprises aren't they, Mr Fellows?'

'They are indeed,' agreed Jack, before asking, 'Did you ever catch even a glimpse of this mysterious boyfriend?'

'*Never*,' answered Gladys with emphasis. 'Even though I didn't visit her anymore, I thought I might see her with him in the village, but never did.'

'And you never asked her directly?'

'I never really saw her again. When the war ended and the old estate workers started returning, I was told Emily had returned to her old life in London and that was the last I knew of her...' Gladys gave Jack a warm smile, '... until now.'

'Well, I'm sorry I can't tell you exactly *what*, just yet,' said Jack, 'but I'm sure that something very significant happened to make Emily abandon your friendship like that.' He gave a small pat of his stomach. 'Time for lunch, I think. You've been so frank and helpful, Gladys. Now let Audrey and me treat you at the *Boot and Oyster*.'

'That would be lovely, Mr Fellows.' Jack helped the old lady to her feet and then followed her to the top of the nearest dune, where she stood gazing at the sparkling sea. 'Emily really did love this spot,' she said once more, with sadness in her voice. 'I hope she found happiness again.'

Jack said nothing as he led the way back to the car, leaving Edward's photograph unseen in his pocket.

* * *

Sitting in *Ace of Hearts'* open cockpit, close to the abbey gateway, Ian and Sally were enjoying their own onboard meal. The sun still shone overhead, but there was a chilly edge to the wind so the mugs of soup, heated on the galley stove, had been a welcome warmer for hands and stomachs alike. Now it was the turn of the cheese and biscuits, simple fayre, but sheer ambrosia after the morning's abundant fresh air and bracing walk.

'This really is quite an enchanted place,' said Sally, slicing herself a wedge of Wenslydale while *Ace of Hearts* rocked gently to the passing of another boat. There had been a steady flow of craft of every type, both up and down-river, but the slight turbulence they caused, far from being an inconvenience, had only enhanced the enjoyment of feasting afloat.

'Yes, Saint Benet's does have an almost tangible atmosphere of its own,' agreed Ian, topping up Sally's glass of Riesling and refilling his own. 'Not surprising really, when you consider the history that's been enacted here and the legends that have entrenched themselves as a consequence.'

'Such as?' asked Sally, ever happy to be immersed in the past.

'Well, one concerns a certain Brother Veritas who, in 1066, was quite ambitious for advancement within his Order.' Ian's voice was suitably intriguing.

'Go on.'

'All myth really,' admitted Ian, 'but the story goes that the besieging Norman army promised him the Abbotship if he treacherously left the abbey gates unlocked at midnight. This he did, allowing the Conqueror's men to enter and gain control, happily, with no loss of life.'

'And did Brother Veritas get his promotion?'

'Oh yes,' explained Ian, 'though he didn't enjoy it for very long. After fulfilling their promise by consecrating him Abbot that same night, they then took poor Veritas, still in his mitre and new robes, straight out and hanged him from the abbey gateway.'

'Poetic justice,' declared Sally.

'If you believe it. There's no documentary evidence to support the story any more than the legend that Veritas's ghost has been seen hanging from the gateway every year since.'

Sally grimaced. 'They certainly like their ghost stories around here.'

'Talking of which, any feelings today that Granddad Charles is still clinging to his earthly toil?'

'No, not at all.' Sally realised she hadn't even thought of it amidst all the excitement of new experiences and blossoming friendship.

Ian grinned. 'Which just goes to prove that it's all a result of sensual influence and, dare I say, an over-active imagination.' He swept his hand around *Ace of Hearts'* classic lines. 'This boat was where your grandfather was always at his happiest and, sadly, it was where he died. Surely, if he were going to linger *anywhere*, it would be here?'

'I know,' said Sally, somewhat reticently, 'but all I can say is that I *sensed* his presence in *Marsh Haven*, at the yard and even in the church. I can't explain it further than that.' Keen to change the subject, she nodded to where, several miles away, a tall square mediaeval tower rose majestically over the flat marshland. 'Which church is that, Ian?'

Ian shielded the sun from his eyes. 'Saint Helen's, Ranworth. It contains the finest rood screen in the country and some artefacts from the old abbey here. We'll go and visit it sometime.'

'I'd love to,' she answered with sincerity, reaching for the binoculars just beside the cabin hatchway. As she focussed them on the tower, she was unprepared for what she saw. 'Ian, there are people up there… right at the top by that big crown-shaped weathervane.'

'Yes, the public can climb right up to the top,' said Ian. '89 steps, two vertical ladders and a trapdoor, but well worth the effort for the beautiful view when you get there.'

'Are the public allowed up All Saints' tower too?' asked Sally, at the same time giving an involuntary shudder at just the recollection of last night's terror and foolishness.

'No, there is a rickety wooden ladder to the bells and an even shakier one to the battlements, but nothing the Health and Safety people would ever allow the public to set foot on.'

'Just as well,' responded Sally with feeling. 'I found the nave terrifying enough without risking life and limb in the heights.'

A different sort of boat was passing Saint Benet's moorings as she spoke. It had sails, but also an enclosed wheelhouse, giving it lines somewhat akin to a fishing boat. Sally returned the wave of the crew.

'A motor-sailer,' explained Ian, with obvious admiration. 'With an electric motor, that would have to be the ultimate eco-boat, just the sort I dream of having myself one day.'

'You will,' encouraged Sally with a loving hand on his arm. 'Oh look… how sweet.' She was pointing to the river where two birds with distinctive feathers on their heads, were systematically passing a stick backwards and forwards to each other's beaks.

'Great crested grebes,' explained Ian, watching them glide by on the stream. 'Imitating each other like that is one of their courting rituals.'

'Whereas, with human couples, it's usually the telephone bill that's being passed backwards and forwards,' observed Sally with a chuckle.

'Money seems to be the source of most arguments.' Ian shook his head. 'Here I am talking about owning fancy yachts, when just achieving some sort of financial security is proving hard enough.' He threw some leftover bread to a passing swan, but his face belied an underlying sadness. 'I watched my own grandfather go through all the trauma of bankruptcy and swore I would never go down that road myself.'

'No, it must have been horrible for you, that and his suicide.' Sally didn't want to open old wounds, but there was something that had been puzzling her. 'Ian, you said your grandfather was a successful naturalist and writer, so how come he got into such financial difficulty?'

'A combination of factors,' answered Ian with a shrug. 'After the war, his popularity waned and, with it, most of his income. He remained a generous person though and I know much of his accrued wealth went in helping others less fortunate. In the end, they bled him dry. He must have found all that so hard to handle and, finally, it drove him to suicide.'

'How awful.' Sally wanted to enquire more, but knew just those admissions had been painful enough for the person who was rapidly edging into her heart. Instead, she brushed the crumbs from her plate into the river and glanced up. 'When do you plan to set sail again, skipper?'

Ian followed her eyes to the burgee and then to the river now starting to flow the other way past the hull. 'Wind's still fair and the tide's turned,' he said with a nod. 'Let's go now and make the most of it.'

'Aye aye.' Sally gave a mock salute. It had been a wonderful day with, perhaps, an even better night to come. She glanced again at the far tower of Saint Helen's and, just for a second, wondered again why Jayne had never kept her appointment at All Saints.

Then she thought of Jack and his visit to Suffolk. She hoped he'd had an enjoyable day too, but more than that, she hoped it had been worthwhile.

* * *

As Sally slipped mooring lines and Ian hauled on *Ace of Hearts'* main halyards, thirty-five miles south, the Fellows were beginning their own journey homeward.

'So, we still have no name or face for Emily's mysterious lover,' said Audrey, as husband Jack swung right off the country lane and onto the busy A12.

They'd had a pleasant lunch with Gladys Evans, enjoyed her stories of growing up on the Suffolk coast, but gained no further clues as to what or who had so changed Emily Halard that night in 1944.

'No, but what we do know now for sure is that Emily did have a man unexpectedly arrive on the scene, and one she was very keen to keep secret,' confirmed Jack, accelerating into fifth gear.

'Hence the sudden breaking up of her friendship with Gladys,' reasoned Audrey, 'but why?'

'Because Emily doubtless had a treasured photo of husband Edward in her cabin,' explained Jack, 'probably this same one of him in uniform that Sally remembered always being on the sideboard in London. Like any proud wife, you can bet she showed it to her friend, Gladys.'

'And if Edward really did survive *Hood* and came home a deserter, Gladys would have recognised him from the photo,' completed Audrey, following her husband's line of thinking. She shook her head. 'Imagine the shock it must have been for Emily, a husband she was sure was dead, suddenly turning up on her cabin doorstep one dark night.'

'If that *is* what happened,' cautioned Jack. 'We'll need more than just suspicion to prove that Edward Halard and Charles McKenna-Hynes were one and the same bloke.'

'Wouldn't DNA do that?' asked Audrey.

'Only if we had Sub-Lieutenant Halard's prior to his supposed death in 1941, which we don't and never will,' said Jack.

'How about his naval medical records; wouldn't they still be available?'

'Probably, but they'd only show his blood group which wouldn't help DNA-wise.' Jack dropped down one gear to accelerate past a heavy lorry. 'Comparing them with Charles' own records would have been an interesting exercise, but we can't do that either because his have been stolen…' He slid once more into fifth, before continuing, '… which makes you wonder why someone did that.'

'Or *who*,' added Audrey. 'Surely that person must also be Captain Charles' murderer?'

'Or, at least, someone who didn't want us discovering his true identity… but, in reality, probably one and the same.'

'Like Edward Halard and Captain Charles,' said Audrey.

Jack nodded. '… but, proving that is going to be a challenge.' He gave Audrey a sideways smile. 'All I need is to find something that those two have in common other than their relationship with Emily, and I'll at least know I'm on the right track.'

'Yes, well, you love a challenge, Jack. I know you. Get your teeth into a mystery like this and you're like a schoolboy on his first date.'

Jack's smile dropped as he turned again to his wife. 'What did you say?'

'… "like a schoolboy on his first date"… it's only an expression Jack but…'

'No, it's no problem,' Jack, gave her hand a reassuring squeeze. 'It's just that you've reminded me of another angle I've yet to check out. If I could find out which school Edward went to, that could be a good start in establishing his change of identity.'

'But how will you do that?'

'By the tie,' explained Jack, 'the one belonging to Charles that I brought home from *Marsh Haven*. If that can lead me to a local school which turns out to be the one Edward Halard went to, it begs the question…'

'… how come Captain Charles owned and wore it?' completed Audrey, seeing now her husband's train of thought. 'A long shot, though, Jack. Where do you start?'

'By simply ringing round likely schools. Mollie Jenkins said Captain Charles went to school in Norfolk so, I'd put money on that being Edward's. It could be a grammar school but the facts point to it being either public or private.'

'How do you figure that?'

'Because, remember, Charles had a slight Scottish lilt in his speech and he used McKenna-Hynes as a surname, which sounds pretty highland to me. If his family really were from north of the border, then his school was probably boarding. On top of that, we know he learned to sail on the Broads through his school.' Jack turned to give his wife a knowing look. 'We're talking about pre-war, Audrey, when state schools certainly didn't offer that sort of facility to their pupils. No, this was an expensive boys' private school and there aren't many of those in the county. If I can find which, it might give us the lead we need.'

'A lead, but not proof.'

'No, but we don't need proof, Audrey. Remember, we're only trying to solve the mystery of who Sally's grandfather really was, not going to court with legal proceedings.'

'Unless it has a bearing on his death.'

'That's Phil Hengrove's problem.'

Further discussion was halted by Jack's mobile phone ringing its urgent tone. Audrey picked it up from its slot between the seats. 'Hello… yes he's here but we're driving up the A12 right now… just a second…' Audrey turned to her husband. 'Jack, it's Mrs Jenkins and she sounds quite upset.'

There was a lay-by just ahead and Jack swung into it, stopped the car and took the phone.

* * *

The sun that had blessed their whole day was fast-setting in a blaze of golden glory, as *Ace of Hearts* glided into home waters. Ian and Sally had hoped that fair wind would carry them right to *Marsh Haven*, but the last few miles found them drifting on the tide and gradually losing steerage, leaving them no option but to drop the sails and start the engine.

'You usually lose the wind at the end of a day like this,' explained Ian from the cabin roof, where he was furling the sails.

'We can't complain.' Sally was beginning to feel a chill in the air and pulled on her fleece. 'A bit noisier, but at least we'll get home before nightfall.'

But, even with the putt-putt of the boat's little engine pushing them along at a moderate but steady pace, it had still been dark by the time the broad and the lights of the distant village hove into sight. 'Almost there,' reported Ian coming back into the cockpit and pointing to the house and mill silhouetted over the reedbeds.

'Good. It'll be nice to get that fire going and snuggle down for the night.' Sally gave a little shiver and, as Ian sat down beside her again, he put a warming arm around her shoulders. She touched his knee gently and said, 'It's been a wonderful day, Ian, one I'll remember always.'

'I'm glad.' He stood up again, opened a locker lid and pulled out two large fenders. 'Harbour stations,' he ordered with a smile.

Sally was putting the helm over now to swing *Ace of Hearts* into the cut leading to *Marsh Haven*'s basin. The house and mill stood stark against the starlit sky. Already she was beginning to feel of this as home, but now, as the basin itself opened out, she saw there was one big difference from the scene they had left just twelve hours earlier. Alongside the jetty was a large orange rigid inflatable boat.

'Hello who's this?' frowned Ian, as a large spotlight illuminated *Ace of Hearts* and her somewhat startled crew, in its all-probing beam.

There was no reason to answer Ian's question; it could be seen all too clearly, emblazoned on the RIB's curving sides.

POLICE

Two uniformed constables jumped ashore to take the sailing cruiser's lines while a voice that Sally recognised as Chief Inspector Hengrove's, came crackling out from a loud-hailer.

'I'm glad you're finally back, Miss Beckett. I've some questions I need to ask you.' As they got closer, he said, 'I couldn't call you because you didn't have this, did you?' He was holding up Sally's mobile phone.

'What sort of questions, Chief Inspector?' asked Sally as she jumped ashore, her hand taken by DC Bailey, who was standing beside his chief. Not for one second did she think this impressive show of force would be solely for the purpose of returning her mobile phone. She had a nasty feeling it might well relate to an unauthorised entry of All Saints Church.

The Chief Inspector came closer. He was a good head taller than Sally and his voice had an altogether more authoritarian tone than the last time they had met at The *Steamboat.*

'Very important questions, Miss Beckett, relating to my investigation into the murder of Miss Jayne Howlett.'

If this day had seemed heaven-on-earth, Sally now knew it's night would be a journey into that other, darker, realm.

* * *

Chapter Seventeen

'Where were you between six and eight o'clock last night, Miss Beckett?'

DCI Hengrove stood with his back to the unlit stove in *March Haven*'s dimly lit lounge, while Sally and Ian sat facing him on the sofa. DC Bailey sat on a hard chair, just to one side, taking notes.

'All Saints Church… I think,' stammered Sally, still not over the shock of the DCI's news and finding it difficult to find words to answer even the simplest of questions. She nodded towards her phone lying on a small table nearby, noticing, for the first time, that it was in a sealed, clear plastic bag. 'But, you know that already, don't you?'

Hengrove nodded back. 'We know your phone was there. Why were you?'

'To meet Jayne.'

'A strange venue.' Hengrove's questions came in a sharp monotone. 'Whose choice?'

'Jayne's,' answered Sally nervously. 'We wanted somewhere confidential to meet and her aunt had the key to the church.'

'So, what was the nature of this secret tryst that needed the loneliest place in the village?'

'She had some things she wanted to tell me… about Full-deck Marine.'

'Your boatyard. She was your bookkeeper, wasn't she?'

'Yes, though I hadn't had time to get to know her at all.'

'But well enough to agree to meet where the only witnesses had been dead themselves for centuries.'

'I'm telling you as it happened, Chief Inspector. I realise it doesn't sound very convincing and you obviously think I'm somehow involved in Jayne's death…' Sally swallowed nervously, '… but, believe me, I'm as distraught as anyone at the thought she met her death trying to tell me something.'

Hengrove maintained his calm monotone. 'I'm not thinking anything, Miss Beckett, until I have more facts. These are just preliminary enquiries though, I have to say, placing yourself at the scene of the crime at the time of death isn't the best of situations for you.' He paused a second before asking, 'So, who else besides you, knew that Jayne Howlett would be at the church last night?'

'Her aunt did, because she loaned her the key,' answered Sally. 'I told no-one else, but my housekeeper, Mollie Jenkins, overheard the arrangement and told Ian here.'

'And Henry Higgs knew as well,' interrupted Ian. 'You remember, Sally, you thought he'd been listening in when you were talking to Jayne on the phone.'

'Your yard manager?' checked Hengrove, turning to Sally.

She nodded. 'Yes. I've got a suspicion, but no proof, that he's been working a fiddle with Full-deck's accounts. I was hoping Jayne was going to give me that proof last night.'

'And he's been having an affair with the girl to boot,' added Ian.

'We don't *know* that, Ian,' cautioned Sally.

'Well his wife does because she's dumped him!' exclaimed Ian, not sorry to expose Higgs' philandering.

'But let's get back to you, Miss Beckett,' said Hengrove, sitting down in the armchair opposite and allowing his manner to mellow just a fraction. 'I want you to tell me *all* that happened last night.'

Sally did as requested, leaving nothing out, including even the embarrassing admission of being panicked by the figures on the tomb. From the corner of her eye, she noticed Bailey, taking copious notes, exchange glances with his DCI when she mentioned hearing the solitary toll of All Saints' bell as she neared the staithe.

'And this figure you say you saw lurking in the churchyard,' continued Hengrove when she'd finished, 'no description, I suppose?'

'No, I'm afraid not. It was only a fleeting glimpse and the next time I looked, the figure was gone. It left me wondering whether I'd really seen something or just imagined it.'

'Not another statue was it?' commented Bailey with a slight smirk.

'No it wasn't,' responded Sally, between clenched teeth. 'It was moving.'

'But you can't tell us whether it was male or female?'

Sally shook her head. 'Poor Jayne; are you telling me she was lying dead in the church at the same time I was groping around in the darkness myself?'

'Probably,' answered Hengrove non-committedly.

'My God.' Sally anxiously ran a hand through her hair, at the same time welcoming the feel of Ian's strong hand in her other. She glanced sideways again at DC Bailey. Was this whole scenario causing her to hallucinate, or did she catch a momentary look of disapproval pass over the young detective's features at this small gesture between her and Ian. If so, it was gone in a flash, though there was little warmth in his voice when he said, 'And how about you, Mr Haverson, can you account for your movements during those hours last night?'

'I certainly can. I was working on a boat downriver.' Ian gave a small smile just to show he wasn't going to be intimidated. 'I've been converting it to electric propulsion. That's my business.'

Bailey didn't return the smile. 'Anyone who can corroborate that?'

'No, the owner has given me a key and I just go and work alone when I can. The boat's moored in a remote stretch so…' Ian shrugged, '… not a soul to vouch for me.'

'Give me the name of this boat,' said Bailey.

Ian provided the details.

'Right.' Bailey closed his notebook and glanced towards his chief who nodded and got to his feet.

'We'll leave it at that for now,' said Hengrove, picking up his coat.

'So, are we suspects or what?' blurted out Ian, with some annoyance.

'For the moment, you're just helping us with our enquiries,' answered Hengrove, 'but don't leave the area without telling me and be ready to make yourselves available for more questioning when needed.'

'You'd be spending your time more usefully interviewing Henry Higgs,' said Ian with feeling. 'I'm sure that man has something to hide.'

'We'll be talking to a lot of people,' responded Hengrove, bluntly, 'but, thank you for the information you have given us. We'll see ourselves out.'

Striding towards the jetty in clear night air that had now chilled to near-freezing, Bailey said, 'Higgs was next on our list anyway, sir.'

Hengrove nodded. 'I know *that*, Bailey, but I wanted *them* to point the finger.'

'If Higgs had been dipping his fingers into Full-deck's till and was about to be found out, it would certainly give him a motive,' said Bailey, buttoning up his overcoat. 'Plus, it sounds like she was his girlfriend, so… romantic jealousy and all that. It could be him, sir.'

'Anyone but your precious Miss Beckett, heh,' teased Hengrove with a sideways smile.

'What do you mean, sir…' but they were at the jetty now, the RIB's engine idling and the two constables preparing to slip lines.

'Right, let's get going,' shouted Hengrove, jumping aboard, 'back to the staithe.' Looking up at the starlit sky, he shivered and said, 'Bloody freezing. Why can't I be home watching the telly like the rest of the nation?'

Half a minute later, the inflatable was surging out of the basin, the disturbed wash left behind, somehow symbolic of all the upheaval she'd brought to *Marsh Haven* this night.

* * *

The village staithe was certainly a place of uncharacteristic activity when Jack walked onto it an hour after the police RIB had returned from *Marsh Haven*.

The urgent call from Mrs Jenkins had told him of Jayne Howlett's murder. She'd been unable to contact Sally on her mobile and had rung the Ranger in desperation, knowing he would find a way to reach her employer.

Jack's first action had been to try Sally's mobile himself with equally futile results. Instead of driving straight home, therefore, he and Audrey had made for the village, parking the car at *The Steamboat*. His intention had been to borrow a dinghy from Full-deck Marine and get to *Marsh Haven* as soon as possible to see Sally and check she was all right. As it was, after leaving Audrey to find warmth in the pub, the flashing blue lights of police vehicles and the Broads Beat RIB alongside, had drawn him straight to the staithe, where he found the serious figure of Phil Hengrove pacing and engrossed in conversation on his own mobile. The DCI switched off as Jack approached, seemingly pleased to see his friend.

'Jack; what brings you here?'

'Trying to find out what's happening, Phil.' Jack nodded towards the round tower of All Saints, peeking above the village rooftops. 'Bad business.'

'Yep, murder is never nice but when it's a young girl…' Hengrove shook his head. 'Her aunt rang us. Apparently Jayne had gone out just before six-thirty last night, supposedly to show some tourists around the church, but didn't come home, which wasn't like her. This morning, when auntie found her bed hadn't been slept in, she went and checked the church herself, found it unlocked, but no Jayne. No-one else had seen the girl and when she still wasn't home by midday, she called us. The church was the first place we checked and that's where we found her body.'

'I know. Mrs Jenkins told me.'

'Sally Beckett's housekeeper?'

Jack nodded. 'She's a friend of Agatha Howlett, Jayne's aunt. Agatha rang her before you. It was Mrs Jenkins who told her to call the police.'

'You know the *real* reason Jayne Howlett was at All Saints Church: to meet Sally Beckett in some sort of secret tryst.' The DCI raised his eyebrows. 'Not good for her, Jack, and she left her mobile phone as proof.'

Mrs Jenkins had already told Jack she thought Sally had been meeting Jayne at the church, so this information didn't surprise him. One aspect, though, did puzzle him. 'You say Agatha Howlett went and checked the church herself, Phil. How come she didn't discover Jayne's body?'

'She probably only had a cursory glance inside but, even if she'd looked under every pew, she still wouldn't have found her niece.'

'Go on…' said Jack, only too aware that already the DCI had told him more than the public would know for a long time.

'Because she wasn't in the church proper but up the tower.'

'The tower!' exclaimed Jack. 'What was she doing up there?'

'Lying strangled is what she was doing,' answered Hengrove bluntly. 'Pathologist reckons she was killed down below and then the body was taken up to the top to delay discovery.'

'Which at least rules out Sally Beckett,' said Jack with considerable relief. 'It would take some strength to haul a body up those ladders.'

'Not if you hoisted it with a block and tackle, it wouldn't,' replied Hengrove with the smug look of one with inside knowledge. 'The rig was already up there for hoisting bells and the like. All the murderer had to do was drag her to where they pull the bells, attach the line and hoist away.'

Jack shook his head sadly. 'Strangled you say?'

Hengrove nodded.

'Not your normal female method,' commented Jack. 'Any sexual motive?'

'None apparent at preliminary examination and we can rule out robbery as a motive too: her jacket pocket was still stuffed with cash.'

Jack's eyebrows rose. 'How much?'

'A thousand pounds in readies.'

'A lot of money for a girl like Jayne.' Jack shook his head thoughtfully. 'What time of death are you estimating, Phil?'

'Between six and eight last night, according to the pathologist. I reckon though that the murderer was hoisting her up the tower about six-fifty.'

'Why so exact?'

'Something your Miss Beckett said,' explained Hengrove. 'She reckoned that when she was crossing the broad that night, she heard All Saints' bell give one single chime. She checked her watch and it was six-fifty. If she's telling the truth, that chime was probably our murderer catching the bell-rope as he hauled up Jayne Howlett's body.'

'Sounds reasonable,' agreed Jack, adding, 'which, of course, rules out Sally Beckett as the perpetrator.'

'Yes, well I'll still keep an open mind until I'm sure, Jack.' Hengrove glanced out at the darkened broad. 'One unexplained death and now a murder. Hard to think the two aren't connected.'

'They have to be,' said Jack. 'What about some of those other names on your suspect list?'

'I've just been interviewing another likely candidate over there.' Hengrove nodded in the direction of Full-deck Marine.

'Henry Higgs; not my favourite sort of person, but whether he's capable of murder… What did he have to say for himself?'

'Not much. Reckoned he'd been out driving around with no witnesses.'

'And you believe that?'

'Not for a second,' answered Hengrove. 'Apparently, since his wife chucked him out, he's been bedding down where he can. Right now he's using one of the yard's boats, so I've got Bailey and a couple of uniforms doing a rummage just to show Mr Higgs that we don't appreciate his silence.' The DCI was interrupted by the ringing of his mobile phone. He turned his back to Jack but his words were still audible. '… hello, Bailey… good work… okay, arrest and caution him, I'll be right over.' He turned again to Jack. 'Bailey's found something.'

With Hengrove gone, Jack continued to hang around by the police cars. In some ways, it gave him a little nostalgia for the old life but, more important, he wanted to see developments for himself. He didn't have to wait long; fifteen minutes saw Hengrove back at the cars but, this time, followed by Bailey, two constables and, between them, a very disgruntled looking Henry Higgs.

'I tell you, I knew nothing about them being there. Your own men must have planted them to stitch me up,' he shouted back as he was ushered into the police van and driven away.

Seeing Jack waiting, Hengrove paused before joining Bailey in their own car and came over. He was holding a large sealed plastic envelope containing some copious paperwork. He glanced around to ensure no members of the public were within earshot and then held them up to Jack. 'Medical records.'

'The ones stolen from the surgery a few days ago?'

'That's them.' The DCI nodded in the direction of the departing police van. 'Our Mr Higgs has some explaining to do.'

'Where were they?'

'Well hidden under some floor access panels. Down there in the… the…'

'… bilges,' offered Jack.

'Whatever you call them, but a good place to hide something you don't want found.'

'What was his reaction?'

'The usual,' answered Hengrove. 'Feigned total ignorance.' He shook his head. 'He's a good actor, I'll give him that.'

'Hmm.' Jack nodded towards the notes. 'Are Charles McKenna-Hynes' records in there?'

'I won't know until I've examined them back at the station,' said Hengrove, turning towards his car. He paused before closing his door. 'I'll let you know, Jack.'

'Thanks, Phil… Oh, one further point; did Higgs appear to have been sleeping on that boat very long?'

The DCI thought before answering, 'Not really. Seemed to be living out of his suitcases, actually, but long enough to fill the boat with fag ash. Why?'

'Oh, just a thought.'

'Right, well let me know if you've got any ideas.'

Hengrove's car sped off leaving Jack to rejoin his wife in *The Steamboat* and ponder this latest development.

* * *

Chapter Eighteen

There was a cool wind blowing up the broad as Jack took his patrol launch across its white-flecked expanse early the next day. This was one of his Sunday duty days, so Spike was beside him in the wheelhouse. Jack never minded working on a Sunday. Audrey had her own commitments as churchwarden of Saint Cuthbert's, and tomorrow off in compensation would be useful for pursuing those elusive loose ends.

Today, though, he was more than happy to be back in an environment he knew and loved. After the trauma of Jayne's murder and all the grief that must be bringing, this special corner of creation seemed like a spiritual sanctuary, a good place to cleanse the soul. He glanced upwards as a flight of greylag geese came winging overhead, squawking noisily, before sliding to formation landing just ahead of his bows.

The turbulence they created reminded him that sometime this day he must visit *Marsh Haven*. In the light of yesterday's developments, Sally would surely be glad of a friendly face and chat. She was obviously becoming quite close to Ian Haverson and Jack was glad she had the young engineer to support her. However, sometimes it needed someone with just a little authority to give the reassurance people needed when they found themselves the wrong side of officialdom.

As the patrol launch's lean bow cut through the gentle waves running up the broad, Jack looked ahead and saw a large traditional sailing cruiser surging towards him. The tan sails were goose-winged out, producing a healthy "moustache" of foam beneath her long bowsprit. There was something familiar about those lines and soon a wave from the crew confirmed his suspicions: it was *Ace of Hearts*.

With the motor brought to 'stop', the launch slowly drifted to a standstill, beam on to the same wind that brought the sailing boat ever closer. It was Sally, he noticed, who was at the helm, but Ian who shouted, 'We'll come alongside!'

Jack lowered his fenders and soon *Ace of Hearts* was rounding up beside him, Sally letting fly the jibsheets and nervously edging in on the last of the boat's weigh, while Ian released the main halyard and brought down the sail. Lines were thrown and soon the Ranger was joining them in *Ace of Hearts'* cockpit, the two boats breasted together and drifting happily before the wind. The only one disappointed was

Spike, ordered to stay onboard the launch.

'It's so good to see you, Jack.' There was sincerity in Sally's voice, but the same face that braved a smile, also held a tiredness that spoke of pent-up anguish and a night with little sleep. 'You know the terrible news, of course.'

Jack nodded and glanced towards the distant staithe. 'Perhaps you haven't heard yet, but Henry Higgs was arrested last night.'

'Thank God for that.' Ian's relief was obviously heartfelt. 'Maybe now we'll learn the truth.'

'Higgs hasn't been arrested for Jayne's murder,' cautioned Jack, 'but they found those stolen medical records on his boat, which gave Phil Hengrove good reason to pull him in for further questioning.'

'Why on earth would he want those?' asked Sally, reaching across to give Spike a biscuit.

'Probably something to do with Captain Charles' murder,' answered Ian, not hiding his transparent dislike of Full-deck's manager.

'But why not simply destroy them,' puzzled Jack.

'Because they might come in handy later. Those records obviously contained confidential details,' said Ian with a knowing look. 'Higgs was probably hiding them down there until he needed something from one of the patients and then use them for a bit of blackmail.'

'Well, the police have both them and him now,' said Jack, taking the mug of coffee Sally had just made. 'The important thing is to connect or eliminate him from Jayne's murder enquiry.'

'Oh poor Jayne,' Sally sighed, 'she was only in All Saints Church to meet me and now she's dead.' She swept her hand across the expanse of broad and reedbeds. 'This place is so beautiful but it seems to be generating so much evil.' She turned to Jack, feeling rather embarrassed and sad, and said, 'It probably looks awfully insensitive, us out here enjoying ourselves sailing so soon after, but...'

'... it was my idea,' interrupted Ian. 'Sally had a terrible night thinking about it all and I felt the best thing this morning was to do something that would get her mind off the whole sad business.'

'Good idea, Ian,' agreed Jack. 'Most problems are at least eased a little with a few hours afloat.' He turned to Sally. 'Audrey and I had a useful day in Suffolk yesterday.'

'Oh, gosh, with everything else, I clean forgot to ask,' she apologised. 'Did you find out anything?'

'Nothing concrete but it's given me a basis to work on. Tomorrow's a day off and I plan to do some calling. I'll let you know when I have some news.'

'Thanks, Jack.' Sally tried to keep the disappointment out of her voice. 'With all these dreadful things happening, it would at least be some comfort to find out where I came from.'

'I know.' Jack glanced at his watch. 'Time for more patrolling.'

'Yep, and we mustn't waste a good wind,' declared Ian, leaping for the main halyard and hauling away.

Jack watched the big tan sail rising slowly to the masthead. Once there and with the still-unsheeted sail flapping and cracking in the wind, Ian rejoined Sally in the cockpit while Jack scrambled back aboard the launch and slipped the lines.

'See you later, Jack, and thanks again for all you're doing,' shouted Sally with a wave, as the two boats drifted apart and *Ace of Hearts*, mainsail now filled, heeled to the wind and gathered speed.

Soon the sailing cruiser was well up-broad and, as Jack eased the throttle ahead, the launch also pursued its own silent passage.

The last few days had produced much to think about and even more now as he continued his solitary patrol.

* * *

'I've already told you, I know nothing about any medical records.'

Henry Higgs had recovered from the shock of his arrest. Sitting in the interview room of North Walsham Police Headquarters, with his solicitor beside him and facing DCI Hengrove and DC Bailey across the table, he was back to his old belligerent self.

'Well, they were on *your* boat,' stated DCI Hengrove, not for the first time this Sunday morning.

'It's not *my* boat.' Higgs wiped his sweating brow. 'It belongs to the yard. I'm just using it for now.'

'... since your wife threw you out for having a bit on the side,' interjected Bailey. 'Was Jayne Howlett that other party?'

'No she *wasn't*,' answered Higgs with emphasis. 'I don't go chasing young girls.'

'That's not what we've heard.' Hengrove looked down at Higgs' handwritten statement. 'You state you were "out" at the time of Jayne's murder, but don't name anyone who can corroborate that.'

'No, because there wasn't anyone.' Higgs shifted in his chair.

'So, where were you?'

'Just driving around.'

'I don't believe you,' said Hengrove, well used to the symptoms of false evidence. 'I think you were at All Saints Church.'

'Don't you try and pin *that* on me,' shouted Higgs.

'All I'm seeking is the truth,' responded Hengrove, calmly. He glanced again at the file. 'Jayne Howlett had a lot of money on her when she died. Do you know anything about that?'

'Why should I?'

'Because you were her supervisor and she handled your boatyard's accounts.'

'Not the cash, she didn't,' corrected Higgs with the assurance of someone back on safer ground, 'and I certainly wouldn't trust her with a thousand quid.'

'Who said anything about a thousand pounds?'

'*You* must have,' retorted Higgs, but with slight consternation clouding his face.

'I only said "a lot of money"?' The DCI nodded towards the tape recorder slowly turning beside them. 'We can play it back if you want.'

Higgs looked sideways at his solicitor who merely shook his head.

'You are…' Hengrove checked his notes, '… the "yard manager" of Full-deck Marine?'

'That's right.' Higgs sounded relieved to be off the subject of the cash.

'Whose owner died in suspicious circumstances just a month ago?'

Higgs groaned. 'Oh, you're not going to drag all that up again. I've already told you a hundred times what I was doing that day.'

'… out on a boat and, yet again, with no corroborating witnesses,' stated Bailey. He leaned closer towards the prisoner. 'Not very good at covering yourself are you, Mr Higgs?'

'You're trying to plant that one on me again are you,' shouted Higgs, jumping to his feet. 'You lot are good at planting aren't you…' he pointed a shaking figure at the medical records lying on the table between them, '… including them.'

'Sit down, Mr Higgs.' There was a forcefulness in Hengrove's voice that, combined with a tug on his client's arm by the solicitor, had Higgs sinking back into his chair. 'According to this…' Hengrove glanced again at his notes, though he knew their contents by heart, '… you were once a beneficiary in your employer's will… all set to inherit a share of the business, apparently.'

Higgs merely nodded.

'And then, just months before your employer's death, you were cut out.' Hengrove looked directly at his prisoner. 'That must have made you pretty bitter?'

Higgs nodded again.

'What reason did Charles McKenna-Hynes give for changing his mind?'

Higgs shrugged. 'I was dead against his electric boat project and he thought I was too tough on the hands.'

'Why didn't he just sack you then?'

'Because, in the end, I got the work done, didn't I?' answered Higgs, the bitterness evident in his voice. 'The gov'nor told me if I changed my ways, he'd put me back in his will.' Higgs looked the DCI straight in the eye. 'So, why would I kill him when I might still have got my share back?'

It was the sort of logic Hengrove didn't want to hear on a Sunday morning when he should have been at home with the wife and kids. Perhaps Higgs wasn't involved in the old man's murder, but he was sure as hell lying about his part in Jayne Howlett's last hour.

The DCI could have murdered someone himself for a cigarette right now. Instead, he sat back, took another swig of his coffee and began the questioning all over again.

* * *

'Jack Fellows, I can read you like a book. You're on to something.'

Audrey Fellows had just put the kettle on when her husband walked in with Spike at day's end. She was ready for a cup of tea, having just fulfilled her own duties at Saint Cuthbert's. She couldn't help noticing Jack had just a little extra spring in his step this evening. Long ago, Audrey had recognised it as a reliable sign of progress with a case. Not that he'd ever admitted it and he didn't now.

'Not really love. Perhaps a bit more to think about, that's all.'

'Hmm; well, we'll see,' said Audrey, pouring some tea into his favourite cup and becoming serious. 'The police need to make some progress soon, Jack. We said special prayers at church this morning for poor Jayne Howlett, but everyone's saying this wouldn't have happened if Henry Higgs had been arrested earlier.'

Jack helped himself to sugar and milk. 'We don't know that Higgs is the murderer, Audrey. He's only in for questioning. It remains to be seen if he's charged with anything.'

'What do you think, then?'

'I'm not sure,' admitted Jack, pausing to give Spike a loving scratch on the head. 'Let's say I'm keeping an open mind.'

Audrey knew better than to push her husband any further on a closed subject. Instead she asked, 'Did you see Sally and Ian today?'

'Yep, they were sailing *Ace of Hearts* on the broad.' Jack explained the couple's thinking and Audrey agreed.

'Yes, it would do them both good to have something to take their mind off Jayne's murder. Sally must feel partly responsible.'

'And is still a suspect in Phil Hengrove's book,' added Jack, helping himself to a biscuit. 'All the beneficiaries of Charles' will are in the frame for *his* murder and, therefore, Jayne's as well.'

'Not poor little Mrs Jenkins, surely!' exclaimed Audrey, shocked that this pensioner should even be considered.

'When big money's involved, the most unlikely people will take a risk,' said Jack, wondering if he himself dare risk taking another biscuit and quickly deciding the odds were against him. 'More than one dear little old lady has been hanged for murder over the years.'

'But Mollie wouldn't hurt a fly, let alone murder Jayne.'

Jack shrugged. 'One thing I didn't mention was that Mollie Jenkins spent the evening of the murder with Jayne's Aunt Agatha. That was why Agatha called her first and it was Mollie who advised her to bring in the police.'

'As would any friend. What's wrong with that?'

'Nothing really,' acknowledged Jack, 'except we know Mollie Jenkins hardly ever goes out at night. It's just another of those strange coincidences that on the one night she does, her host's niece gets murdered.'

'What are you saying, Jack? Surely, being with Agatha Howlett at the time of Jayne's death gives Mollie the perfect alibi.'

'Yep, you're right, love. It's just that Mollie seemed a bit… well, secretive when she told me about being at Agatha's and when murder is involved, I don't believe in coincidence, as you well know.'

'Only *too* well,' Audrey replied, smiling, 'which is why I know you are so keen to discover the truth about Captain Charles.' She reached for the teapot and poured herself a cup. 'Do you really think that Edward Halard survived *Hood*, eventually made his way back to Emily and started a new life as Charles?'

'It sounds far-fetched, I grant you,' admitted Jack, 'but sometimes it's the most way-out theories that prove correct.'

'So, how do you prove this one?'

'Well, the stolen medical records have turned up now, so we might eventually be able to compare Charles' with Edward's naval ones.'

'Won't that take time?' asked Audrey.

'Yep, a long time if I know the authorities.' Jack nodded for a refill. 'That's why I've got more immediate plans. Tomorrow I'm going to get calling all the private boys' schools in Norfolk. If I can find the one whose colours match Charles' tie, we've got a start.' Jack sat back, stroking his chin. 'My feelings, though, are that the ex-pupil we're looking for is Edward Halard.'

'I thought it was Charles McKenna-Hynes?' queried Audrey, slightly confused.

'One and the same, if I'm right,' said Jack, 'because, if *I* were starting a new secret life, I'd try and use as much of the old one as possible. Lying is a pretty difficult exercise at the best of times. Using as much truth as possible always makes your story more credible.'

'But you all think Charles had a Scottish background?'

'And we don't know that Edward Halard didn't have also,' countered Jack. 'I bet this school, whichever it is, is the one Emily's naval officer husband went to.'

'Yes, but Charles never did talk about his school. It was only Mrs Jenkins who got that information out of him, and she, bless her, may have misunderstood him anyway.'

'I know,' admitted Jack, 'but we've got to start somewhere.'

'But not until tomorrow,' stated Audrey. 'What are your plans for the rest of this day?'

'To take old Spike for his walk,' answered Jack, amused, as always, at the way his Border Collie's ears picked up at just the mention of the magic word.

'Well, relax and enjoy your tea before you go.'

As she went to fetch Spike's lead, Audrey hoped Jack's theories proved correct. She knew what the truth always meant to him.

* * *

Truth seemed to be something ever more elusive at North Walsham police headquarters. After another hour's fruitless questioning, Hengrove had sent Higgs back to his cell to reconsider his attitudes and contemplate a future behind bars.

'What do you think, sir?' asked Bailey as he and his chief sat unwinding with mugs of coffee.

'He knows something about the circumstances of Jayne Howlett's death, I'm sure of it.' The DCI sat back and took a long drag on his cigarette. Personnel weren't supposed to smoke in the HQ any more but this was Sunday, he'd lost a day with his family and, quite honestly, right now, he didn't give a toss.

'Me too.' Bailey took another swig of his coffee and waved away some of his DCI's smoke. 'He dropped himself in it with that cash amount, and the overwhelming impression I got was that he was shielding someone.'

'Yep, so did I.' Hengrove stubbed the butt of his cigarette. 'But who?'

'The real murderer?'

'Possibly,' Hengrove sighed. 'We'll try and find out tomorrow.' He stood up. 'Perhaps I might even yet salvage a bit of home-life from this otherwise waste of a day, but first…' he paused to fish out his mobile phone, '… I'll give Jack Fellows some bad news.'

Bailey followed his chief from the building. Hengrove always complained of work conflicting with home-life.

At least, thought Bailey, he does *have* a home-life. It was something the young Detective Constable wondered if he'd ever know himself.

* * *

Jack was out walking the riverbank when his mobile rang.

'Jack, Phil Hengrove.'

'Hi, Phil. What's happening?'

'Not much… or at least nothing I can discuss now.'

'Right, why are you calling then?'

'Just to let you know one bit of unwelcome news…'

'Go on…'

'McKenna-Hynes' medical records weren't amongst those we found on Higgs' boat, Jack.'

'You don't say.'

'You don't sound surprised, Jack.'

'Not totally.'

Jack switched off his phone and threw another stick for Spike. Just across the river, a grey heron stood immobile on the bank, its bead-like eyes searching for the next unwary prey. Last night, Hengrove's news would have been a disappointment. This afternoon, if anything, it went to reinforce a rapidly forming conjecture.

The heron lifted off with a lazy beat of its wings, gradually retracting its neck, and legs straight back.

To the west, the sun started its graceful descent below the horizon. Another Broadland day was ending.

* * *

Chapter Nineteen

Monday morning found the workshop hands of Full-deck Marine in something of a quandary. By now, all knew of the circumstances of their manager's absence. Normally it was a great relief to the yard hands when Henry Higgs' overbearing personality was elsewhere, but Jayne Howlett had been well-liked and her death, together with Higgs' possible involvement, were hard to comprehend. Coming close after the boss's death, all were now wondering how long Full-deck itself might survive.

The fact was that Higgs, for all his bullying ways, was a man who always knew what needed doing and how to get it done. Now, without his commanding presence, the workforce stood around in undirected peace, wishing his rasping voice could direct them back once more to meaningful productivity.

It was only eight-thirty, but already coffee flasks were almost empty and the main topic of conversation was rapidly becoming old. Eventually, only the hammering of rain on the corrugated roof broke the bored silence which had descended like a cloud on Full-deck's despondent shop floor. When the main door flung open with a bang they jumped as though the devil himself had descended upon them.

Not Satan but, as they all spun round, they feared it might be "Hollering Henry" himself who had unexpectedly returned to "sort them". There was a sigh of relief when they saw it was Sally. That was cut short just as quickly as her caustic words ripped across the workshop. 'Have you lot nothing to do but stand around and chat?'

The new owner of Full-deck Marine surveyed the reddening faces around her, but the only response her question produced was a shuffling of feet. 'Right,' she said in a rather gentler tone, 'gather closer, we need to sort things out.'

With the workforce forming a half-circle around her, Sally knew it was a time for reconciliation. 'It's been a bad weekend for the yard,' she said, satisfied that this, at least, produced a reaction of nodding heads. She went on, 'Our bookkeeper Jayne, who I know you all thought a lot of, has been tragically killed, and Mr Higgs is in police custody helping them with their enquiries.' She paused a few seconds before continuing, 'But that must not affect the day-to-day operation of the yard. The main season will soon be upon us and there's still much work to do. So, who's the senior man here?'

The awkward glances and shaking of heads showed that delegation of authority had not been one of Henry Higgs' greatest strengths. Sally scanned the bewildered faces and selected the one that looked the most competent. 'Who are you?' she asked, ashamed that she still didn't know the names of all the men working for her.

'Fred Blowers, miss.'

'Right... Fred... I'm appointing you charge-hand.' Ignoring the startled look on his face, Sally went on, 'There'll be a few more pounds in your pay at month's end but, right now, I want you to organise the rest of the team here as you think fit.' She nodded towards the two cruisers that dominated the shop-floor. ' Which one is due out first?'

'*Three of Diamonds*, miss.'

'Good. Well, I'm sure you know what tasks you were all busy on last thing Friday, so I suggest you start there. During the morning, though, I'm going to have you in the office, one by one, and get to know each of you personally.' Once more, she dropped her tone to almost-motherly. 'Full-deck has had more than its share of tragedy these last months, but I want to assure all of you that I have every intention of bringing it back to prosperity. I can't do it without your help. I know what a great team we have here and that you won't let me down...' she glanced at her watch, '... so let's get cracking.'

As the hands went about their labours, Sally could already sense a change in atmosphere. In spite of the tragedy hanging over the yard, some hands were even whistling. Everyone just seemed relieved to know that some things were not going to change. Even young Tom Brewer seemed a happier lad. Sally called him and he followed her into the manager's little shack of an office.

'Tom, you'll find Mrs Jenkins waiting on the end of the jetty. Take the dory and run her out to *Marsh Haven* for me. Later on I'll need you to bring her back because I'll be going into Norwich for a new phone.' She nodded outside to the yard car park. 'I'll use the company van so I need the keys.'

Tom took the set off the line of hooks and handed them over. As he went to leave, Sally said, 'Now, please ask Fred Blowers to come in.'

As she waited for her new charge-hand, Sally looked out of the office's grimy window. In the rain, cruisers yawed and snubbed at their moorings, seemingly impatient to start their season's cruising. One, however, had black and yellow police tape blocking its every entry. This was the cruiser that Henry Higgs had been using for his own unauthorised accommodation.

There was a tap at the door and the new chargehand walked

uncertainly in. Sally turned from the window and smiled. 'Take a seat, Fred, and let me tell you all the things that are going to change around here.'

* * *

It was luck in his investigations that Jack hoped would change this rainy morning, as he settled down for a session on the telephone. His intention was to call every private boys' school in Norfolk until he found the one sharing the colours of Charles' old tie… if, indeed, one did.

There were only half a dozen such establishments now listed in the county, but the nineteen-thirties could well have seen double that number. Possibly, Charles' old school no longer existed, which would certainly frustrate further research. Nevertheless, he got dialling and hoped for the best.

It was a hope fulfilled, and quickly too, when he struck gold with just the third name on his list. The female bursar of Saltmarsh College was very happy to confirm that yes, yellow, green and black always had been, and still were the school colours. She was a friendly lady and keen to help in any way she could, but what she couldn't do, as she explained to Jack, was discuss any past pupil over the telephone, even ones from almost eight decades before. Instead, she made an appointment for Jack to visit and talk to the Headmaster late that same morning.

Jack sat back with the contented feeling of at last making progress. Then he flicked through his road atlas to check the location of this select-sounding school that could well hold the key to this whole puzzle. He saw, with satisfaction, that the college was situated in another area that he and Audrey loved to visit.

'Hi, love,' he shouted downstairs, 'do a flask and some sarnies; we're off to the North Norfolk coast.'

* * *

Pleasant contemplation of destination was not something Doctor Helen Newson shared with Jack this stormy morn. In truth, she dreaded what she had to do, a course of action that could ruin her reputation, professional integrity and financial security all in one foul sweep. But it had to be done.

First thing this morning, the police had called to say they had found her stolen medical records. She had tried to sound relieved and grateful and agreed to come and identify them, but in reality, that call was the last thing she wanted to hear and merely represented a foreboding of disasters to come.

So, once again, she sat in her consulting room, wondering how she had worked her way into such a corner and dreading making the next irrevocable move. Determination, though, was something she had inherited from her father, got her through medical school and given her that extra boost when the situation demanded.

It demanded from her now, more than ever before. She got up, put on her coat and went out to reception.

'No more calls today, Annette,' she instructed the receptionist. 'I'm going to be away for some time.'

'When can we expect you back?' asked Annette, well aware of the doctor's distraction this last week, but still unsure how to handle these unpredictable movements.

'Not sure,' answered Helen as she went out the door. 'Get someone to cover for me.'

I might never be back again, she thought sadly as she started her car and drove away from all she had built over the years, to a future that could only get worse before it got better.

* * *

'What a wonderful location, Headmaster.'

From the Victorian bay window of the head's first floor office, Jack looked out over typical north coast scenery. Beyond the seemingly endless, dyke-crossed expanse that gave Saltmarsh College its name, he could just make out the rolling grey of the North Sea with a large ship slowly edging its northern fringe. Jack could well understand any pupil spending formative years in such a maritime environment, choosing it as a career.

He and Audrey had arrived at Saltmarsh just before midday, his wife content to remain in the car reading while he made contact with the bursar. Soon a senior pupil was leading Jack across a stone quadrangle and into the forbidding main college building, passing on the way, groups of male and female pupils cheerfully going about their studies. They all wore green sweatshirts with the college badge depicting a black cormorant over yellow sand. The same colours as Charles' old tie.

Apart from sport, Jack had unashamedly hated his schooldays, and just being back in this atmosphere with its smell of polished wood and school dinners was enough to rekindle many an unpleasant memory. Such negative attitudes, however, did not appear to afflict the pupils of Saltmarsh College, who came across as a singularly cheerful bunch. It was a characteristic that seemed to run through the whole establishment.

Much of this was probably due to the Headmaster, a surprisingly young man who introduced himself as Graeme Capel. Obviously a freethinker who inspired the young people under his care with the same philosophy, he ushered Jack into a chair and asked, 'So how can I help you, Mr Fellows?'

'I'm trying to trace an old pupil of the school,' said Jack, briefly explaining the background to his research and, at the same time, showing his Ranger's ID card. It didn't carry quite the same weight as his old police warrant but, nevertheless, established his credentials.

'Well, let's see what we can do.' Capel clicked some key words into his laptop. 'We've put most of the college records onto computer during the last few years so, if your man did attend here, we should soon find him. What's the name?'

'Halard.' Jack, spelled out the surname. '… Edward Halard, and he probably attended in the late thirties.'

'Hmm, a long time ago.' The headmaster clicked in the names and frowned. 'No record here of a Halard, Mr Fellows. Are you sure of the spelling?'

'Absolutely,' said Jack, feeling dismay already eating away at his conviction.

'No, I'm sorry,' Capel seemed genuinely upset, 'no Edward Halard ever attended Saltmarsh College.' He saw Jack's obvious disappointment. 'Is there any other way I can help you?'

'Well,' said Jack resignedly, 'you could just try McKenna-Hynes… Charles McKenna-Hynes.' He spelled out these names, though he was just as sure this would be another futile search.

Capel clicked away again before taking a closer look at the screen and smiling. 'Yes, he's here: Charles McKenna-Hynes, attended as boarder from 1933 to 1939.'

* * *

'Oh dear; not good results?' Audrey had immediately detected her husband's downcast expression as he climbed back into the car beside her.

'We got *a* result, but it puts us virtually back to square one,' answered Jack, giving a deep sigh and explaining how the search had produced findings the very opposite of what he expected.

'Well, at least we know that poor Edward Halard's soul can rest easy in *Hood*,' said Audrey, thankful that, at least, one man's honour was preserved. 'So, Captain Charles really was who he said he was.'

'Charles never did *say* who he was which is why we're here,' said

Jack grumpily and, for once, careless of his dear wife's feelings. 'I still want to know more before I write him off as just a casual love of Emily's.'

'And how will you do that?' Audrey was all too well aware of her husband's stubbornness.

'By talking to someone who actually knew him when he was a boy.' Jack nodded towards the college buildings. 'They only have the bare details relating to past pupils, but the college does have a very active Old Boys' Association with members' names maintained on computer file. The headmaster kindly looked up four from Charles' class who are actually still living.' Jack brought out his notebook and checked the names. 'Two abroad, one in failing health, but one well worth calling tonight.'

'Good, that will keep you out of trouble,' said Audrey with feeling. 'Where to now?'

'Norwich...' Jack started the car, '... a couple of things there I need to check.'

'So much for our picnic in North Norfolk,' thought Audrey, as they pulled away, leaving Saltmarsh College and its beautiful setting soon far behind.

* * *

'Doctor Newson. Good of you to come in.'

At Police Headquarters, Detective Constable Bailey had come through to reception to meet his visitor who had already given her relevant details and been issued with a pass. Most people seemed ill at ease in a nick, but he was surprised that a professional such as Helen Newson would appear quite so intimidated. There was even a slight tremor in her voice when she said, 'That's all right, officer. There's something else I want to discuss anyway.'

'Well, the medical records won't take long,' Bailey reassured her cheerfully, trying to diffuse the tension this senior, but still attractive, woman obviously felt. 'All we need is for you to formally identify them as your stolen documents and check they're all there.'

'Of course...' Helen Newson paused, as though inexplicably searching for her next words, '... and then do you think I could have a word with Chief Inspector Hengrove?'

'He's pretty busy right now,' explained Bailey, ' but if it's important...'

'... it is,' interrupted Helen, the stress of the circumstances already eroding her normal authoritative calm.

'Then you'd better come with me.' Bailey led her through the double doors into the inner offices. He'd learned long ago not to expect any thanks from members of the public being re-united with stolen property, but there was something far deeper on this lady's mind. He knocked on his DCI's door.

The barked, 'Yes … come in!' might have been a death sentence, judging by the look on Doctor Newson's drawn face.

*   *   *

Chapter Twenty

Beyond its bustling main thoroughfares, Norwich has another far more interesting and atmospheric world of narrow, often cobbled streets, joined by even narrower, more interesting alleyways. In one of these hidden corners, Jack found the little shop he remembered from a previous shopping excursion with Audrey.

He glanced up at the shop sign: *Garner Collectibles*. Stuck into one of the small panes of the bowed Georgian window frame was written STAMPS & COINS BOUGHT FOR CASH. Ducking through the low doorway, his entry was accompanied by the jangle of an ancient bell.

Behind the counter was an elderly man with spectacles balanced on thin grey hair. He was holding a stamp with small tweezers and studying it through a magnifying glass. When he turned, the glass magnified his eye, giving the appearance of some squinting Cyclops. The face surrounding that eye was tired and world-weary with a voice to match. 'Can I help you?'

'I hope so. Are you Mr Garner?' asked Jack, taking out his notebook.

'Yes, I am.'

'Good.' Jack took Sally's two pristine banknotes from the notebook and handed them over. 'What can you tell me about these?'

The shopkeeper squinted as he studied the notes at arm's length. 'Obviously pre-war sterling but hardly used… if ever at all.' He was feeling the texture of the notes as well as studying their appearance. Then he placed one note under a desk lamp and scrutinised it with the lens. 'Very interesting.' In the backlight from the lamp, Jack caught a momentary tremor of excitement pass over the dealer's otherwise expressionless features. After studying the other note with equal intensity, Mr Garner switched off the light and looked up. It was obvious he was striving to suppress excitement, but unable to control the slight tremor in his voice as he asked, 'Where did you get these?'

'They belong to a friend who found them in a book.'

Mr Garner nodded slowly and Jack could see the knuckles on the hand holding the notes had whitened slightly. 'Would your… friend… be interested in selling them?'

'Possibly… later.' Jack leaned across the counter. 'Mr Garner, what I need to know right now is, are those notes what I think they are?'

'And what do you think they are?' countered the dealer, playing the game to the end.

Jack told him.

The dealer rubbed his chin. 'I think you may be right, but I need a second opinion. May I keep them to show to an associate.'

'How long?'

'Twenty-four hours,' answered Mr Garner, all pretence now gone in exchange for what might be the opportunity of his lifetime.

'Twenty-four hours, then.' Jack slipped his card onto the counter. 'Here's my number. Would you please call me this time tomorrow with the result.'

Mr Garner nodded and wrote out a receipt. 'And if they *are* what we think, may I have first opportunity to purchase?'

Jack shrugged. 'That's the owner's decision.' He handed back the receipt. 'Just put the serial numbers on this, will you.'

'Why, don't you trust me?' asked Mr Garner in a suitably injured tone but, at the same time, copying the numbers as requested.

Jack placed the receipt into his notebook and turned towards the door, where he paused. 'Mr Garner, I was a policemen most of my life and I don't trust *anyone*.'

* * *

The rain had stopped now, the pavements drying in the weak afternoon sun. Jack strode along them, deep in thought. He was heading for the Cathedral where he'd arranged to meet Audrey for tea. Busy city life went on around him, but his own thoughts were with those banknotes. Where did they fit into this whole strange equation? Passing under the Ethelbert Gate and into the Cathedral grounds, he decided to postpone that question until he received confirmation from Mr Garner. Walking through The Close towards the new refectory, a voice suddenly shouted, 'Jack!' He turned, looked, and saw a familiar face.

* * *

Sally had spent the rest of her morning interviewing the workforce of Full-deck Marine. She'd spent about twenty minutes with each hand, learning of their backgrounds, personal circumstances, their strengths, weaknesses and ambitions. She'd also asked each their own ideas for improving the yard. Not all were practical, but many were good suggestions that she'd written down for future study. The important thing was that every man went away feeling he was someone who mattered.

Without appearing to interrogate, Sally had also probed into their relationship with Grandfather Charles. To a man, they'd spoken warmly of their late boss, though it was evident his apparent dementia had begun to put a strain on relations in the last year. It was all the more tragic that they felt he seemed far more like his old self in the weeks before his death.

All in all, it had been a productive morning and Sally felt she had finally got to know each of her employees personally. She'd driven the company van into Norwich feeling Full-deck Marine, at least, was perhaps a little better for her presence. Her appointment in the city was for mid-afternoon so, as a little reward, she planned to make the most of the few hours in-between.

Like Audrey, Sally had enjoyed browsing around the shops and visiting the famous market she'd heard so much about. She was pleased to find several bargains to supplement the rather limited wardrobe she had brought in her rucksack, but was otherwise content to just soak up the atmosphere of this historic and finest of cities. Strange to say though, she already found herself missing the desolation of the marshes and the peace of the Broads. As she walked the busy streets, they seemed like a film speeded up. Short visits like this would always be enjoyable, but more than ever, she knew her soul was amongst the reedbeds and wildlife of her new home.

Feeling tired and now burdened by several bags, Sally glanced at her watch and realised it was time to be heading towards her meeting. She made her way to Cathedral Close and, while ambling pleasantly through its tranquillity, glanced across the cobbled way and saw Jack Fellows.

* * *

'Sally…' Jack was taken aback, '… what are you doing here?'

'On my way to the solicitors, Landers, Simpson and Hedges.'

'What, old Herbert Blenkinsop?'

For a second, Sally was surprised that Jack knew the elderly lawyer, but then realised he would have met him at the inquest on her grandfather. 'Yes, that's right…' she paused, before continuing, '… I didn't tell you, Jack, but at my meeting at Full-deck the other day, I found out that the yard no longer holds the freehold.'

'Really; who does?'

'That's the problem,' explained Sally, 'I don't know exactly. Apparently it's some local investment group by the name of Marine Development Holdings, but who the individuals are is a mystery. That's why I've made an appointment with Mr Blenkinsop. Hopefully he'll be able to shed some light on it all.'

'I'd be glad to know myself.' Jack glanced towards a seat beside an expanse of well-trimmed grass. 'Can you spare a minute?' Sally nodded and they sat down together. 'I'm glad I met you,' admitted Jack, 'because I was going to call old Blenkinsop myself tomorrow. As you'll be seeing him shortly, could you ask him a question for me?'

'Of course. What do you need to know?'

Jack explained his question.

'Do you think that's important?' asked Sally.

'It might be.'

'How about your other enquiries, Jack? Any luck with finding out who Granddad Charles really was?'

The Ranger shook his head, sadly. 'Afraid not. Every time I think I've made a breakthrough, it takes me into another dead end.' He told Sally of his findings at Saltmarsh College and how he'd hopefully soon know more about the origin of the banknotes.

'And perhaps this old classmate of Granddad's will be able to tell you more tonight,' Sally suggested, hopefully.

'Perhaps he will,' agreed Jack, but without quite the same optimism. He glanced at his watch. 'You'd better be off, Sally, or you'll miss your appointment.' He nodded over in the direction of the refectory. 'Why don't you join Audrey and me for a cuppa when you've finished, and then you can update me on what you've found.'

'A good idea. I'll see you in about forty-five minutes, Jack.'

He watched her striding off down The Close to her three o'clock appointment, a gutsy girl not likely to flinch from taking the odd risk. Jack wondered if he really had the right to ask her help in the devious plan his mind was already hatching.

* * *

The first-floor refectory of Norwich Cathedral was only a few years old, but already with a charm of its own, having seemingly soaked up the atmosphere ingrained into the nine hundred year-old place of worship it served.

Jack and Audrey always made a point of visiting the Cathedral whenever they visited Norwich. This forty-four acres in the city-centre was like a haven of peace amidst the turmoil of commercial life, and the refectory, a good place to rest and recuperate. With three of its walls comprised of floor to ceiling glass that overlooked the Cathedral precincts and its fourth, the mediaeval flint of the south cloisters, the refectory represented a brilliant union of award-winning design and ancient beauty. The tea was good too.

Jack took another sip of his as he looked up into the open roof, which always reminded him of the inside hull of an upturned Viking ship.

'It will be lovely to meet Sally at last,' smiled Audrey, pouring herself another cup.

'Well you won't have long to wait because here she is,' replied Jack, noticing the girl herself, still laden with her carrier bags, elbowing her way through the east entrance. After stowing her shopping and making introductions, he went off to get the promised tea while she and Audrey got to know each other with casual chat. When he returned, it was to find them discussing the Cathedral itself.

'It's such an impressive building,' enthused Sally. 'I'd love to look around it properly sometime.'

'We'll make a point of doing that,' assured Audrey, pouring Sally's tea. 'Let's have a day here together just as soon as you're sorted at home and at the yard.'

'Talking of which,' interrupted Jack, seizing the moment, 'how did the meeting go?'

'Not quite as successfully as I'd hoped,' answered Sally with a slump of her shoulders. 'Mr Blenkinsop had no information on the sale of the freehold. Apparently, the exchange was handled by another solicitor, appointed for that one transaction.'

'That's strange in itself,' commented Jack. 'Charles had a good personal relationship with *LSH*, built over decades. Did Blenkinsop have any idea why he suddenly switched?'

Sally shook her head. 'No, he was just as baffled, though he did say he thought it was during the period when Granddad seemed increasingly vague about everything.'

'We all worried about his change in behaviour at that time,' remembered Jack. 'It was finally diagnosed as simple vitamin deficiency, which Mrs Jenkins sorted out by making sure he ate proper meals again.'

'Yes, I know. The sad thing is, everyone tells me he was just starting to recover when he died.' She shook off that thought with a bright smile. 'The good news is that I got the answer to your question, Jack.' She recounted Mr Blenkinsop's reading of the will, adding, 'and, even better, with me finally in the loop, the executors are ready to finalise everything and pay us all our inheritance.'

'When?' asked Jack.

'Wednesday.'

'The day after tomorrow?'

'Yes.' Sally detected a slight reservation in the Ranger's acceptance of this good news. 'Any problem with that, Jack?'

'Just a little soon, that's all,' he answered, without further enlightenment.

'Well, it will at least make Mollie Jenkins *very* happy,' broke in Audrey, smiling. 'She's so looking forward to being able to buy *Lichens* from her landlord.'

'Yes, and Ian needs his to pay off some of his accumulating debts as well,' added Sally. 'I can't wait to give him the good news.'

'You and that young man are becoming quite close aren't you?' Like most women, Audrey's feminine intuition had read the signs when Sally mentioned the young engineer's name.

Sally blushed slightly. 'I suppose we are, though both being suspects in Chief Inspector Hengrove's enquiry, isn't exactly the best atmosphere for romance to flourish.'

'That's only because you're both beneficiaries in the will,' explained Jack. 'Even Mrs Jenkins falls under that umbrella of suspicion.'

'Which just shows how ridiculous the whole thing is.'

'Just standard police procedure…' Jack paused, '… but, Sally, having asked one favour of you today, I'm now going to ask a much, much bigger one.'

'Go on…'

'Well, you know as well as I do,' said Jack, 'that there are so many unresolved questions hanging over this whole affair. It was bad enough for you when it was just the mystery of your granddad's death and his place in your family history. Since the weekend, though, we've suffered Jayne Howlett's murder as well.' He leaned closer. 'Sally, am I right in assuming you'd like to bring this whole business to some sort of conclusion as quickly as possible?'

'Of course.'

'Even if it involved an element of risk?'

'Jack!' broke in Audrey. 'You really have no right…'

'It's all right, Audrey,' Sally laid a reassuring hand on Audrey's, 'Jack's right; we need to get this whole horrible nightmare sorted once and for all. And as for risks,' she smiled weakly, 'what's life without the odd bit of excitement.'

'Let's be clear on this though, Sally,' said Jack, fixing the young woman's eyes with his own, 'we're dealing with a murderer who's struck twice already and who could well try for a third time. Excitement's one thing,' he observed, with a slight lifting of his brows, 'but life-threatening situations are another. Are you quite sure you're prepared to accept the risks I'm asking you to take?'

'Absolutely, Jack,' replied Sally, stoically. 'What do you want me to do?'

Jack sat back. 'Well, for starters, I want you to stop at Mrs Jenkins' on your way home tonight and tell her about the will being settled on Wednesday.'

'No problem, but why the urgency? I'll be seeing her tomorrow morning.'

'Just trust me,' reassured Jack, before further discussion was cut short by the ringing of his phone. He excused himself and went out onto the stairwell to take the call.

Through the glass doors, both women could see him involved in some animated conversation. Jack never lingered over phone calls so, in the few seconds she knew she had, Audrey leaned across and said, 'I don't like this taking of risks, Sally, but what I do know is that Jack won't let you down.'

'Thanks.' Sally squeezed Audrey's hand just as Jack reappeared at the table.

'That was Phil Hengrove with some significant news. Henry Higgs has just been released from custody.'

'Why?' asked both women simultaneously.

'I don't know yet,' answered Jack, 'but I will shortly. Phil's asked me to call and see him a.s.a.p.' He picked his coat off the back of his chair. 'I'll drop you at home on the way, Audrey.' He turned to Sally. 'I may not be able to speak to you again for a little while, but just behave naturally and take the situations as they come.'

Sally gave a little gulp. 'Whatever you say, Jack.'

They all left together, Audrey still worried, Sally excited and Jack, not surprised by the DCI's call, but well aware he was taking a lot on his broad shoulders.

He just hoped he wouldn't regret it.

* * *

'Thanks for coming in, Jack.' DCI Hengrove stood up and shook his friend's hand before ushering him into the seat opposite. 'Bit of a turn in events, we've had today.'

'Tell me about it.'

Hengrove explained before concluding, '…so we had no alternative but to let the blighter go.' He turned a twelve-inch ruler over in his fingers as he spoke. 'Still plenty of questions for Mr Higgs yet, of course, regarding those medical records, but they can wait for the moment.'

'But at least you've got them back,' said Jack, trying to sound positive.

'We've got *some* back...' the DCI shook his head in frustration, '... but not McKenna-Hynes'. That's still missing.'

'Hmm.' Jack stroked his chin thoughtfully. 'So, any further thoughts on the murder of this poor Howlett girl?'

Hengrove shook his head again. 'None, other than it's surely connected to old McKenna-Hynes' death.'

'You say her body was hoisted into the belfry with a block and tackle?' checked Jack.

'Yeh, it's a permanent rig set up for any bells they need to hoist up or down.' The DCI reached into his drawer and brought out an already bulging file from which he extracted half a dozen colour prints, which Jack immediately recognised as crime-scene photographs. Before passing them over, Hengrove looked his friend in the eye. 'You haven't seen these... right?'

'Of course not,' agreed Jack, taking the prints and examining them carefully. Years with Scotland Yard should have made him immune to the trauma of violent death, but seeing these images of young Jayne Howlett's life so brutally extinguished still filled him with abject sadness. Flicking through them, he finally found the one shot he needed. Luckily, it was a close-up. After careful scrutiny, Jack handed the photos back to the DCI. 'That lifting rig has a four-part block and tackle, Phil. One man could lift a bell with that, so a woman would have had no problem lifting a slim girl like Jayne.'

'I agree,' nodded Hengrove who had been watching Jack study the photos, 'but that wasn't the image that most interested you.' The DCI held up the large colour print that had most absorbed Jack. 'It was this one wasn't it?'

'Yep.' Jack leaned back in his chair. 'Let me tell you what I think, Phil.'

'Go ahead.'

Jack explained his own theory and was pleased to see Hengrove nodding agreement. When he'd finished the DCI said, 'For once I think we may be on the same wavelength with this one, but how do we go about proving it?'

'I've got an idea about that too,' continued Jack, with a twinkle in his eye.

Hengrove shook his head. 'I have a horrible feeling I might regret this, but tell me your plan Jack.'

It was a good hour before Jack finally made his way out of police headquarters. Hengrove saw him through to reception and shook his hand. 'Thanks, Jack. I'll get our side organised and be in touch.'

'Right, Phil.'

At the door the DCI suddenly remembered, 'By the way, I never asked if you've made any progress in finding out about McKenna-Hynes' background?'

'A little,' answered Jack cagily, 'but I'm hoping a phone call tonight might throw a bit more light.'

'Let's hope so. Do you still think it'll have a bearing on the case?'

'It has to, Phil.'

Driving home, Jack thought about his last statement. Like so many police investigations, there'd been a mountain of work with precious little result. But now things might finally be moving.

In fact, they might be moving just a little too fast.

* * *

Mollie Jenkins was positively ecstatic when Sally stopped at *Lichens* on her way home and gave her the news of the impending payout.

'Oh, how wonderful!' she exclaimed, clasping her hands to her breast in that way of hers, and glorying in the thought that her days as a tenant were down to one. 'Thank you so much for coming especially to tell me, my dear,' she said gratefully, with tears welling in her eyes. 'Will you have a cup of tea before you go home?'

Sally shook her head. 'Thanks anyway, Mollie, but I must get going. I just wanted to be sure you got the good news from me.'

Driving on to the yard, Sally wondered just what reaction Jack had expected of her housekeeper, on receiving such welcome news. It was exactly what *she* would have anticipated.

At the yard, Sally posted the van keys through Full-deck's letterbox and transferred her shopping to the dory lying at the end of the jetty, where young Tom had been instructed to leave it. Soon she was motoring across the moonlit broad on the now-familiar route to home. A week ago, this would have been an epic adventure. Now it was a routine part of her everyday life. She smiled at the thought that some things, at least, had been achieved.

That satisfaction might well have been dimmed, though, if she had been aware of the hooded figure in the open boat, secretly watching her from the isolation of the reedbeds. As the dory slid through *Marsh Haven*'s entrance, the figure lowered binoculars and keyed a familiar number on the mobile phone.

Fifteen seconds later, a mile away in *Lichens*, Mollie Jenkins put down her own phone and smiled.

* * *

'Tyndale here.'

The voice booming over the phone gave no impression of extreme age, even though Jack knew this old classmate must be equal to Charles' eighty-six years. It carried a military authority in keeping with rank but, just to confirm, Jack asked, 'Major Tyndale... Major Toby Tyndale?'

'That's right; who's that?'

Jack identified himself and said, 'You don't know me, Major Tyndale, but I was given your name by the headmaster of Saltmarsh College which, I believe, is your old school.'

'Saltmarsh... God, yes.' If anything, Major Tyndale's decibel count had peaked even higher with mention of his old Alma Mater. 'Long time ago though, old boy.'

'I realise that, sir,' said Jack, 'but the reason for my calling is about an old classmate of yours.'

'Not many of them left,' conceded Tyndale with a laugh. 'Which one?'

'Charles McKenna-Hynes.'

'What old Mac?' There was no hesitation in Tyndale's reaction. 'Yes, remember him well.'

'Excellent,' said Jack with relief. 'He was a friend of yours, then?'

'Can't say he was a friend as such,' explained the major. 'Bit of a sickly chap was poor old Mac.'

'Really?' This was a surprise to Jack who remembered Charles as always remarkably physically fit for his age. 'Sickly in what way?'

'Oh, you know, chesty and wheezy which stopped him playing most sports and being one of the lads. Only sport he did was sailing and that was with Erich.'

'Erich?'

'Yes, Erich Baden, German lad, son of a diplomat or something. 'Course, this was before the start of the unpleasantness in thirty-nine.'

'Did you keep in touch with Charles at all after you left Saltmarsh?' asked Jack, hoping the major might give him some pointers. In this, though, he was doomed once more to disappointment.

''Fraid not,' shouted Tyndale. 'As I said, we weren't that close. Erich was his only real friend.'

'The Erich Baden he went sailing with?'

'That's right,' thundered the old major. 'Sailing and rowing were *the thing* at Saltmarsh. Used to do it right there on the coast or, if the weather was a bit fierce, on the Broads, which weren't too far away. I know Mac particularly liked it there.'

'Indeed he did.' Another thing was puzzling Jack. 'Major Tyndale, you keep referring to Charles as "Mac" but wasn't his nickname actually

"Caloy"?'

'Caloy... Caloy,' the major repeated loudly, 'never heard that one. No, he was always "Mac" to us.'

Perhaps Mrs Jenkins got that wrong, thought Jack. The major seemed very certain of his facts so, perhaps, it was time to bring him up to date. 'Well, it's good that you remember him so well,' said Jack, before adding, 'but I'm afraid I have some sad news. Charles died just over a month ago.'

'A month ago... a month ago!' roared Tyndale, 'no you've got that wrong, old boy.'

'I think not, major,' assured Jack as diplomatically as he could. 'Charles actually died in a boating incident on his beloved Broads.'

'Impossible,' blasted the major.

'Why impossible?'

'For the simple reason,' said the major with fast-reducing patience, 'that Charles McKenna-Hynes died in Germany in 1940.'

* * *

Chapter Twenty-One

'In Germany... in 1940... that can't be,' said Audrey in disbelief, after her husband had explained the shock of this last call.

'I'm afraid it is.' Jack stretched his legs in front of the fire. 'Major Tyndale was quite specific.'

'How would he know anyway?' asked Audrey. 'He admitted himself that he hadn't kept in touch with Charles since leaving Saltmarsh.'

'No, but he did attend all the reunions and some of the other lads from the class had kept their fingers on the pulse. In addition, Charles' family posted a full explanatory obituary in the college magazine at the time, so there seems very little room for doubt.'

'But, what on earth was *that* Charles doing in Germany during the war anyway? This Tyndale himself said the Charles he knew was a very poorly lad.'

'... which *was* the reason.' Jack rubbed his toes against the sleeping form of Spike. 'Charles' best friend was this Erich Baden whose father was with the German Embassy in London, hence his son being sent to an English public school. His father was posted back to Germany shortly after the boys left Saltmarsh and the family invited Charles to go and holiday at their home on the Baltic. They hoped some healthy sea air might help his condition and, apparently, for a while he did show some signs of improvement.'

'The Badens must have been a very kind family,' said Audrey, ever conscious of goodness in others regardless of international boundaries.

'Yes, but, sadly, events soon overtook them. Britain declared war on Germany within the year and poor Charles was interned. Later, his family heard through the Red Cross that his condition had worsened, and that he'd been admitted to a sanatorium. In 1940, they received word that he'd died.'

'How terrible for them, but surely they made enquiries after the war ended?'

'Oh yes,' said Jack, pausing to put another log on the fire, 'but it was years before they found out anything. The old East Prussia was now in the control of the Soviets who had little interest in the fate of one English boy.'

'And what about the kind Baden family? Couldn't they help?'

'There were none of them left to help anyone,' explained Jack sadly.

'Apparently, Erich was killed during the war and the rest of the family were lost in the *Wilhelm Gustloff* disaster, when the Germans were evacuating the Baltic, in the face of the Soviet advance.'

'Oh dear,' uttered Audrey, always uncomprehending of man's inhumanity to man. More immediate problems, however, were still to be resolved. They'd hoped this old classmate would give some clue to Charles' early life, but now another avenue seemed to have closed as it opened, unless... 'Jack, do you think there's any possibility that this Charles didn't die in 1940 and, instead, returned to a place he'd loved in his schooldays?'

Jack shook his head. 'I've already given that a lot of thought, love, and I think it's highly unlikely. The Red Cross were usually pretty careful about such things, added to which, this sickly lad who went to Saltmarsh is very different to the healthy octogenarian we knew as Charles.'

'And we can't check in his medical records because they're still missing.'

'Exactly.'

'So, who really was the Charles we knew?'

'Goodness knows,' said Jack, forlornly. 'I'm beginning to think we'll never find out.'

Like everyone else in the area, Audrey had always felt great affection for the kind old man who ran Full-deck Marine. The thought that he should now rest in obscurity, was almost as sad as the young Charles dying alone in Germany. 'Poor Captain Charles,' she said out loud, 'his whole life seems doomed to remain a total enigma.'

Jack sat in silence, a frown on his brow, but some of the despair seemingly leaving his face.

'What are you thinking, Jack?' asked his wife, conscious of the change in attitude that had just come over her husband.

'Oh, only about what you just said,' explained Jack.

'Which bit?' asked an increasingly bewildered Audrey but, already, her husband had retreated back into that deep contemplation which, so often in the past, had solved the most perplexing of crimes.

* * *

Sally stood on top of *Marsh Haven*'s lookout tower. An easterly wind was ruffling her hair and bringing with it, an enticing scent of the sea. Behind the house, the giant sails of the mill creaked their incessant revolutions but, perhaps, a little faster now in the freshening wind that was causing the reedbeds to sway and moan as if in mourning for the lost souls that Mollie Jenkins said still lingered in these marshes.

This was not the first time that Sally had ventured up the tower after her first rather scary night in *Marsh Haven*. She'd since come up here nightly, somehow finding great peace, but also secretly hoping she might get another glimpse of the mystical "corpse candles". She was quite prepared to believe in happenings beyond our earthly realm, even though she was sure Ian's rational explanation of these strange lights was probably nearer the truth. So, each night she'd climbed the tower with her grandfather's binoculars, hoping for a closer study of the phenomenon and, each night, was disappointed. Either the corpse candles were spiritually discerning in their visitations or, more likely, this spontaneous combustion of marsh gases required certain specific conditions that had only been present that first night. Despairing of ever seeing them again, Sally turned her attention back to the mill.

This was a scene that never disappointed her. Day and night those great sails rotated, and watching them was an absorbing sight that never lost its fascination. This background sound and movement had already become an accepted part of her everyday life, and the thought that this graceful working structure should also be powering her home, was something she found intrinsically satisfying. So too was the thought of sharing with Ian, his dream of restoring dozens of such mills to provide, at least locally, emission-free power and light.

Man-made light was all that was available this dark night. Above the mill cap, clouds still covered the sky, blocking out the starlit heavens and "Parish Lantern" that Sally had grown to know and love as never before. Now the only illumination to be seen from this lofty perch was the distant pinpricks of the village, and the sweeping arc of the lighthouse further up the coast. It was only when she glanced back to the darkened reedbeds, close by the basin, that she saw the other light.

It was just the briefest of flashes, but Sally eagerly leaned out over the lookout guardrail and focussed her binoculars on the location of its source. Perhaps, tonight, she would see again the illusive "corpse candle". The light flashed again and she brought it into sharp focus, only to feel thwarted. The light was a torch and it was being held by the man in the boat.

She had seen him before on her lone night vigils in the tower, thinking with each glimpse of the light that it was a reappearing corpse candle, but discovering it was only this lone figure sitting silently in the small clinker dinghy. Who was he and what was he doing, spending hours in the cold night air for, seemingly, no purpose?

Jack had assured her he'd check it out, but told her not to worry as it was probably a naturalist, perhaps watching out for otters or owls.

Whatever, the figure was here again, a hooded mysterious entity making no sound and little movement. Was this the "ghost" she had seen the first night at *Marsh Haven*? If so, it was very real, but nonetheless, slightly disturbing.

Then more lights appeared, gliding silently up the channel and turning into the basin. These, she recognised and welcomed because they revealed the distinctive lines and spinning wind turbines of Ian Haverson's *Electrifier*.

Corpse Candles and mysterious night-watchers forgotten, she ran down the steps and out onto the jetty to greet him.

* * *

'It's so good to have you here, Ian.'

They were snuggled together on the big lounge sofa, the spitting flames of the log fire once more casting dancing images over the book-lined walls and wood-beamed ceiling.

'I'd have been here earlier,' Ian gave her shoulder an extra squeeze, 'but a bungalow downriver had a minor electrical problem.' He gave a small sigh. 'Not really the sort of work I find professionally rewarding, but it does provide the odd crust.'

Sally sat upright and turned to face him directly. 'Well, there I might have some good news for you.' She told him about the imminent payout of the will. '... so, one more day and then you'll have all the cash you need to pay off those debts.'

'That will certainly take a huge load off my shoulders,' replied Ian, his face glowing with excitement, '... and, who knows, there may even be enough left over for me to develop some of my new ideas.'

'You mean your water-pumping scheme?' Sally remembered Ian's idea for replacing the batteries.

'That and a better component arrangement by placing the gearbox and generator in the cap,' answered Ian. 'It would do away with the need for the vertical shaft, improve reliability and reduce maintenance costs.'

'So, could you modify this mill for those systems?'

'I could,' answered Ian, hesitatingly, 'but it would be expensive. A more cost-effective way would be to install them in an existing mill that hasn't yet been converted.'

'Are there other mills that would be suitable for conversion to wind turbines?' asked Sally, the germ of an idea already turning in her head.

'Lots,' said Ian, 'but it would take thousands just to convert *one* and, even with your granddad's kind legacy, I won't have that sort of dosh.'

'No, but *we* will,' said Sally coyly.

'We?' Ian had turned to look straight into her eyes.

'Yes, I've been thinking…' Sally took Ian's hand in hers, '… after the payout, I'm going to be pretty well off myself. I don't believe in money sitting idle so, why don't I buy another suitable mill and you convert it?'

'You mean a partnership… a… business partnership?'

'Business to start with but, who knows…' Sally looked into Ian's eyes and saw already an acceptance of her thoughts, '… perhaps a personal one as well.'

'It sounds wonderful, Sal,' said Ian, taking both her hands in his. 'There's so much we could achieve together… eco-wise and… well, who knows.'

'Well, have a good think about it and don't decide too soon.' Sally was trying to keep her feet firmly on the ground, despite the surging emotions plying her soul. Outside, a gust of wind rattled the window frames and tinkled the wind-chimes. She smiled and gave Ian's hands another squeeze. 'For the moment though, I'm just glad you're going to be around.'

Ian caught just the hint of unease in her voice. 'Anything specific worrying you?'

She told him of Jack's impression that events would soon be coming to a dramatic head. 'I'm not sure how,' she admitted, 'but whatever it is, it will be good to have you close for support.'

'No problem,' he said, reassuringly, 'I was planning to be here a few days anyway. There's some work I need to do on the induction generator so I won't be further away than the mill.'

'Great.' Sally didn't try to disguise her relief. 'There are spooky things going on here,' she shuddered as she glanced outside to the darkened reedbeds, 'like that creepy boatman out there.'

'What boatman?'

'The one who hangs around out there in the marshes.' Sally frowned. 'You must have seen him when you came in just now.'

'I didn't see any boat or any*one*, Sal.' Ian gave her a playful rub on the shoulder. 'You sure you're not imagining things again?'

Sally ignored this typical male condescension; she knew what she had seen. Just the same, she'd be glad to get solutions to just *some* of the strange things happening around her.

* * *

Chapter Twenty-Two

Even the ducks seemed to be staying at home next morning as Jack's launch threw back sheets of spray as it punched through the even choppier waters of the broad. Dawn, this morning, had found the night's strong wind increased to near-gale.

Jack's main concern was that no anchored boats had dragged their mudweights and ended up grounded or blown into the reedbeds. Luckily, there were few hire boats out at this time of the year and those that were, had listened to the forecast and found themselves a snug berth in the various public moorings off the broad. He moored his own launch at the larger of these and went along the row of boats, checking ropes and answering the odd question from concerned crew. The forecast was for this weather to last another twenty-four hours, but clearing rapidly on the morrow. Reassured, most hirers retreated back into their cabins for a day of comfortable warmth with book or television. It was nine o'clock now and Jack had his own itinerary.

Back on his launch, he rang a London number and was put through to the relevant department. He asked for the person he hoped would supply the information he needed.

'Oh yes,' answered a pleasant sounding female voice, 'I'll just get him for you.' He heard her take a few steps across the office floor and say, 'A telephone call for you, Caloy.'

Jack pulled up the collar of his waterproof and smiled. At least, now, he knew he was on the right track.

* * *

"The right track" might not have been the way the hands at Fulldeck's yard would have described their morning's happening. With corrugated roofs rattling and loose panels banging, the cold sheds had become even chillier with the return of Henry Higgs.

After Sally's pep-talk and personal interest, they'd hoped this event would be a long time coming, if ever at all. Now the taskmaster had returned and they feared the worst.

It was a worry unfounded. To everyone's amazement, the returning yard manager was a much-subdued version of his former self. Apparently, a short sojourn as guest of the local constabulary had produced a sobering effect on the previously blustering character of

Henry Higgs. Instead of shouted orders, his response to the few begrudging calls of "Morning Boss" from the shop floor was an almost-imperceptible silent nod. In fact, the only hand he spoke to was young Tom Brewer.

'Come outside a minute, Tom.'

There was a moment of shocked disbelief as each hand looked from one to the other. No-one had ever heard the yard manager call *anyone* by their first name before, let alone this most junior of their team. The lad himself followed his old boss out onto the jetty in stunned silence.

'Right, Tom,' said Higgs, when they'd reached the end of the jetty, 'I'll be needing *Dealer* tonight.' He indicated the hefty open boat that Full-deck used as its tug. 'Get her checked over, bring her round to here and…' Higgs looked around sheepishly, '… don't tell *anyone* it's for me.'

'Right.' This new-found mellowness in his yard manager gave Tom Brewer the nerve to ask a question he would never have dared a few days before. 'Will you be working here again now, Mr Higgs?'

For just a second, Henry Higgs tottered on the verge of telling his dogsbody to mind his own bloody business. Then he looked out over the broad, shook his head and said, simply, 'Perhaps none of us'll be working here after tonight.'

Then he stormed off leaving young Tom Brewer to wonder just what that meant.

* * *

It was mid-morning when Jack's mobile rang once more. He was motoring across the broad and, in spite of the worsening weather, keeping to his usual allotted patrol.

'Fellows. Go ahead!'

'Hello, Mr Fellows,' said the excited voice at the other end. 'Henry Garner here.'

'Ah, good. What have you found, Mr Garner?' asked Jack.

'That our suspicions were correct,' answered the stamp and coin dealer, before giving Jack a full report on his findings. 'I think you'll agree, it's good news.'

'It's *interesting* news,' declared Jack, before thanking the dealer for his help and continuing up the broad.

Another piece of the jigsaw had just been found. Whether he could find where it fitted, depended on another call tonight.

* * *

In the tower of the mill, Ian finished his morning's work on the induction generator. In the cap above, the wind screamed through every aperture while intermittent gusts shook the tower, causing the ever-turning blades to groan in protest. Beside Ian, the vertical shaft revolved steadily and with it, the drive belt feeding all that natural power to the gearbox and generator. Those gusts must be producing great torque fluctuations and extra stress on the whole system. He glanced again at the drivebelt.

He'd chosen it in preference to a gearwheel for reasons of pure economy, though, he had to admit, it did appear quite archaic for such a futuristic concept. Once more, his mind played on all the advantages of having the shaft of the blades drive the gearbox and generator directly. The cost of the equipment would be surely less than this system, and the result would be more efficient and safer, without the exposed vertical shaft running right through all the levels.

Direct drive would eliminate that risk, but it would take time and money. Charles would have provided that funding if things hadn't taken such a disastrous turn. Dreams had been put on hold but now, with Sally prepared to step in and take over where her grandfather had left off, they could yet come true.

Ian threw his tools back into their bag and turned to leave, but not before checking that all was as it should be. Another gust hit the mill and he winced at the thought of all that extra torque.

Up in the cap was the brake, which could be applied to stop everything.

If the winds increased tonight as forecast, he might have to use it.

*   *   *

Mollie Jenkins looked out of the window of *Lichens* and saw Henry Higgs driving furiously by. She'd already heard on the grapevine that he'd been released from custody. Like the rest of the parish, she knew what she'd like to do with Henry Higgs, and could well understand him wanting to put as many miles as possible between himself and the village.

Another gust of wind, this time leaden with rain, struck the windows of the cottage making Mollie content that, this morning at least, she would not be venturing far from home. Sally had rung early to tell her to take the day off. No domestics at *Marsh Haven* were urgent enough to warrant a crossing of the broad in force six winds, so Mollie had lit the fire and settled down for an easy day. Not until mid-morning did she struggle out of her favourite chair to make a phone call.

The person she wanted answered straight away and Mollie quickly explained her plan.

The person on the other end was very agreeable to Mollie's

suggestion and confirmed this night would indeed be a good time.

'Right, I'll see you then.' Mollie replaced the receiver and returned to her comfortable chair. In some ways, she felt almost guilty at the way things were working out. So many poor souls had suffered and others were due to make amends but, for her, the future seemed so fair. She looked around the walls of her sitting room and contemplated again the delightful prospect of being an owner instead of a tenant.

By this time tomorrow, so many things would be changed beyond belief.

* * *

True to forecast, the wind and rain were as intense as ever as Jack made his sodden way home. The only good thing that could be said about weather like this was that it made domestic comfort all the more blissful. Once through his front door, Jack wasted no time in getting out of his wet clothes and into the warmth of the kitchen, especially as the enticing aroma of homemade bread was already wafting into his nostrils. Settled into his favourite chair, he stretched his legs beneath the table and felt a wet nose nuzzling his knees.

'Not just yet, Spike,' he soothed, giving the collie's head a scratch and stroke, 'at least not before I've had some tea and a slice of that loaf.'

'Made this afternoon after getting back from the library,' explained Audrey, cutting some generous slices and slipping two in the toaster.

'So love, did you manage to get the book I wanted?'

'I hope it's the right one.' Audrey passed across a fairly large volume.

'Perfect.' Jack flicked through some pages. 'Hopefully this might give us some pointers.'

'But will they be relevant, Jack?' Audrey placed the toast in its rack and went to the fridge for the butter. 'Surely this is all a bit obscure.'

'Not after my call this morning. I'm sure I'm on to something.' Jack layered his toast with a generous coating of butter before starting to work his way through the book. The slice was actually in his mouth when an illustration stopped him in mid-bite. He put the toast back on his plate and pushed the book across to Audrey. 'Look at this, love. What does that tell you?'

It took much to stop Jack Fellows eating, so Audrey didn't hesitate to suspend pouring the tea and look at the page indicated. Immediately, she realised what had caught her husband's imagination. 'Good heavens, Jack, it's certainly a coincidence, but will it help?'

'It will when I've rung this,' said Jack, bringing out his notebook and the number he'd obtained that morning. A paw settled on his knee. 'Right, Spike, let's get you walked, because I need to get phoning.' Between mouthfuls of tea and toast he said, 'I'll skip supper tonight. I think my call will be a long one.' Even rushing his tea for the prospect of a blustery walk in the rain hadn't dulled Jack's new-found optimism.

'But you can have a late bite if nothing else,' said Audrey.

'Actually, I can't,' said Jack, realising he hadn't yet told his wife the full plan. 'After the call I'm off out again.'

And the sooner the better, he thought, as he went and fetched Spike's lead. There was a lot hanging on tonight, not least a young woman's life.

* * *

An hour later, similar thoughts were dictating Doctor Helen Newson's actions. Back at the Health Centre, with evening surgery over and the staff all gone, she quickly changed from designer two-piece into more practical jeans, thermal tee-shirt and thick sweater.

This was apparel far more acceptable to Helen than the formal dress her profession conventionally demanded. She still had a sincere interest in medicine, but part of her would always be amongst the wood, tar and varnish of the boatyard where she'd spent her childhood years. She was proud of her medical career, but now she longed for time to hold a tiller and mainsheet in her hands once more, to feel the surge and heel of a boat meeting the wind and know again the exhilaration that always brought.

A sudden lash of rain against the surgery window brought Helen's dreams back to imminent reality. After pulling on her padded oilskin, she took a powerful torch from the desk drawer and checked it worked. It did and all she had to do now was get on with it. Switching off the lights, she made her way through reception and out into the car park.

Was it only yesterday that she had thought she might never return here again? A lot had happened since then and a lot more would follow.

Helen pulled up the hood of her jacket and ran to her car.

Swinging out of the car park, her headlights reflected off rain carried almost horizontal on the piercing wind. The elements were in a truly nasty mood.

So too was human nature.

* * *

Lights were also shining at Full-deck Marine, outside lights that illuminated driving rain made all the worse by clouds from *Dealer*'s exhaust. The boat had been left lying on the jetty as Henry Higgs requested and now the man himself was giving it a good run before venturing out onto the broad.

It was a prospect with limited appeal. Looking out into the blackness of that now-hostile expanse, Higgs could make out only the white tops of water driven into curling waves by the unrelenting wind.

'Why tonight?' he asked his troubled soul, but he knew the answer, just as he knew that the events of tonight could well decide whether he spent time behind bars or not.

He glanced at his watch and climbed aboard the tug. The engine was warm now, its rpm settled into a smooth rumble, as if impatient for the off.

Higgs wished he felt the same.

* * *

At *Lichens* Cottage, Mollie Jenkins pulled her front door just inches ajar and took a furtive glance outside. As if detecting just this chink in the home defences, a bitter wind iced its way into the living room warmth, causing Mollie to flinch and draw back. She gave the long, hand-knitted scarf around her neck another turn, snuggled deeper into her thick overcoat, opened the door fully and ventured out.

The wind and rain were driving straight down the main street of the village, all the stronger and colder after a free flow down the broad. Mollie lowered her head and battled straight into its teeth. She'd known it was going to be a bitter trek, before even opening the door for that first brief glance. The purpose of that recce had not been to check the weather, but rather to make sure there were no witnesses to her night-time excursion. In a village such as this, very little went unnoticed and an elderly lady leaving the comfort of her cosy home on the stormiest night of the year so far, was bound to raise questions later.

Questions about what she was doing this night were ones Mollie certainly didn't want to have to answer to anyone. Scuttling through the darkness, she was relieved that most curtains were firmly drawn and all good villagers, presumably, comfortable in their armchairs. Just the same, she kept her coat collar well up and her face towards the ground.

As she passed the churchyard, the howl of the wind in the surrounding trees made it an even eerier place than usual on a cold dark night. In this setting of swaying branches and scudding clouds, the tower of All Saints stood rock-like, as it had through a thousand storms before. The solid fabric of the church and all it stood for had always been a comfort to Mollie, but now she couldn't pass without thinking of poor Jayne Howlett. That she should have met such a brutal and untimely end was appalling enough, but that evil should stalk the consecrated hallows of their church was shocking beyond words.

All Saints had been the scene of much activity in the days following that foul deed, with blue flashing lights, young fresh-faced constables and people in white hooded overalls kneeling and searching every square foot of church and graveyard. Now all had gone and only a remnant strip of yellow and black tape bearing the words, POLICE – DO NOT ENTER, flapped noisily by the gate to show this had so recently been a place of tragedy.

What would poor Captain Charles think of it all, wondered Mollie with a quick glance towards his grave under the far row of tall poplars. She'd find out tonight after she'd talked to him.

Mollie, hurried on towards her night's work.

* * *

Within the wooden walls of *Marsh Haven*, Sally listened to the storm outside and wondered what else this night would bring. Although not specific, she'd gained the firm impression from Jack that whatever was going to happen would be before tomorrow.

She'd been totally sincere in saying she wanted an end to this whole unsettling business, but now, with strange creaks and groans coming from mill and house, she began doubting her own nerve to see it through.

If she'd known what to expect, it would have helped, but Jack had been reticent on this point, doubtless unsure himself of the actual course of events. All she could do was take it as it came but, for no other reason than to do something, she went over to the window for the umpteenth time that night and looked out.

Out on the jetty, the boats moved and strained at their moorings, little *Joker*, bobbing and twisting and the wind turbines of *Electrifier* buzzing away as never before. Even *Ace of Hearts* was heeling slightly as gusts struck her tall mast and rigging before shrieking their way onward over the marshes, where the tops of the reeds swayed like an oily sea. The scene was made more unreal by light from the mill being intermittently blocked behind its turning sails. The result produced an effect something akin to a slowed down old movie made all the eerier by whatever menace loomed beyond in the darkness.

Ah, the mill. She knew Ian was concerned about the effect of this gale on the sails and the rest of its mechanism. He was up there now checking things yet again, hence the lights. A bang from the back door made her jump.

'Ian, is that you?' She'd tried to keep the tension from her voice, but the words still came out like a schoolgirl's cry.

'Yep.' He came striding in, towelling wet hair and flashing a reassuring smile.

It worked because she had some of her old composure back when she asked, 'How's the mill?'

Ian made a shaking movement with the flat of his hand. 'Touch and go. I'm trying not to shut her down but it may come to it yet.' He shook his head. 'Going onto limited battery power is the last thing we need tonight.'

In her bones, Sally knew some hostile force was out there intent on evil. She couldn't have agreed with Ian more.

* * *

Forces were indeed at work, and closer than Sally imagined. Just short of *Marsh Haven*'s basin, the hooded figure in the small boat shut down the engine and allowed it to ghost into the lee of the reedbeds.

It had been a horrendously wet passage across the broad, but now the basin entrance was just ahead and, through it, the house. Beyond that, the mill stood stark against the night sky, its sweeping sails seemingly scraping the low stratus scudding overhead. Another gust of wind hit the little boat, swinging it beam-on and stopping it dead in the water. The figure picked up the oars, slipped them into the rowlocks and then paused before continuing on into the basin.

It was vital this entry went unseen, but lights still burned in the mill as well as the house, which could only mean someone was still about. For how much longer? It was a question answered by the mill lights suddenly switching off and the exiting figure of a man running back to the house, his torch beam forming a cone of illuminated rain.

Now was the chance to go in and land. Ahead lay the jetty with the usual boats alongside. Half a dozen good pulls and the dinghy was with them, the creak of the working rowlocks effectively blanketed by the cacophony of slapping halyards, straining mooring lines and the continual clunk of the turning mill. There was also a strange buzzing sound and it took the figure a few seconds to work out its source.

It came from the small wind-turbines of *Electrifier*, moored at the end of the jetty. This was Ian Haverson's boat, so it must have been him leaving the mill. Hopefully, he would not be returning, for this was where the rower wanted to land, well clear of the jetty and boats and shielded from the view of the house. With long bow-painter in one hand and a torch in the other, the figure leapt ashore.

The torch remained unlit. Star or moonlight would have been the greatest of aids tonight but, instead, blackness lay heavily over all, making any other light all the more conspicuous to anyone taking a glance outside. Using stealth instead, the figure edged slowly and carefully along the wooden walls of *Marsh Haven*, the eerie tinkling of wind-chimes indicating the entrance near at hand.

Close by was the open bunker storing logs for the stove. Even in the blackness it stood out clearly, but what didn't were the scaffolding poles, used previously in the mill, standing against it.

The figure only nudged them, but it was enough to send the lot crashing noisily to the ground.

*   *   *

'What was that?' asked Ian, looking up as the ominous clatter sounded outside.

Sally had heard it too, almost jumping out of her skin at the sudden crash which, to her already-stretched nerves, sounded as if half the house had fallen down. She had a good idea, though, of the cause. 'I bet it was those scaffolding poles by the log store. The wind must have blown them down.'

'I'm sure you're right,' agreed Ian, 'but I'll go and check.' The thought that the gusts had reached a strength sufficient to blow down steel had given him more immediate concerns. 'I reckon we must be close to having to shut the mill down, Sal.'

'Couldn't we give it just a little longer?' pleaded Sally, making no effort to disguise her dread of a blackout.

'I'll go and check the workings and make a final decision there,' he said, looking into her eyes and placing an affectionate hand on her cheek. 'If I can avoid it, I will.' He went through into the hall, slipping on his already wet oilskin as he did so and grabbing the torch off the shelf.

'Can I come and help you?' Even the atrocious weather seemed preferable to being alone.

'No, you stay here.'

'How long will you be?'

'Not long.'

'Please don't be.'

'Five minutes,' he reassured her as he made his way to the back door and pulled it open. A blast of bitter air came flooding in, the slanting rain outside illuminated by the escaping light from the hall. Then he was gone.

Sally shut the door and with it, the hideous moan of the wind and the demon-like rattle of everything loose. She went back into the lounge, poured herself a drink and settled down before the log fire. At least Ian would only be five minutes.

But, twenty minutes later, he still hadn't returned.

*   *   *

In *Marsh Haven*, the lights still burned but Ian Haverson appeared to have vanished. Particularly unnerving was the mill remaining in darkness. The light switches were right by the entrance door and Ian's first action on entering was always to switch them on. Sally kept checking every few minutes, but still the sails continued slicing through the relentless rain while the tower itself stayed ominously unlit.

'Where are you, Ian?' she thought anxiously, wondering why, even if there was a problem with the mill lights, she couldn't at least see his torch flashing through the small tower windows. Thoughts of him lying injured, perhaps caught in that horrible central shaft, decided her to disregard his orders and to go and search. She'd just turned from the window when the lights of *Marsh Haven* suddenly went out.

Standing there in the darkness with the storm winds screaming, Sally experienced a second of sheer terror. 'Get a grip, Beckett,' she said to herself out loud, clasping the back of a dining chair for reassurance and support. For a full minute, she just stood there, breathing deeply and deciding what to do. Outside, she could hear the mill still turning, so its stoppage was not what had caused the blackout.

By now her eyes were adjusting to the darkness, the log fire throwing a light that, in other circumstances, would have been gently romantic. Now it served sufficiently for her to go to the desk, pull out her torch and switch it on. With thoughts only on discovering what had gone wrong, Sally didn't even pause to put on her coat, but plunged out into the night, sprinting straight to the mill.

Even that short distance had her woollen jumper hanging sodden against skin already numb with the cold. She hardly noticed, wrenching open the mill door and groping for the light switch. She found it and switched on. Nothing. There must be a problem with the internal electrics.

'Ian,' she shouted up the wooden steps. No reply came save the incessant creek and grind of the turning machinery above. Pointing her torch beam up the steps, Sally slowly climbed upwards, pausing only to wipe rainwater running from her sodden hair and into her eyes. 'Ian,' she shouted again, but her calls seemed as futile as her search. Emerging through the trapdoor of this first level, it was only to find it empty, save for the turning central shaft and stored redundant mill machinery.

Above this floor was the generator room, the hum of its motors and ancillary equipment audible, despite the scream of the wind and thump of the sails. There was light there too, the red and green lights of the switchboard panel casting an eerie glow down the steps and giving the impression of entering the domain of some demon king, as Sally slowly made her way upwards.

In her heart was the dread that she would find Ian here, unconscious or worse after some catastrophic contact with the voltage. As her head came level with the floor, she scanned its small surface. Beside her, the shaft continued turning, its drive belt powering the gearbox and generator alongside. On the other side was the control cabinet with its dials and flickering array of lights. Everything as normal, but no Ian.

His tool bag was there though, lying by the cabinet and evidence that he had been this far. Everything within this vital compartment seemed to be humming healthily enough, so why the blackout in *Marsh Haven*? Sally flashed her torch over the panel, particularly the lights shining red. One was labelled HOUSE and the other MILL. There were largish switches below the lights that were in the OFF position. Tempted to simply move them back to ON, she stayed her hand, fearful that if Ian was working on equipment elsewhere, she could well cause the electrocution she'd initially feared. But where else could he be? The question automatically continued her scan upwards to the next level, immediately below the cap. The trapdoor that normally blocked this off was open.

Sally went to the foot of the near-vertical ladder up into this topmost level. Here the drive from the sails was geared to the vertical shaft. She could hear the wheels grinding away up there and remembered Ian's warning of the danger of those gears. Had he gone up there to apply the brake and been dragged into it himself? Pocketing her torch, she climbed the ladder into the darkness above.

Once again, she stopped, waist level with the floor. Close by, the vertical shaft turned, the noise ever-greater in the confined space of the clinker-built cap. Driving it here was the huge angled gear wheel, seemingly only inches from her head, its revolving teeth like the snarling mouth of some demented creature. Sally was reaching down for the pocketed torch when vicious arms grabbed her from behind and brutally pulled her the remaining feet into the cap.

Shock and confused thoughts desensitised immediate reaction, but then self-preservation took over and she struggled to free herself from arms that seemed like the jaws of a vice around her slim frame. Through a wave of mounting horror, she knew she was being dragged towards the hungry teeth of the gears.

* * *

In those desperate seconds, kicking, screaming, struggling, Sally fought for her life. Still her head was being forced ever closer to the turning cogs of that ghastly wheel. Inches now would see life extinguished in the most horrendous way imaginable. With the grinding wheels almost touching her nose, she heard steps on the ladder and sensed another figure leaping into the cap.

Whoever was holding her, flung her to the floor, her head striking the revolving vertical shaft with such force that she ended prostrate, with senses dulled to near-oblivion. Through a veil of partial-consciousness she heard, rather than saw, two figures fighting within the confines of that awful cap. Thank God, Ian had arrived to save her. She knew she should be doing something to help rather than lying there helpless. She tried struggling to her feet, but a wave of nausea seemed to overwhelm her just at the very moment she heard one of the figures fall heavily to the floor. The fight was over, but who had won; Ian or her attacker?

As if in answer, a figure came straight to her and she knew that movement *wasn't* Ian's. The figure bent down and she knew it was all over.

A torch was shone in her face. Blinded as she was, it created enough background light for her to see the hooded outline of the person so intent on her immediate destruction.

'No… please… don't.' Even as she pleaded, Sally realised her words were just mouthfuls of air, her voice going the way of reason as she sank into blissful oblivion once more. As consciousness drained away on a cloud of despair, her last image, her last on earth, was of the man she knew was going to murder her.

*   *   *

Chapter Twenty-Three

'Sally… SALLY.'

The face behind the voice shouting into her's slowly came into focus. Sally blinked twice and brought the even features of Helen Newson into sharper focus. She tried to sit up. 'Doctor Newson…'

'It's all right.' Helen pushed Sally gently back into the sofa. 'Just relax. You've had a terrible experience.' Sitting beside her, the doctor placed a tumbler of brandy close to Sally's lips. 'Take a sip of this.'

The fiery glow of the alcohol quickly restored both awareness and spirit, enough for Sally to glance around and take in her surroundings.

She was in the lounge of her own *Marsh Haven*, a warm blanket wrapped around her and the room seemingly full of people she knew. Facing her was Jack Fellows, his face a mixture of relief and concern. To one side of him was Chief Inspector Hengrove, serious as ever but a reassuring presence nonetheless. In the background, standing between two uniformed constables, immobile and expressionless, was the hooded figure. 'Oh no…' Sally started up, just the sight of her assailant recalling that last horrifying image. It was Jack this time who placed a comforting hand on her shoulder.

'Take it easy, Sally. You're amongst friends now.'

Sally mentally questioned that description for *everyone* present. Apart from her attacker, she could make out the figure of Henry Higgs, skulking in a dark corner of the room. What on earth was he doing here? It didn't really matter though because Ian was close by, slumped in a chair with a young female constable dabbing a bleeding wound on his forehead. Though obviously feeling much the worse from his own encounter, he gave her a reassuring smile. 'Thank God you're safe,' she uttered, trying to rise and just as quickly sinking back down as light-headedness and Helen Newson's hand forced her back into the cushions. Once again, it was Jack, who spoke.

'I'm sorry you've had to go through this, Sally.' The Ranger shook his head. 'We never intended things should go so far, but an accumulation of factors caused events to get rather out of hand.'

'You… you mean you planned all this?' Through groggy mental processes, Sally was trying to bring some order and logic to this whole evening's nightmare.

'We had to let the murderer try for you and show their hand,' admitted Jack, lifting the fringe of hair covering Sally's forehead. The blackness spreading from the bruise above her right eye was evidence of the battering she'd taken. 'If we'd known it would be as close as this, though…' He nodded towards the figure standing between the two policemen. 'You were very lucky.'

'*He* tried to kill me,' cried Sally.

'I know', said Jack. 'Chief Inspector Hengrove and I have had our suspicions for some time now, but we had to have proof.'

'… and my near-murder gave it to you!' exclaimed Sally, struggling to remain calm. She turned and gave Ian a smile of absolute gratitude. 'Thank goodness I had someone looking out for me.' The thought of that gallantry was almost as warm as the brandy and with it, the realisation that the final outcome had probably been worth it. 'Well, at least you've now got your man.'

'We have indeed,' said DCI Hengrove, stepping forward, 'thanks to your guts.'

He walked over to Ian, and Sally was glad the man in her life was going to get the recognition he deserved. 'Ian Haverson, I'm arresting you for the murder of Charles McKenna-Hynes and Jayne Howlett and for the attempted murder of Sally Beckett. You don't have to say anything but…'

* * *

At a nod from the Chief Inspector, the two constables moved to either side of Haverson, the young engineer remaining immobile and seemingly oblivious to the drama being enacted around him. Sally was less accepting.

'No… not Ian… you've got the wrong man!' she exclaimed, pulling herself to her feet and standing between Haverson and the DCI. Jack gently pulled her back.

'No, Sally. Believe us, it was Haverson here who tried to kill you and who murdered your grandfather and Jayne Howlett. Bailey was here to keep an eye on you, and, even then, only got to you just in time.'

Sally looked up to see the figure at the back of the room had removed his hooded jacket, revealing the face of the smiling Detective Constable.

Jack put a comforting arm around Sally's shoulders and guided her to a chair.

She stood for a second, looking at Ian and hoping against hope that he would reassure her that this was all some terrible mistake. Instead, he remained in sullen silence, head lowered to his chest. Sally slumped into the chair and shook her head before looking up and asking, 'Could someone here just tell me what's happening and that this isn't all some sort of horrible dream?'

'It's all too real, I'm afraid,' frowned Jack, 'but as to the facts... we know some and have to surmise others.'

'But why would Ian want me dead?' She looked again at the man she had loved, but again got no response.

'For the oldest murder motive in the world,' explained Hengrove, taking a seat of his own. 'Money.'

'But Ian was going to get his share of the inheritance tomorrow...'

'... which was why you had to be got rid of tonight,' completed Jack. 'Tomorrow, the executors would have wound up the estate and any event after that would have been *sub judicae*.' Jack knew there was no easy way he was going to explain all this, but he kept his tone as fatherly as possible. 'Sally, you remember I asked you to check something with your solicitor. I got you to ask what would have happened if you hadn't been traced. Blenkinsop's answer was that if any beneficiary of the will failed to inherit, the estate would be shared by those remaining. In other words, with you out of the way, Haverson here would have got half of your cash, the yard and this house.'

'But Mrs Jenkins would have got the other half,' reasoned Sally, still clutching at straws.

'But for how much longer?' asked Jack, rhetorically. 'Mrs Jenkins is an elderly lady with a soft spot for Master Haverson. Something tells me it wouldn't have been long before he managed to separate her from the bulk of her money.'

'That can't be right,' pleaded Sally in a voice that failed to convince even herself. 'We... we had such plans.'

'No, it was Haverson who had the plans,' stressed Jack, firmly, 'and they were for your death before the estate was wound up...'

'... in what would just seem a tragic accident,' completed Hengrove, glancing towards the mill.

'But Ian is too clever to think he would ever get away with a scheme as brazen as that!' exclaimed Sally. 'The coincidence would have been too much for any coroner to accept.'

'But how would we have proved otherwise?' countered the DCI. 'Haverson wasn't to know Bailey would be there to put the kaibosh on his plans. A coroner's jury could have all the suspicion it wanted but...' the DCI held out his hands in supplication, '... without proof...'

'But the other murders... Granddad and Jayne...' Sally rubbed a confused hand over her forehead, '... Ian himself says Granddad Charles treated him like a son... I don't understand.'

Jack sat down beside her. 'It's a long story, Sally. Do you feel up to hearing it now?'

Sally merely nodded.

'Okay then,' said Jack, 'here we go.'

* * *

'Put simply, Ian Haverson needed money and knew he was a beneficiary in your grandfather's will. But, for how much longer? It was that question which precipitated Captain Charles' death.' Jack turned to Sally. 'You, yourself, found evidence of embezzlement of Full-deck's funds. Mr Blenkinsop also told you your grandfather had made an appointment to see him just the day before his death and that he sounded distressed.' Jack glanced towards the silent figure of Ian Haverson. 'It's my surmise your grandfather had just realised who was pilfering big sums of company money and, in spite of the heartache this must have caused him, decided to have Haverson cut out of the will.'

'Yes, there were certainly large sums being paid out for components that seemingly didn't exist,' agreed Sally, turning over the distasteful facts in her own mind, 'but surely it was Higgs who was working that fiddle.' From the corner of her eye, Sally could see the figure of her old yard manager move a little closer.

'No,' said Jack. 'Higgs had already been cut out of your grandfather's will because he violently disagreed with the electrification project and Charles also questioned the way Higgs bullied the hands.'

Higgs listened to this but said nothing.

'But the sort of embezzlement you're accusing Ian of couldn't have happened without the help of Higgs' girlfriend...'

'...Jayne Howlett,' completed Jack for her, 'except she wasn't Higgs girlfriend, Sally, she was Ian's.'

'Ian and Jayne... together...' gasped Sally, sitting upright with all her own pains forgotten, '... no, Jack, that can't be right.'

'I'm afraid it is... or *was*, until you came on the scene.' Jack laid another fatherly hand on Sally's shoulder. 'Cast your mind back to when Jayne wanted desperately to talk and was going through some great mental turmoil. You assumed it was guilt, but that was only the half of it. She was also feeling the heartache of a young girl cruelly dumped and finally realising that all those promises of a life together after they'd ripped off your grandfather, were just the smooth words of a conniving schemer, who'd used her from the first.'

'Is this true, Ian?' asked Sally, but Haverson's silence was the answer she didn't want. It was Jack who spoke again.

'Jayne was a pretty girl and it wouldn't have been difficult for a relationship to flourish between the two of them at the boatyard. As Jayne took over more of the yard's accounts, the two must have quickly seen the possibilities of sidelining Full-deck funds, especially when your grandfather started having mental problems, and the whole scheme became easier than they'd ever imagined.'

'But, Granddad's memory problems were only temporary,' queried Sally. 'When he started getting better, they must have known they'd be found out.'

'But we didn't think he *would* get better.' It was Helen Newson who had stepped forward now, still an elegant figure in spite of casual dress and wet hair in disarray. 'I made what turned out to be a wrong diagnosis.'

There was silence in the room broken only by Jack saying, 'Go on…'

Doctor Newson paused, aware that her professional reputation was about to be compromised. 'I was sure Charles had developed Alzheimer's disease. The symptoms were classic and I had no hesitation in treating him accordingly.'

'And you told him this?' asked Jack.

'Yes, of course. The diagnosis was given in all good faith.'

'How did he take that?'

Helen shrugged. 'As anyone would take such devastating news, but the confusion he was already experiencing probably dampened extreme reaction.'

'And then he started getting better?' stated Sally.

'Yes. Sometimes we can be blinded by science and miss the obvious,' admitted the doctor. 'It was Mrs Jenkins who was sure Charles was just not eating properly. She started cooking him real meals and he began to recover.' Helen Newson shook her head. 'Just simple vitamin deficiency.'

'Not an insignificant misdiagnosis,' observed Jack.

'But quite a common one,' defended the doctor.

'Well, it must have been a relief to Charles,' said Jack, before continuing, 'so, feeling gradually better, he starts to get his hands back on the controls of Full-deck Marine, only to discover that, while he's been ill, someone has emptied his coffers and sold the freehold of the yard.'

'You must have known about all this,' accused Sally, turning towards the shadowy figure of her old yard manager. 'Why didn't you do something about it?'

'Why should I?' said Higgs, stepping forward. 'Yes, of course I knew that Haverson here was working a fiddle, supposedly buying components from imaginary firms and getting Jayne to make out the cheques which went straight into his own coffers. So what? The old man had cut me out of his will and wouldn't listen to me when I spoke out against that crazy idea of converting the whole fleet to electric, so I just turned my back and let things ride.'

'Yes, but there was more to it than that, wasn't there Higgs?' Jack leaned forward and faced the big figure of the manager. 'It served you well, didn't it, if Full-deck got into difficulties.'

'What, and lose my job? Don't be daft,' said Higgs dismissively.

'I think you planned to have a better job,' countered Jack. 'If cash became a problem, it would be only a matter of time before the yard had to be sold and that was where you could step in.'

'You're joking,' scoffed Higgs. 'You think I'd have that sort of money to spend.'

'No, I don't,' answered Jack calmly, 'but I think your girlfriend did.'

'But I thought you said Jayne wasn't…' broke in a confused Sally.

'And she wasn't,' said Jack. 'We all knew that Mrs Higgs had thrown her husband out over yet another woman and, somehow, assumed it was Jayne. But it wasn't. Higgs had a ladyfriend all right, but it was…'

'… me.' Helen Newson uttered the word, knowing it would leave her personal reputation in tatters.

'You… and Higgs?' Sally couldn't believe what she was hearing.

'You don't have to sound so shocked, Sally.' The doctor's voice was surprisingly calm, as though relieved at their secret being finally out. 'Henry might appear a blustering bully to most of you, but he's a man who's good at his job and with depths of warmth and kindness you wouldn't dream of.'

'Plus, by befriending him, you'd have inside knowledge of all that was happening at the yard,' added Jack.

'What do you mean?'

'I mean that you had a continuing hankering for the yard your father had sold to Charles all those years ago. Now a situation was evolving that you must have found almost irresistible. Here you had the present owner suffering, what you were sure, was progressive mental illness. Through your manfriend, Higgs, you knew that Haverson and Jayne were defrauding it. By getting Higgs to turn a blind eye, the yard was fiddled to the point of cash bankruptcy at which point, a confused Charles was easily persuaded to sell its freehold to Marine Development Holdings.' Jack looked Helen straight in the eye. 'A fancy name, Doctor Newson, but I have little doubt a search at Companies House will find it registered in your name. It was surely only a matter of time before your man Higgs was Managing Director and you had control over your father's old yard once more.'

'I paid a fair price for that freehold,' defended Helen. 'No-one can say I cheated Charles.'

'I'm glad to hear it,' conceded Jack, 'and we'll leave it to the medical council to decide the ethics of manipulating a patient in your care. No doubt they'll want to study just what medication you were prescribing through that period, when Charles seemed so confused.'

'If they ever find Charles' medical records,' butted in Sally. 'Presumably, when I turned up, she must have worried I'd delve deeper into my grandfather's condition and faked that break-in as an excuse to destroy his file.'

'No, actually, they really were stolen,' corrected DCI Hengrove. He cocked his head towards Ian Haverson. 'He was the one who burgled the surgery.'

'Why, for heaven's sake?' Sally was, by now, prepared to think the worst of Ian, but there were others here just as culpable.

'As an insurance against being handed in,' answered Jack. 'Haverson here was very happy to have the yard sold because it freed up more cash for him to embezzle. Helen was content to let that extortion continue because she'd got what she wanted and, in her medical opinion, Charles wouldn't need his cash for much longer anyway. Then Charles started recovering, discovered what was going on and got murdered.' Jack turned to Helen. 'Underhand deals were one thing but murder was another, and I'm sure that was where you started falling out.'

Doctor Newson nodded. 'I told Haverson I knew he must have murdered Charles and that I was considering going to the police. He threatened to say in court that I had *caused* Charles' condition with aggressive drugs. I told him I could prove otherwise from my records…'

'… which therefore drove him to steal them in that night burglary,' concluded Jack.

'But why steal *all* those records and why did Higgs hide them for him?' asked Sally, finding the intrigue of this whole business starting to neutralise some of the shock.

'Stealing a bundle of records was simply to cover the intent of the basic theft,' answered Jack, 'but they did serve also to throw us a red herring.' Jack turned to Ian Haverson and raised questioning brows.

The young engineer raised a weary head, shrugged and said, 'Yes, you're right, Higgs knew nothing about the records.' He turned and faced the yard manager, 'I thought if I hid them in the bilges of his boat when he wasn't there, it would take the heat off me and give him some agro in return.'

'You bastard!' Henry Higgs sprang forward, but DC Bailey quickly stopped him with firm hands.

'You're a lucky man, Higgs,' said DCI Hengrove. He nodded towards Helen Newson. Your ladyfriend here decided the truth of the whole thing was the only way you'd avoid the rap. Her coming in and giving that statement set us on the road to solution.'

'And, hiding those records in Higgs' boat was what made me suspect Haverson in the first place,' said Jack. He turned to the engineer. 'I'm afraid, your false trail got me right onto yours.'

Haverson looked up. 'How?'

'The day after Jayne Howlet's murder, when I met you both sailing on the broad,' explained Jack, 'we were discussing Higgs being arrested for the discovery of the records on his boat and you used the phrase "down there". Neither I nor anyone else had told you those records had been found in the bilges, so why say that if you didn't already know?'

'Just an expression,' sneered Haverson. 'It would never stand up in court.'

'Possibly not,' agreed Jack, 'but it doesn't matter now anyway. The important thing was that it put you in my sights and when you hoisted *Ace of Hearts*' sails a few minutes later, I observed the knots you used in belaying the halyards.'

'Knots?'

'Yes, you know perfectly well that my evidence at the inquest was based on my conviction that someone else had been on *Ace of Hearts* the morning of Charles' death. I told the coroner that *most* sailors used two "eights" and a half-hitch to secure cleated halyards, but that Charles never did. What I wasn't specific on were the knots I did find that morning: one turn, no eights and *three* half-hitches. Now that really is a weird way of belaying halyards, and I'm sure you were careful to avoid them in future when you were teaching Sally.' Jack fixed Haverson through his own narrowed eyes. 'But that morning we met on the broad, you forgot and that's when I knew who'd murdered Charles.'

'Just because I was on the boat, doesn't mean I murdered him.' Ian Haverson smiled as he added, 'You'll never prove that.'

'No, but juries don't believe in coincidence and that same knot put you at the scene of Jayne Howlett's murder also,' said Jack. 'Jayne was about to expose you. You assumed her devotion would keep her quiet, and it would have done if you hadn't started courting Sally here. Then Jayne's love turned to jealousy and she decided to come clean and shop you. You knew from Mrs Jenkins about the secret meeting at the church, got there before Sally and strangled the poor girl who you'd taken advantage of from the start.'

'You mean, the shadowy figure I saw in the graveyard was Ian?' shuddered Sally, remembering all the details of that horrifying night.

Jack nodded. 'He must have had a busy time. He only had minutes to strangle her, hoist her body to the top of the bell tower and make his getaway.'

'But why only "minutes"?' queried Sally. 'Ian left *Marsh Haven* well ahead of me and Jayne said she would be there from six-thirty, so there was plenty of time to do his worst.'

'Not as much time as he'd planned. He probably got there at six-thirty only to find others already with Jayne.'

'Others?'

'Yes,' intervened Helen Newson. 'Henry had overheard Jayne arranging to meet Sally and knew it must be to disclose all the fraud going on in the yard. He told me, and together we went to All Saints to buy Jayne's silence.'

'Which accounts for the thousand quid we found in her pockets,' said Hengrove. 'The poor kid still had her price right to the end.'

'You mean, she wasn't going to talk anyway?' The irony of his situation was falling upon Haverson like the sword of doom.

'No, you committed a foul murder for no reason,' answered the DCI, adding, ' and then gave yourself away again with your strange knot.'

'...the three half-hitches, which you re-secured the bell rig with after you'd used it to hoist Jayne's body up the tower,' explained Jack. He gave Haverson a grim smile. 'You may as well have left your signature scrawled on the church door.'

Ian Haverson placed his head in his hands and DCI Hengrove seized the moment.

'I think it would be better for you, Haverson if you told us, in your own words, just how you murdered Charles McKenna-Hynes.'

'I didn't murder him... or at least I didn't mean to murder him,' said Haverson, looking up and scanning the faces before him. He turned to meet Sally's own accusing stare. 'I just wanted to talk to him.'

'Go on,' said Hengrove.

'Well, he'd found out everything, hadn't he,' said the accused, 'all about the way Jayne and I had been getting his money for non-existent components and the yard being sold while he was mentally vulnerable. Charles called me from his boat to say he was going to his solicitors the next day to have me struck from his will, and also to instigate legal proceedings against us both.' Haverson looked about him, trying to discern a sliver of sympathy from those listening, and finding none. 'So, knowing he was probably waiting for the fog to lift, I went looking for him next morning and found *Ace of Hearts* anchored on the broad. I tied up alongside, went on board and pleaded with him to change his mind. I promised I'd repay all I'd taken, but he wouldn't hear any of it, just kept reminding me of all he'd done for me and how he would now see me in gaol. Things got pretty heated when I told him he'd got enough blood on his own hands not to be accusing others. He stood on the cockpit side-deck and ordered me off the boat. So, I jumped back across to *Electrifier*. Just that sudden shift of weight and the rock of the boat was enough to throw him overboard.'

'So, you had an eighty-six year old man struggling in icy water with no lifejacket. What did you do to help him?' asked Hengrove.

Haverson thought for a few seconds before shaking his head and saying, almost to himself, 'Nothing.'

'In other words,' said Jack, 'you left him to drown?'

Haverson nodded. 'Yes, but no jury will convict me of murder. The most I'll be tried for is manslaughter.'

'And I hope that will be a comfort to you as you serve life for murdering Jayne Howlett,' said Hengrove, before turning to DC Bailey, who'd been busy taking notes, and asking, 'You got all that?'

Bailey nodded and flipped closed his notebook.

'Right, I think we've heard enough,' said the DCI, nodding to the two constables, 'Take him away.'

But Haverson hadn't finished yet. 'Don't you all look at me like I'm a common criminal,' he shouted, pointing a shaking finger at the encircling group. 'Your precious "Captain Charles" got what was coming to him. I didn't steal that money from him. He took all *my* grandfather's money and drove him to suicide. I was just recovering what should have been mine anyway.'

Sally stood up, but Jack held her back, shaking his head. Then Ian Haverson was marched out of *Marsh Haven* and, seconds later, from the jetty came the sound of a powerful outboard bursting to life. Hengrove glanced at DC Bailey. 'Go with them. I'll see you there later.'

'Right, sir.'

As the young DC went to leave, Sally got unsteadily to her feet and went up to him. 'You saved my life, Bailey, and I probably haven't shown the gratitude I should.'

'That's okay,' responded the DC, 'all part of the job.'

'Just the same, I wish I'd known you were here.' She raised her eyes to the ceiling. 'It would have been a bit less scary knowing the strong arm of the law was so close at hand.'

'If you had, Haverson would have sussed it too,' said Bailey. 'We needed you to act as natural as possible.'

'I was natural all right,' agreed Sally with a mirthless smile, 'naturally terrified.' Her next smile was one of genuine warmth. 'Next time don't leave it until quite so late.'

'No, sorry for that,' he apologised. 'I arrived in what I thought would be plenty of time. The plan was that I'd stake out the house and generally keep an eye on the situation. Then Haverson came out and went into the mill, so I concluded you were safe for that time at least and relaxed my guard. When you eventually ran to the mill yourself, it caught me by surprise and, by the time I followed you in, I was one floor behind. At least that meant I wouldn't give my game away if nothing happened.'

'... and when it did, it was almost over before you realised,' admonished Sally, smiling.

Bailey nodded, apologetically. 'Yes, I heard you struggling up in the cap. By the time I got there he'd almost got your head in the gears...' He stopped, noticing the whitening in Sally's already drawn features.

'Yes, spare her the details,' tutted Jack, passing Sally the half-drunk tumbler of brandy before turning back to Bailey. 'The main thing is, you floored Haverson and saved Sally's life.'

'For which I'll be eternally grateful,' said Sally, giving Bailey another smile and, for the first time, noticing his own waterlogged state. 'You're still soaking wet.'

'Just a bit,' he shrugged. 'I was like this before I started. Small boats can be pretty wet in weather like this.' Outside, a gust of rain-laden wind striking the window served to emphasise this obvious understatement.

'You came here in a small boat in tonight's gale?'

'And every night for the last week,' interrupted Hengrove. 'Bailey here has been keeping an eye on you since you got here.'

'What, in that black rowing boat?' asked Sally incredulously, realising this was another mystery about to be solved. 'So, the strange hooded figure was you all the time?'

'Afraid so,' admitted Bailey. 'I was here in the village that first day you arrived. I thought you'd actually seen me when you came out of the Post Office.'

'I saw *someone*, but you were too quick for me to identify the face behind the hood,' said Sally. 'Fancy you being out there in the reedbeds in all weathers, you poor thing.'

'Don't worry; surprisingly, it was one duty he never complained about,' grinned Hengrove with a wink before becoming his old serious self. 'You see, Miss Beckett, you three beneficiaries were the logical first suspects, but it didn't take long to narrow that down to Haverson who had the means, opportunity and motive. As soon as we knew you were coming to live at *Marsh Haven*, we knew we had to look after you.'

'Even if, at times, your presence *was* more scary than the perceived threat,' Sally stated, glancing out of the window where rain slanted across the lights of the RIB awaiting its final passenger. It wasn't difficult to recall another frightening episode. She turned to Bailey again. 'When you turned up here that first night, I really thought the ghosts of the abbey had come to haunt me.'

'Ah, that wasn't me, actually, but I do know who it was because I was watching from my own boat through the binos.'

'And who did you see?'

Once again, DC Bailey glanced outside to the RIB and its occupants. 'Ian Haverson.'

'Ian?' Sally frowned. 'But he didn't even know I was here until he came the next morning.'

'It wasn't you he'd come to see,' explained Bailey.

'Who then?'

But, before the DC could answer, Hengrove said, 'On your way, Bailey.' The DC, somewhat reluctantly, exited the warm lounge and, minutes later, the RIB was speeding out of the basin, sheets of spray flying back on the wind to show where its bows had struck the small waves rolling in from the broad.

'Yes, good question; who had Haverson come to see?' said Hengrove, resuming the discussion. He turned towards Henry Higgs, nervously drawing on a cigarette at the back of the room. 'Perhaps you could answer that, Mr Higgs.'

Realising there was yet more to explain, the yard manager stubbed his half-smoked cigarette into an ashtray and stepped forward.

'It's true,' admitted Higgs, 'he'd come to see me.'

'But why here?'

Higgs hesitated enough for the DCI to answer for him. 'Because Higgs had been living here since Charles died.'

'I had to live somewhere after my wife threw me out, didn't I.' protested Higgs, finally finding his voice again. 'The old man had gone, the place was empty, so why not make use of it?'

'I could give you some reasons,' said Hengrove cynically. 'What did Haverson want to see you about, Higgs?'

The yard manager shrugged. 'He'd heard the guv'nor's granddaughter had been located and wanted to talk to me about it.'

'Probably to work out how you were going to cover all those shenanigans you'd both indulged in,' added the DCI, before nodding towards the door. 'Okay, clear off, but don't plan on travelling far in the immediate future. There are a lot of questions I need to ask you yet.' He turned to Helen Newson, who was demonstrating her own loyalties by edging close to Higgs and holding his hand, '... and that goes for you too, doctor.'

Without further comment, the pair left and soon another engine was starting and fading into the distance.

'Higgs and Doctor Newson... whoever would have thought it?' sighed Sally, flopping back into a chair. She turned to Jack. 'How did you get them to come out here tonight?'

'Just a phone call.' Jack gave a little chuckle. 'I made it quite clear there would be accusations to answer and that it would be to their advantage to defend themselves.'

'Which they may have to do again in court,' completed Hengrove with a satisfied smile. He turned to the Ranger. 'Pretty buttoned-up, I think, Jack...' he glanced at his watch, '...and time I was home. I'll ride back with you, if that's okay.'

Jack nodded. '... but, I want to make sure Sally's okay first.' She was sitting quietly now, periodically wiping reddening eyes with a tissue. Jack put a firm hand on her shoulder. 'It's been a pretty rough night for you one way or another.'

Sally nodded and gave a weak smile between wipes and sniffles. 'You could say that.' She glanced upwards. 'Jack, I think some fresh air is what I need right now. Will you come with me?'

'Of course.' He helped her to her feet and as they walked towards the door, Sally fought back another tear. Then she suddenly stopped in her tracks.

'There it is again.'

'What?'

'The impression that Granddad is here in this room. I've kept sensing it at different times since I came here: this house, the yard office, even All Saints Church that night.' Sally gave another sniff. 'It's that smell isn't it, the odour of Henry Higgs' cigarette?'

'Yes, he rolls his own.' Jack picked up the cigarette end from the ashtray and smelt it. 'Dutch tobacco, the same brand Captain Charles used to smoke...'

'... in his pipe. Of course!' Sally slapped her forehead. 'Not only was Higgs squatting here, he was helping himself to Granddad's baccy as well.' She gave a smile of heartfelt relief. 'No ghost, just another mystery solved.'

Jack smiled in return and nodded upwards. 'Let's get you that fresh air.'

* * *

'The wind's dropping.'

Aloft in *Marsh Haven*'s lookout tower, Sally stared out across marsh and broad. There was definitely less force behind the gusts.

'Yes, and the rain's stopped too,' observed Jack beside her. He turned and looked again at the bruise on Sally's forehead. 'Are you sure you're feeling okay. That was a nasty knock you had in there.'

Sally nodded. '... and my poor old heart has taken a bit of a bashing as well.' She leaned out over the guardrail and wistfully scanned the choppy waters of the broad where, just days before, she'd learned to sail with Ian. 'I really did love him, you know.'

'I know you did.' Jack leaned out with her. 'And I think he had genuine feelings for you, but something drove him to be the way he was.'

'Greed, by the sound of it,' said Sally, bluntly.

'Perhaps,' agreed Jack, 'but I think there was a strong element of bitterness there too.'

'Why, and what was all that talk of Granddad stealing all *his* grandfather's money? I don't understand any of it,' she protested. 'From all I've heard, Granddad Charles treated Ian like a son.'

'It's a long and murky business,' countered Jack, 'and all connected to Charles' previous life.'

'You mean you've finally discovered something!' exclaimed Sally, brightening again. 'Who was he Jack? What is all this about?'

'I'm still waiting for the confirmation,' answered Jack, with a twinkle in his eye. 'I'll wait until then before committing myself.'

'All right, I'll wait,' agreed Sally with a smile before looking out again over the broad. It didn't take long for her thoughts to stray to ones which brought the shadow back to her pretty face. 'Ian would have been getting his own money tomorrow. I wonder what will happen to that now?'

'Held by the executors pending the outcome of his trial, I should think,' guessed Jack. 'If he's found guilty, he'll be disinherited and his share split between you and Mrs Jenkins.'

Mention of the housekeeper's name sparked another question. 'Why did you ask me to let Mollie know about tomorrow's payout, Jack? Did you think she was involved in any way?'

'Only in that she could never keep a secret,' smiled Jack. 'We obviously wanted Ian to know the estate was being wound up, but couldn't be sure you'd be telling him. We had to keep it natural and telling Mollie was a sure way of doing it. My bet is she was on the phone before you were out of the garden gate.'

'You can be sneaky when you want, can't you?' Sally chuckled.

'You're not the first to tell me that, but I get results,' laughed Jack.

'You certainly do.' Sally looked out across the broad to where the distant lights of the village pierced the darkness. She'd certainly have news for Mollie when she picked her up tomorrow. Her gaze continued scanning out over the marshes where something had just caught her eye. Gasping, she grabbed Jack's arm with one hand and pointed into the marsh with the other. 'There… Jack… do you see them?'

'What?'

'There, just in those reedbeds… two lights.'

Jack followed her outstretched arm and saw for himself the two wavering flickers that moved silently through the reeds. 'Corpse Candles.'

'Yes, and surely they can't be natural because they're floating *against* the wind.'

Sally was right and, hard as he looked, Jack could see no human hand behind those strange pulsing glows that had now ceased their drift and, instead, were hovering motionless in almost direct line with the house.

'I wonder what Mollie Jenkins would make of this?' he whispered.

'I wonder.' Sally leaned further out over the rail and kept her eyes firmly on the lights.

* * *

As Sally whispered those words, Mollie Jenkins was sitting warm and snug in the home of her friend Agatha Howlett. Outside, the remnants of the storm still rattled on the tin roof of the garden shed, but it was obvious that the rain had stopped and the worst of the night's weather was over.

That display by the elements had made the warmth of the sitting room all the cosier. Both Mollie and Agatha sat sipping mugs of cocoa in front of a flickering fire, the only source of light playing over the rather dated furniture and decor of Jayne's old home.

In spite of the pleasure of shared company, both women had the undeniable feeling that this evening had not produced all they had hoped for.

'Did they speak to you?' asked Aunt Agatha in a hushed voice.

Mollie shook her head and turned to her friend. 'Or you?'

'No, I was so hoping Jayne would come to me tonight.'

'Yes, so was I,' said Mollie. 'I tried speaking to Captain Charles again but his soul must still be journeying to that higher plane. He didn't come to me either.'

Both women had been sharing these spiritual evenings as long as they could remember. Sometimes strange things happened and they were sure voices came to them, but it was not something they talked about with the rest of the village. They were well aware that they were called "witches" by some, but also knew the help and comfort they had often provided to the bereaved.

It was sad then, that at this time when they both needed to reach out to those they had held dear, contact with "the other side" seemed so painfully illusive.

'I'm sure they will come to us eventually.' Aunt Agatha placed a kindly hand on that of her friend.

But Mollie wasn't listening. Sitting immobile, she was seemingly miles away, the firelight flickering on a face stilled but for the smile of surprised pleasure playing over its otherwise inert features.

'Mollie... Mollie... are you all right?' pleaded an increasingly concerned Agatha.

Mollie Jenkins suddenly sat up, as though awaking from a sweet dream.

'Oh yes, dear, I'm fine,' she said, turning to Agatha and beaming a contented smile. She reached across and squeezed her friend's hand. 'Don't worry anymore, my dear...' Mollie looked up and said a silent word of thanks, '... I know now they're both at peace.'

* * *

'They've gone.'

High in *Marsh Haven*'s lookout tower, Sally grasped Jack's arm as the two lights flickered and died.

'Yes, and perhaps we should be gone as well.' Jack turned to the young woman at his side. 'Are you feeling better now?'

'Much,' said Sally with sincerity. 'I feel as though a huge load has just been lifted from me.' She cocked her head towards the French windows. 'Let's go down and join DCI Hengrove for a stiff drink.'

'Good idea.'

As Sally went to close the window behind them, she glanced again to where the two lights had flickered so meaningfully just minutes before. She hadn't liked to tell Jack, but, in that moment of their extinction, she'd had the delightful sensation of her grandfather finally at rest and her own future, content and fulfilled, here amongst the rivers and reedbeds.

'Goodnight, Granddad,' she whispered quietly and then closed the window and followed Jack down the stairs.

* * *

Chapter Twenty-Four

All Saints Church looked at it most beautiful as Jack walked through the lych-gate and up the graveyard path to the tower. By now the early morning sun was filtering through poplar treetops disturbed only by the gentlest of easterly breezes and the incessant squawk of rooks. The storm of two days previous was but a memory now, the deep depression filled by cold polar air that brought with it, the blissful freshness of the spring awakening.

Jack paused at the base of the tower, taking in deep breaths of the nectar-like air and wishing human nature could recover as quickly as the world it lived in. In the far corner of the graveyard, a young woman stood up beside a wooden cross, gave a smiling wave and ran to meet him.

'Sally, I thought I'd find you here.'

'Well it's such a beautiful morning and…' she glanced towards the grave, '… I wanted to bring Granddad some fresh flowers and do a bit of tidying.'

'He'd like that,' said Jack, 'but not those.' He was looking at the bruises still evident on her forehead. 'How are you now?'

'Fine physically…' she shrugged, '… but the heart might take a bit longer to heal.'

Jack looked upwards to a sun now reflecting off stained glass windows and giving just a hint of the warmth the day might bring. 'Summer's coming. Get sailing those boats of yours and life will be good again.' He deliberately brightened into a smile, produced a letter from his pocket and waved it in front of her nose. 'Got the reply this morning.'

'Great…' Sally was trying hard to contain her excitement, '…and…?'

'… and it confirms all I suspected.' Jack indicated a bench seat by the base of the tower. 'Do you want to hear this?'

'Of course I do!' exclaimed Sally, sitting down. 'Good or bad, Jack, I need to know.' She took a gulp. 'So, who was my grandfather?'

'Difficult to know where to start,' he conceded, 'so first let me tell you who he *wasn't*.'

'Go on.'

'Well, for a start, he wasn't Emily's husband, Edward Halard, who, sadly, we now know really was lost with *Hood* in 1941 and…' Jack raised his eyebrows, '… he wasn't Charles McKenna-Hynes either.' Jack went on to explain all he had learned from Major Toby Tyndale, the old Saltmarsh classmate.

'My goodness,' said Sally, running a hand through her hair, 'so, if Granddad wasn't Charles after all, who on earth was he?'

'Erich Baden.'

'Erich Baden,' she repeated, 'the young German lad who took the real Charles sailing on the Broads?'

Jack nodded. 'The only good friend that Charles McKenna-Hynes had at Saltmarsh, and whose family he went to stay with in Germany.'

'But… how… why?'

Jack laid a reassuring hand on her shoulder. 'Brace yourself for this, Sally. Your grandfather's life was more intriguing than any of us ever imagined.'

* * *

'How on earth could Granny have ever got involved with the enemy?' Sally shook her head in disbelief. 'And grandfather Charles, German when everyone thought him as British as you and I.' She turned and faced the Ranger, not prepared to accept this incredible statement without question. 'Are you quite sure of this?'

'Yes,' declared Jack, well aware that his findings weren't particularly welcome. 'It was a couple of small things combined that set me on this trail. Your grandfather had mentioned handling *boats* during the war, which I assumed, had been in our own coastal forces. After I'd learned of the German connection, my wife Audrey used a word which got me thinking.'

'A word…?'

'Yes, she described Charles' life as being a complete *enigma*. Used in another context, "Enigma" was the codeword for British research to break the German codes in World War Two. The association got me wondering if the unthinkable might be possible. Audrey got me a book from the library and in there was an illustration that convinced me I was on to something.'

'A book? What book, Jack?' Still sceptical, Sally was nevertheless, fascinated.

'A book on German E-boat operations in the North Sea. We called them E-boats but to the *Kriegsmarine*, they were *S-boots*, short for *Schnellboot*, and their equivalent of our MTBs. Within a minute of opening that book, I saw a photo and knew we'd cracked it.'

'Not a photo of Granddad?' By now, Sally was prepared for any revelation.

Jack shook his head, smiling. 'No, I wasn't that lucky. What it did show, though, was a type S100 *S-boot* of the second *Schnellboot* Flotilla based in Ostend. Like our MTBs, *schnellboots* had numbers rather than names but they did use codenames for radio work and the 2.SFltl had a unique system.'

'Which was...?'

'Playing cards,' answered Jack. 'Each boat had a playing card insignia painted on its bridge coaming and that was the name it went by in action. The photo showed the boat of the flotilla commander and guess what his insignia was?'

Sally's answer was almost instantaneous. 'Ace of Hearts?'

'Right in one,' acknowledged Jack, 'but I had to be sure. For confirmation, I needed to contact the *S-boot* Association in Germany, and to get their details I rang the German Naval Attaché in London. I was pretty sure, by now, that I was on the right lines, but something happened during that phone call that absolutely confirmed it.'

Sally was hooked. 'Go on...'

'The switchboard put me through to the Assistant Attaché's office,' continued Jack. 'The secretary called him to the phone and said something that set my pulse racing. She said, "Call for you, Caloy".'

Sally sat bolt upright. 'Caloy... that was *Granddad*'s nickname.'

Jack nodded. 'The very one, but, as the attaché explained, Caloy is more than just a nickname in the German Navy. Their equivalent of our rank of Lieutenant Commander is *Kapitanleutnant*. They abbreviate that to *Kaleu*, pronounced "Caloy", which became the standard crew name for anyone holding that rank. By a slip of discretion, your grandfather had given away his old rank, which meant he had probably been a flotilla commander. So, I wrote to the German association asking the name of the commander of 2.SFltl in 1944 plus some other details as well.' Jack held up the letter. 'And their answer was...'

'... Kapitanleutnant Erich Baden?'

Jack slowly nodded.

Sally shook her own head in admiration. 'You're a wonder, Jack...' she paused, some concerns obviously still troubling her, '... but all you've done is trace the old school friend of *our* Charles. What makes you think my grandfather was the same man and why, for goodness sake, would he want to steal another man's identity anyway?'

'It's a weird jigsaw, I grant you,' admitted Jack before once more holding up the letter he'd received that morning, 'but this gives us the clues to all the missing pieces.'

* * *

'I'd already got my suspicions because of those banknotes you gave me days before,' explained Jack.

'The banknotes?' queried Sally, remembering the old five-pound notes that had slipped from her grandfather's book.

'Yes, but more about those later.' Jack tapped the letter once more. 'It's here we have the meat to the theory.' He handed the letter across to Sally and continued, 'I asked also for any service history they had on the flotilla commander. That reply details Erich Baden's career. It shows he joined the Kriegsmarine early in the war and rapidly earned his own command of an *S-boot*. With his knowledge of our east coast from his own school sailing days, he must have been quite an asset in North Sea operations and it wasn't long before he was commanding the 2.SFltl.'

'Obviously a skilled sailor and able commander,' acknowledged Sally, 'but…'

'I'll come to that. The significant thing in that record is that in early 1944, Erich was relieved of flotilla command and called to the *Seekriegsleitung* – the Naval War Directorate – for briefing on "special operations".'

'That sounds rather ominous,' observed Sally.

'For Erich it was,' agreed Jack. 'The German High Command knew our invasion of occupied Europe was imminent and they needed accurate intelligence. Sources already here had reported forces massing in preparation, but SKL needed someone with naval experience to supply a learned evaluation.'

'And that man was Erich Baden,' surmised Sally, following the logic of this whole incredible tale. She gave a slight nod as she said, 'I can see why. Having been to school here and speaking perfect English, he must have been the logical choice.'

'I think it went deeper than that,' said Jack. 'Much of our preparation and most of our air support was based here in East Anglia, an area that Erich knew all too well. This, I'm sure, is where they sent him and, not only that, they had a ready-made cover identity that he could slip straight into.'

'Charles McKenna-Hynes?'

'Exactly. Charles had died in internment in Germany, they had his passport and personal details and, even better, someone who'd known him personally and could talk with authority of his background.'

'They were taking a risk though,' said Sally. 'We know Erich's English must have been grammatically perfect at that time, but surely he would have had *some* accent?'

'He did,' agreed Jack, but remember, he was impersonating a lad from Scotland. It's a fact that English, well spoken by Germans, has the same guttural intonation as Scottish. Often the two can be almost indistinguishable.'

Sally nodded acceptance. 'And, of course, Charles being from Scotland meant there were no local family members around here to even suspect someone was using his identity.' Sally leaned her head on one side. 'So, if things really were as you suspect, how did Granny Emily get to meet him?'

'This is where we start running out of facts and have to surmise,' admitted Jack. 'Let me give you my theory and see what you think.'

* * *

'Some things we do know for certain,' said Jack, tapping the letter again. 'When you read that, you'll see that the operation didn't go to plan. The flotilla war diary shows that in May 1944, Kapitanleutnant Baden sailed from Ostend in S-141 together with two other *schnellboots*, bound for the Thames estuary. As planned though, Erich's boat separated from the other two en route and headed, independently, on a more northerly track for the East Anglian coast. A few hours later, the other two boats received a garbled message from S-141, saying she had struck a mine. Nothing more was ever heard and, eventually, the boat, crew and Erich were all listed as "missing in action, presumed lost".'

'So, that's *it*? The story ends right there?' asked Sally.

'The official one, yes,' agreed Jack. 'From now on I'm guessing, but I'd put money on it being the right one.'

'I'm listening,' said Sally. 'Go on.'

'Right. Well, according to the boats that picked up her call, S-141 must have been somewhere between The Wash and Thames estuary when she struck. My guess is she was just off the Suffolk coast.'

'The Suffolk coast,' repeated Sally. 'You mean close to Emily's nature reserve?'

'That's exactly what I mean. Gladys Evans, who knew her during the war, reckons that after Edward was lost, Emily used to spend many lonely hours just walking the seashore. It was a restricted area, but she'd got to know the local sentries who were happy to let her.' Jack turned towards Sally. 'Now, let me paint a little scenario here and tell me if it rings true. Let's imagine Emily, in May 1944, taking an early morning walk on her favourite bit of beach, the area depicted in that painting hanging in *Marsh Haven*. Suddenly, she sees the body of a man, perhaps in a dinghy, who's washed ashore during the night. She runs to investigate and finds he's still alive... just. She helps him back to her cabin and tends his wounds, intending to call for help when she can. The survivor speaks perfect English and perhaps even indicates a knowledge of the local area, so she probably assumes he's one of ours.'

'But, wearing civvy clothes, not uniform?' queried Sally. 'That must have made her a bit suspicious.'

'Yes,' agreed Jack, 'and somewhere, or somehow, the truth must have come out. We have to assume, though, that there was an early attraction between the two and that Emily made a conscious decision to nurse and conceal him.'

'I still find it hard to believe that Gran, of all people, would harbour an enemy agent,' argued Sally. 'Surely she must have still been feeling some bitterness over the loss of her Edward?'

'She probably was, but perhaps not the bitterness you assume. Look at it another way,' suggested Jack. 'Emily has lost a beloved husband at sea. Yes, she might well have been bitter but against *war* rather than the enemy. Here is another young man, probably about the same age as Edward, another victim of the war and, this time, given up by the sea virtually into her arms. If she found immediate attraction for a man who, we know, was gentle and kind, she might well have thought this was some sort of compensation for all she'd lost. And, remember, it wasn't simply a matter of handing a man over as a prisoner-of-war. In those days, spies were hanged. Can you see your granny allowing that?'

'No I can't,' conceded Sally. 'So, Emily tended Erich's wounds, fell in love with him, and decided to conceal him in her cabin. I wonder for how long?'

'Probably until the war ended,' answered Jack. 'It was a big estate, remember, so it would have been relatively safe to enjoy secret walks in the woods. Gladys Evans said her friendship was shunned from this time on so we can assume Emily was pretty discreet. We know her job ended with the war and that she returned to London. But, by this time, there was a much greater complication in her life.'

'She was pregnant with Mum,' reasoned Sally.

'Which might have taken some explaining to friends and family so, she changed the facts of poor Edward's death from *Hood* to D-Day and saved her reputation and Erich's cover.'

'So what about Erich,' asked Sally. 'Surely, with the war now over, he could have given himself up without risk or retaliation?'

'Yes, but to return to what? Germany was in shambles, his family were all dead and their old home in East Prussia now in Soviet hands. Erich, on the other hand, had all the documents to continue a life here in England with a ready-made identity to assume. Your grandfather told Mollie Jenkins that, from his schooldays, he always wanted to live in Broadland. Manpower was still short and he was handy with boats so what could be more logical than that he simply come here, get a job and make himself a new life.'

'But I still don't understand. If he and Emily were so much in love, why didn't they eventually get married and be together?' asked Sally.

'Probably a combination of reasons. As we discussed before, marriage would have entailed awkward questions from registrars, but we do know that Emily visited your grandfather regularly until your mother's death. The devastating loss of their only child probably had a stymieing effect on their relationship, or, at least, as far as your granny was concerned. Money was probably another factor. On her own, Emily would be getting a naval pension for Edward, whereas Erich had only a boatbuilder's pay. In those days, that was hardly enough to bring up a family and I can imagine Erich, ex-naval officer, being too proud to offer Emily anything other than a good life. By the time he'd bought the boatyard and become better off, your gran had built her own life in London, the initial passion had probably passed and her priorities been reassessed. There only remained that enduring memory and lasting affection.'

'How sad. So, that was why Gran had written "To my darling E" on the portrait of herself. It wasn't for Edward, but for Erich.' Sally wiped her cheek before shaking away emotion with thoughts of another unresolved problem. 'That money for the boatyard, Jack; where did that really come from?'

'That,' said Jack, 'is the most intriguing point in this whole odd tale.'

High above, the rooks continued their interminable squawking.

* * *

'The answer's in there,' said Jack, tapping the report in Sally's hand. 'The bit about "sources already here reporting troop buildups". It's those first three words that are the most significant. Who were those sources? We know Germany must have had several agents and informers about the country and, I'm sure, they had one right here.'

'Isn't this getting a little far-fetched?' asked Sally. 'I can imagine German agents operating in military and industrial areas, but why would the enemy be interested in sleepy old Broadland?'

'Look at a map,' answered Jack, 'and you'll see disused airfields all around us. This was an area of intense air activity, plus ports and havens right down the coast with constant naval movements. That was why Erich was sent here. But why an informer already in place? For that you'll need to cast your thoughts back even earlier to when the boot was on the other foot.'

'You mean to 1940, when it was *us* facing invasion,' surmised Sally.

Jack nodded. 'Hitler's "Operation Sea Lion", but one problem he faced was the same as ours on D-Day: how to get troops off the beaches and into the interior as quickly as possible. In this area, he had a ready-made solution.' Jack swept his hand in the direction of the shimmering expanse of water, just visible through the village.

'You mean they would have used the rivers and broads?'

'They would indeed,' confirmed Jack. 'If invading troops had got into these waters, they could have spread over a huge area. But they needed accurate data on depths, bridge heights, landings and the like.' Jack looked straight at Sally. 'And there was one man in this area who had already done the survey and given them the information they needed.'

'You don't mean…?'

Jack nodded. '…Howard Haverson, grandfather of Ian and renowned Broadland naturalist.'

Sally threw her head back in disbelief. 'Now you really have gone too far, Jack. According to Ian, his grandfather was a local icon, a writer of cruising guides, not a data-collecting traitor.'

'Why couldn't he be both?' countered Jack. 'I've looked into his antecedents and he was certainly an acquaintance of Sir Oswald Mosley and probably a member of the BUF.'

'BUF?'

'British Union of Fascists, the so-called Blackshirts. Quite a few prominent Brits were, though most swallowed their convictions once we'd declared war. Some never did though and you can bet they would have been the first to crawl out of the woodwork if Hitler had ever invaded.'

'But Howard Haverson was a successful man in his own right,' argued Sally. 'Why would he risk it all for mere political leanings.'

'Money,' answered Jack, bluntly. 'Even before the war, I bet the Germans had paid for his survey of the Broads and all the data it supplied them. Ian told you himself, his granddad was a wealthy man until he lost it all, which is where Erich comes in.'

'But you're saying my granddad was a common blackmailer,'

protested Sally.

'I'm sure he didn't see it like that,' said Jack, appeasingly. 'He would have known the name of the German informer here, who he was supposed to contact. That was hot stuff. When the war finished, Erich himself would have simply been another prisoner to be repatriated. Traitors, on the other hand, were still being readily hanged and, years later when Erich needed money, disclosure would still have meant imprisonment and social ruin. Newson's boatyard, where Erich was working, was being offered for sale. He wanted to buy it, but where to get the money? Down the road was a man with plenty of the stuff but with a secret he would want to preserve at all costs.' Jack shook his head. 'Erich, as an ex-officer who'd served his own country, would have had little time for traitors prepared to sell their own. I'm sure he wouldn't have felt too much guilt separating Howard Haverson from his ill-gotten wealth.'

'And so, my granddad prospered and Ian's committed suicide,' summarised Sally.

Jack nodded. 'But, I suspect the one guilt your grandfather did feel, was seeing Ian suffering as a consequence.'

'Which is why Granddad treated him almost as a son himself.'

Jack nodded. 'But it wasn't enough to stem Ian's bitterness because, I'm sure he never understood *why* the man he knew as Charles McKenna-Hynes, was in a position to do what he'd done.'

'Only that it had driven his Grandfather Howard to an early death and robbed him of his own inheritance. I suppose, in Ian's eyes, he was only taking back what had been his, by rights, anyway,' concluded Sally. She looked towards her grandfather's grave. 'Let's hope Ian doesn't try and bring all this up at his trial.'

Jack shook his head. 'Not much chance, I should think. Ian must have realised there was *some* reason Howard Haverson paid up and I'm sure his defence council will be reluctant to risk any further family dirt coming up in court.'

Sally smiled. 'So, I now have to rewrite my life yet again, as the granddaughter of a German spy.'

'And a brave sailor and kind man,' added Jack. 'Don't forget all that he and his family did to help the real Charles.' Jack suddenly remembered something, pulled out his notebook and removed the two old five-pound notes that Sally had given him only days before. 'Let me give you these back, Sally. They were a big factor in setting me on this trail to begin with.'

'Two old British banknotes… how could these have been significant.'

'Because they're not British,' said Jack.

'But…?'

'They were produced in Germany during the war.' He handed Sally the notes. 'In 1941, the Third Reich had the bright idea of ruining the British economy by flooding it with forged five-pound notes. They called it "Operation Bernhard", forced Jewish craftsmen in Sachsenhausen concentration camp to make the plates and then printed off a hundred and thirty million quid's worth of the stuff. They might have got away with it if the notes had been perfect.'

'But they weren't?'

'No, those Jewish engravers bravely slipped in little defects.' Jack pointed to the depiction of Britannia. 'Her eyes were made a little duller on the forgeries. That allowed our experts to tell the difference. So, the Nazis abandoned their original plan, but still used the counterfeits to finance intelligence operation overseas. I'm sure Erich had a bundle, but kept just those two fivers for souvenirs.'

'And the rest?'

Jack shrugged and smiled. 'Burnt in the boatyard stove, probably.'

'Good for Erich.' It was Sally's turn to smile. 'You see, I'm already thinking of Granddad now as Erich, rather than Charles.' She raised her eyebrows. 'And now I even know how I got my middle name… Erica.'

'Your whole life seems to be coming together now,' smiled Jack, before tapping the banknotes still in Sally's hands. 'Take care of those, they're quite valuable to collectors.'

'Good,' she said, placing them into her rucksack, 'because I've already decided to sell them and use the money to buy Granddad a proper headstone.' She glanced again towards the grave. 'No man should rest under any name but his own.'

'I agree,' said Jack before glancing at his watch. 'Time for me to be off.' He stood up. 'More river to be patrolled yet before lunch.'

'I'll walk with you,' said Sally.

As they made their way back down the churchyard path, Jack asked, 'So, now we've sorted the past, what about the future. Any plans?'

'My first job will be to get the yard operating profitably again,' explained Sally. 'There's a lot to be done and I might even get Helen Newson in to help.'

'Doctor Newson!' exclaimed Jack. 'But she bought your grandfather's freehold under very dubious circumstances.'

'But all in good faith in her own mind, I think. She really did think Granddad had Alzheimer's, as she's explained…' Sally pulled a letter from her pocket, '… in the same handwriting as that other note saying

"Sorry" on the wreath on Granddad's grave.'

'Well, she's still going to have to explain to the medical council why she took advantage of a patient's condition for her own commercial gain,' said Jack.

'Yes, and she may not be practising medicine much longer,' agreed Sally, 'but she did pay a fair price for the yard, and she *is* my legal landlord with a sincere and personal interest in the business, so I think we'd work well together.'

'You probably would,' agreed Jack, 'and it's good to have someone to share ideas and responsibilities.'

'And I haven't got anyone else now,' she said, a sadness very quickly returning to her face and voice.

'Not true. You've Audrey and me and other friends too…' Jack looked towards the lych-gate, where a car had just drawn up. 'In fact, here's one now.'

The driver's door had opened and a fit-looking young man emerged, blinking into the sunshine. Sally recognised him immediately.

'It's DC Bailey.'

'I wonder what he wants?' queried Jack, trying hard to keep a smirk off his face.

'Hello, Miss Beckett,' said Bailey, a little self-consciously. 'I just wanted to see how you were. I rang the house and Mrs Jenkins said you were here so…'

'I'm fine thank you, Bailey,' said Sally, with a freshening glow coming to her pale cheeks, 'but how are you?'

'Oh… fine,' said the young DC, fingering his own bruises. He glanced uncomfortably towards Jack. 'Actually, there was something else I was going to ask…'

'I really must get going,' said Jack with a nod towards the staithe. 'I'll leave you two to… to discuss business.'

'Thanks, Jack,' said Sally, with sincerity. 'Yes, I'll sort some things out with… with…' she turned to the young detective. 'I can't keep calling you "DC Bailey". What's your first name?'

Jack didn't wait to hear the reply. He was already striding back towards the staithe where his launch reflected the morning sunshine. Letting go the lines, he climbed aboard and was soon motoring away.

Sliding out of the dyke, he passed the yard of Full-deck Marine where they were launching a cruiser under the direction of Fred Blowers. He gave them a cheery wave.

Just beyond, a large private cruiser, obviously going too fast, swung round in a half-circle and headed back up the broad. Wash from its passing came rolling back to rock Jack's launch and disperse as small waves against bank and quay-heading.

The helmsman was probably oblivious to the disturbance he'd caused and, within minutes, the commotion had gone and all around was peace and stillness once more.

Just like life, thought Jack, as he headed up the broad in pursuit of the other boat.

THE END

Author's Note

Most works of fiction contain much that is true and separating the two can be as challenging as solving the plot. To find out which is which in this story, visit my website *www.chriscrowther.co.uk*

If you've enjoyed *STILLWATERS*, you may want to read *WATERPROOF* my first 'Jack Fellows' murder mystery on the Broads.

If you are unable to obtain these books from your local bookseller, you can obtain them direct from me by either visiting my website: *www.chriscrowther.co.uk*

or writing to:

Chris Crowther
PO Box 1239
Norwich
NR12 8XF

WATERPROOF

Patrolling the Norfolk Broads as a Navigation Ranger is, to ex-Scotland Yard detective Jack Fellows, the perfect job.

That's until the cold hand of violent death touches even this idyllic corner of East Anglia. Murder on the Broads is rarer than a bittern but the police soon have their man. Or have they? Jack is sure they've got it wrong and sets out to prove it. Amongst the tranquillity of this unique setting he discovers a simmering cauldron of bitterness and deceit with suspects aplenty.

Relationships, livelihoods and reputations are in jeopardy but whose will be sacrificed as he pursues the truth?